ELLE GRAY

BLAKE WILDER

FBI MYSTERY THRILLER

HER
PERFECT
CRIME

 Created with Vellum

PROLOGUE

Speedy Check Cashing & Payday Loans; Bellevue, WA

"You ready?" I ask.

"You know I am, baby."

Sasha gives me that wild-eyed smile I love so much; that smile that sends that familiar thrill surging through me. My veins crackle with electricity and a smile that matches hers crosses my face. I've never felt as alive as I do when I'm with her. I guess you could say she brings out the animal in me. However you describe it, I like it. And I love this woman.

Before I met Sasha, I was simply drifting through life. Each day simply blending into the next. I had no stability and I sure as hell had no sense of excitement. There was absolutely nothing in my life I looked forward to. I stole simply to survive, always hitting the easy marks, and never really pushing or challenging myself. But then I met Sasha, and everything changed. Since we got together, life has been exciting. Every day is an adrenaline rush. For the first time in my life, I feel as if I'm truly alive. And that's because of her.

"They should be closing up now," she says, practically bouncing in her seat. "Place should be clear of customers."

"Time to get into position."

We get out of the car and walk to the employees' entrance at the rear of the check cashing store. I pull her to me and press a firm kiss to her mouth, both of us trembling with excitement. Stepping back, I pull the balaclava down over my face, leaving only my eyes exposed. Sasha follows suit and stands beside the door, clutching her Glock 19 in the ready position. I reach out and push the bell and wait. And when the door's opened by a tall, lanky guy with long hair who looks half-stoned, I drive the butt of my AR-15 into his face.

The guy staggers backward, blood erupting from his nose, and I move in through the door, my weapon at the ready. The back hall is clear, though – save for the guy bleeding profusely from the nose. I drive my foot into his groin and the air explodes from his lungs with an audible gasp. He doubles over, clutching his wounded jewels and I bring the butt of my weapon down on the back of his neck. It connects with a crunch and he collapses into a heap on the floor.

I lean over him, chuckling to myself. "Didn't your boss tell you that you do not open the back door around closing time?" I crow. "Or are you just that stupid?"

When Sasha steps into the shop, she closes the door behind her and leans against the wall beside it, her eyes flicking from the unconscious man at my feet back to mine. Her eyes sparkle with the light of excitement. I tip her a wink and move to the door that separates the back from the front of the store.

I glance back at her. "Stay put."

"Do your thing, baby."

I approach the door and take a deep breath, so much adrenaline flowing through me I'm shaking. I grab the handle and pull the door open, moving into the front of the store fast and low. There's a heavyset guy with long hair, standing with his back to me at a table, counting out the night's cash. As I close in on him, he turns and sees me, his eyes growing wide. I flip my weapon around again and slam the butt of it into his face.

He grunts and staggers back but rebounds off the tall table where he was counting and remains on his feet. Blood flows from a gash on his forehead and we stand there, staring at one another for a moment. He tries to run, so I slam the butt of my weapon into the side of his head and this time he does go down. He rolls onto his side, clutching his head and writhing on the ground at my feet, a high-pitched keening wail coming from his throat.

"Shut up," I growl.

He doesn't, though. He keeps wailing and crying, which pisses me off. I draw back and deliver a vicious kick to his midsection. He screams and thrashes around, flinging blood from the gash on his forehead all over the place.

"I said, 'Shut up!'" I scream at him.

As he continues to scream, I kick him again. And again. I keep kicking him, the sound of his screaming only fueling my anger. I drive my steel-toed boot into his face and hear a nasty crunching sound. But the guy is still and he's not screaming anymore, so it's all good. That task done, I hang my weapon from its strap around my back. Then I slip a can of spray paint from my pocket and move about the store, blacking out all the cameras I can see.

Knowing there's a possibility there are hidden surveillance cameras in the store, I keep my balaclava on as I conduct my business. Taking a black canvas bag from my pocket, I shake it out then move from station to station, taking all the cash out of the drawers. I've just finished emptying the last drawer and am about to turn and go when my eyes fall on the tall safe that's sitting against the back wall and a smile crosses my face.

"I must've done somethin' real good in my life. Not sure what that could be, but whatever," I say.

I move to the safe and pull the door, which had been cracked already, all the way open. And when I see what's inside, I laugh to myself. I reach in and start pulling out the stacks of bundled cash inside, dropping them into my bag. As the bag gets heavier with the thousands of unexpected dollars, I get giddier and giddier, laughing to myself.

With the safe cleared, it's time to head out. But I stop next to the man on the floor and can see he's still breathing. I consider putting a round through him, but think it would be gratuitous, so instead, I squat down and yank his wallet out of his back pocket. I open it up and pull out his driver's license, library card, and an old condom.

"Wishful thinkin', huh bud?"

I toss them all to the floor, then pull out the cash and drop the wallet. It bounces off his head and lands in the small puddle of blood forming around his head. He groans but doesn't wake as I count the cash in his wallet.

"Twelve bucks? Seriously?" I ask.

He groans again and seems to be on the verge of waking up. I get up and walk to the door that leads to the back, open it, and step through into the back of the shop. I pause just inside the doorway when I find Sasha crouched down over the man on the floor with a bloody knife in her hand. She looks up at me guiltily, a flush crossing her face.

"What are you doing?" I ask.

"Makin' him prettier."

I walk over and see that she's been using the tip of her knife on the flesh of his cheeks. She's carving a flower into his skin, making me purse my lips as I look at her.

"That's going to leave a nasty scar," I comment.

"That's kinda the point," she replies. "Now, whenever he

wakes up in the morning, he'll get to see somethin' beautiful. Daisies. Who doesn't like looking at daisies?"

I arch an eyebrow at her. "Was that really necessary?"

"Necessary? No. Fun? Absolutely," she replies. "So, did you get the goods, baby?"

I dangle the bag. "You know I did."

"Then let's go party," she says. "We can't keep our guest waiting."

"Lead the way."

Sasha skips out of the store, pausing only when I stop to close the door behind me. She takes my hand, swinging it wildly as she skips along. I drop the bag into the back seat, and we climb in. Sasha gives me a hard kiss, then drums her hands on the dashboard excitedly.

"I love you," I tell her.

"And I love you, baby."

I start the car and drop it into gear, pulling out of the lot, and take care to drive like a normal, law-abiding citizen. Ten minutes later, we're parked and are walking into the apartment complex. Walking hand in hand, we find our destination, letting ourselves in with the key we'd procured earlier in the day.

"Honey, we're home," I call out.

Sasha giggles as she races ahead of me, bounding down the hallway. I set the bag of money I retrieved from the trunk down on the dining room table. There was no way I was leaving that in the car. The world is full of thieves, after all, and I don't trust anybody. I pull a small leather bundle from the canvas bag and then walk into the kitchen. Opening the fridge, I lean down and frown when I don't see any beer.

"Who doesn't have any beer in the house?" I mutter to myself.

I grab the open bottle of chardonnay and pull the cork out

with my teeth, then spit it across the room and take a big swallow of it. A healthy belch escapes me as I wipe my mouth with the back of my hand. Grinning and feeling good, I saunter down the hallway to the bedroom where she's waiting for me. I lean against the doorjamb and look at the scene before me, my smile growing even wider.

"I hope you girls are having a good time getting to know each other," I say.

Sasha looks up at me, her lower lip stuck out in a pout. "She's not much of a talker."

"No? Well, that's alright," I say.

She gets off the edge of the bed and walks over to me, giving me a long, sensual, lingering kiss. I feel my arousal growing as I gaze at the brunette we'd picked out a couple of days ago when we planned the robbery. She's naked and laying spread eagle, her ankles and wrists bound to the four posters of her bed.

Sasha walks back over and drops down on the bed next to her. She traces the tip of her finger around the brunette's stomach. The girl, probably no more than twenty-one or twenty-two and a student at the University of Washington, is stunning. Sasha always picks out the pretty ones for me. Tears spill from the corners of the brunette's eyes and her entire body trembles as Sasha plants a gentle kiss on her stomach.

Sasha sits up and turns to me, giving me a wink. Then she walks over to the tripod and starts messing with the camera, making sure it's all in frame. She looks at me and smiles.

"All set here," she says.

I lay the leather bundle down on top of the girl's dresser, untie it, then roll it out. I got this shortly after Sasha and I met and started doing our thing. A kit like this became necessary. The light in the room gleams off the razor-sharp edges of the different blades in my kit and I reach for my favorite, holding it up for the brunette to see. Her eyes grow wide and she starts to scream, but the gag in her mouth muffles her cries.

I turn to the brunette, feeling my arousal growing. But Sasha puts her hand down over mine and shakes her head.

"Not yet, baby," she whispers. "You know what to do. Give me what I want before you get what you want."

"Of course, my love," I grin.

She smiles at me then reaches down and unbuckles my belt. As I set the blade down, Sasha unzips my pants and gives me a swat on the butt. The brunette is trying to scream through her gag and is thrashing wildly on top of the bed, trying to break her bonds. But I know how to tie a knot and she's not going anywhere.

"Get on over there and give her what she wants, baby," Sasha says.

I give her a smile as Sasha starts recording, then jump up onto the bed with the brunette and smile at her. She's sobbing wildly, her eyes are red, and she keeps pulling at her bonds. The frustration and fear on her face are so thick, I can almost smell it – and it's a heady aroma that fuels my arousal. I look down at the brunette and smile.

"Don't use up all that energy right now. We're only just getting started," I tell her. "And we've got a long night ahead of us."

ONE

THE MURMUR of Mark's voice drifts to me in the bedroom.
The acoustics in this place do weird things. Even though he's
out in the living room, I can hear him all the way back here. But
I can tell he's keeping his voice low, as if he doesn't want me to
overhear what he's saying. I'm not a jealous woman by nature,
but the fact that he seems to be deliberately hiding his conversation from me is a bit irksome. It's not jealousy. It's that I don't
like liars, and I dislike cheaters even more.

Mark and I have been seeing more of each other lately,
even though I told him up front that I wasn't looking for
anything serious. I told him that my job comes first. And yet, he
spends most nights here with me. And the real kick in the butt
is that I like having him here. I'm more attached to him than I
ever wanted to be. I'm probably more attached to him than I'm
willing to admit – even to myself.

Mark is a doctor who patched me up after one of my more

exciting adventures a while back. We started seeing each other after that, until I transferred to New York. But eventually, I grew tired of the Big Apple, and with the help of my good, well-connected friend, Paxton Arrington,I was able to finagle a promotion and transfer back here to Seattle. Then, as luck, or fate – or whatever you want to call it – would have it, our paths crossed again. And here we are.

I walk into the bathroom and pull my hair back, tying it into a tight ponytail. After that, I finish buttoning up my cream-colored shirt and tuck it into black slacks. I walk back into the bedroom and sit down on the edge of the bed, slip on my black ankle boots, and then pull the hems of my slacks down over them.

I grab a black jacket off a hanger in the closet, slip it on, and look at myself in the mirror. I'm sure I'll never be invited to walk a runway in Paris, but then, those waifs aren't likely going to be kicking in doors and taking down killers anytime soon, either. So, it's a wash. Like my boots, I'm not overly stylish, but I'm functional.

"Good enough," I mutter to myself.

I walk out of the bedroom and down the hallway to the living room. Mark is standing at the window that overlooks the city with his back to me. He must hear me coming, because I see his shoulders tense. It's very subtle, but I'm not only very observant, I'm also very well trained to look for the subtle things. He clicks off his call and slips the phone into his back pocket, then turns around.

"Hey, good morning," he says brightly. "I didn't hear you get out of the shower."

"Yeah, you seemed pretty involved in your phone call," I reply.

"Coffee's in the kitchen."

"Oh, thanks."

I walk in and grab my travel mug out of the cabinet, then fill it up and dress it. I stir it all up and then put the lid on. I turn around and find Mark leaning against the wall, mug of coffee in hand, looking at me. I take a sip of my coffee and return his gaze in silence for a moment.

"Who were you talking to?" I ask.

"Oh, it was a call from the hospital. They just wanted a consult on a case. Nothing big."

"Oh, yeah?"

He nods. "Yep."

"What was the case?"

Mark cocks his head with a crooked grin on his face. "Are you flashing those impressive FBI interrogation skills for any particular reason?"

I chuckle softly. "Believe me, if I were actually interrogating you, it would sound much different."

"So, what's going on, then? Why are you acting so weird?"

"I'm not acting weird," I reply. "What's weird is your feeling the need to take a call and whisper all secretively."

It's Mark's turn to laugh softly now. "Are you jealous? Is that what this is?" he asks. "Do you think I was talking to another woman or something?"

"Were you?"

I hear myself talking and my brain is telling me to shut up, but my mouth isn't listening. And the more I hear myself rambling on, the more I cringe. I swear to God, my foot is so deep in my mouth I'm choking on it. But I just can't seem to stop.

"What's going on here, Blake? What is this all about?"

I shrug. "Nothing. Forget it."

"Seriously, Blake. What's up here?"

I lean against the counter and take a drink of my coffee, silently wishing that the earth would open up and swallow me whole. I've told myself over and over again that I will not let myself get this attached to Mark. That I'm not in a place where I should even be thinking about being seriously involved with anybody. Mark has honored that and hasn't pressured me to put a label on what it is we have or demanded more of my time – nothing like that. So why am I acting like a crazy woman?

"Are you seeing somebody else, Mark?"

He shakes his head, a bewildered expression on his face. "What?"

"I mean, it's fine if you are. We're not exclusive or anything," I say. "But I think just as a matter of respect, you'd tell me. Especially if you're sleeping with –"

"Whoa, whoa, whoa. Slow down. Let's back that pony up. I'm not seeing, let alone sleeping with, anybody else," he says. "And correct me if I'm wrong, but wasn't it you who said you didn't want anything serious right now? I mean, maybe I'm crazy, but I seem to recall your telling me that your job comes first."

I gnaw on my bottom lip, knowing everything he's saying is true and that I have no defense for my neurotic outburst. But it just felt as though he was sneaking around behind my back with his whispered phone call. And it's not the first time he's done it. He's usually a little bit more discreet about it, but he's had those sorts of whispered conversations before.

"That was you, right? That was you who said that?" he presses.

"Yeah, it was. And I stand by that," I tell him. "But if you're in a place where you want something serious right now, that's fine. It's alright. You just have to tell me that's where you're at, rather than sneaking around behind my back."

"I'm not sneaking around behind your back, Blake."

"Yeah well, these secretive, whispered conversations kind of make it seem as if you are."

He sighs and pulls out his phone. He taps a few keys on it and holds it out to me. "Go ahead and look at my call history. Look at my text history, too, if it'll make you feel better," he snaps.

I don't reach for the phone though, because I know it's a trap. I can't take the phone without looking like a possessive, crazy person. And he knows that, which is possibly why he's offering me his phone in the first place.

"Go ahead," he says. "Search my phone to your heart's content."

"Just forget it."

He walks over and grabs my hand, pressing his phone into it. I roll my eyes with a sigh and thrust the phone back at him. But he doesn't take it, gesturing to it instead.

"Look at it, Blake. I've got nothing to hide," he says earnestly.

I know the root of this explosion of neuroses – I've been cheated on before. And for most of my life since then, it hasn't really affected me. I haven't really thought about it since it happened. But that speaks to the fact that I'm more attached to Mark than I should have ever let myself get. The idea that he could be cheating on me hurts because I actually care. Because it feels as if I actually have something to lose.

My mind is screaming at me to not look at the phone. To not give into my insecure, paranoid brain. But my eyes betray me and move downward despite my best efforts to resist. The name on the most recent call is Dr. Frank Schmidt. I note the time and duration of the call and feel like the biggest idiot in the world. I hand the phone back to him silently.

"So, unless you're accusing me of running around with Frank behind your back..."

He gives me a smile as his words trail off. My cheeks flare with heat and I'm sure I'm turning an unnatural shade of red.

"I'm sorry," I say. "I don't know what's going on with me."

"It's alright," he replies graciously. "Just know that I'd never disrespect you that way. If I felt as if I wanted something more, or met somebody else, I'd give you the respect of telling you, Blake. I care about you and I'd never do that to you."

I feel like such a fool that I have no words. All I can do is nod. Mark takes my hand and gives it a squeeze, making me look up at him. His smile is soft, his expression kind. He'd have every right to go off and scream like a banshee, but he's gracious. He's always gracious and kind to me. And it's times like these when I feel as if I don't deserve it.

"I don't have to be in for rounds for a while yet," he says. "How about some breakfast?"

I give him a sheepish smile. "I actually need to get to work," I say. "How about I make up for my barrage of idiocy with dinner tonight?"

"That sounds great. Text me later."

"I'll do that," I tell him and raise my travel mug. "Thanks for the coffee."

"Hey, anytime."

I give him a peck on the cheek and start to head for the front door but stop and turn around. He's taking a drink from his mug, watching me.

"I'm sorry for being an idiot," I tell him.

"We all have our moments. But hey, silver lining... at least I know you care," he says and tips me a wink.

I laugh. "Yeah, well, don't let that go to your head or anything."

"Too late."

I roll my eyes and laugh as I walk out of my apartment and head out for the day.

TWO

"SOMEBODY SHOOT YOUR DOG THIS MORNING?"

I look up to find the tall, elegant runway-ready Astra leaning against my office doorway, a grin on her face. Her silver-blue eyes are framed by her long, midnight-black hair and tawny skin that is utterly flawless. She's lean, but has the kind of curves that can make a grown man blush. I drop the pen I'm gnawing on and sit back in my seat, trying to ignore how positively ordinary I feel next to her. I mean, I think I'm attractive enough, in that girl-next-door kind of way. But standing next to Astra, I feel like a total Plain Jane.

She's also brilliant, has bigger stones than most of the boys, and is one of the best field agents I've ever worked with. Astra is intuitive and almost has a sixth sense about her that's usually so accurate, it's kind of spooky sometimes. She was the first person I picked when I was given the green light to put my team together. Most assume it's because we're best friends, but the fact of the matter is she is simply one of the best in the entire Bureau, as far as I'm concerned. Having her in my unit makes us that much better.

"Don't have a dog," I say.

"Somebody pee in your Cheerios?"

"Don't eat Cheerios."

Astra walks in and drops down into the chair on the other side of my desk. She crosses her legs and folds her hands in her lap, never taking her eyes off me.

"So, what has you looking like such a little ray of sunshine this morning?" Astra asks.

I drain the last of the coffee in my travel mug and frown, trying to decide whether to go get a refill or not. It's probably too early for anything stronger.

"Come on, Wilder," Astra presses. "What's going on with you this morning?"

"Nothing," I reply. "I'm fine."

"That's garbage. Remember, I'm a highly trained federal agent and am far more observant than the average bear," she says with a grin on her face.

That finally gets me to crack a smile. "Unfortunately for me, that is true."

A look of triumph crosses Astra's face as she settles back in her seat and looks at me expectantly. Astra and I have been best friends since the Academy, and she's one of the few people who can read me like a book. It's something I appreciate about her – and something that irritates me at the same time.

"So, spill it, Wilder. What has you looking so constipated this morning?"

"I do not look constipated," I reply with a laugh.

"Your face is all pinched and tight. Your eyes are all squinty and your lips are pursed," she notes. "Yeah, you totally look constipated."

A laugh bursts from my throat. "Okay, can we stop using that word? It's disgusting."

"Would you prefer stopped up? Obstructed?"

"I'd prefer you don't use metaphors like that at all."

"Well, you're no fun," she huffs.

Astra is one of the only people in the world who can pull me out of a funk and get me laughing like this. Her sense of humor is irreverent, borderline offensive, and has a lot in common with the mindset of teenage boys. But she can always manage to lighten the mood and make me feel as if my world isn't actually crashing down around me.

It's a rare skill and a gift. But it makes sense, and I cherish it. Astra is one of the very, very limited number of people I allow myself to be vulnerable around. With her, I feel as though I can be myself, for the good, bad, or indifferent. I don't have many good friends, mostly because people don't usually get me. Astra does. Has since day one, and I've always been grateful that she's part of my life.

"Mark and I had an argument this morning," I finally relent.

"Oh?" she asks, arching an eyebrow. "Did you at least get to have some mind-blowing make-up sex afterward?"

"Unfortunately, no."

"So, what did you do?"

"What makes you think it's something I did?" I ask.

"Because if it was something Mark did, you'd be more than willing to share," she replies. "But because you're sitting in here looking angry with shades of guilty, it's easy to see that it's something you did."

I shake my head, grinning at her. "You're far too smart for my own good."

Astra taps her temple with a fingertip. "It's more than just a hat rack, my friend."

"Clearly," I say with a sigh.

I drum my fingers on my desktop and feel my smile slipping. But then I tell Astra everything that happened this morning. And as I talk, I see her smiling wider with every word that falls out of my mouth. When I'm finished, I narrow my eyes and glare at her.

"What?" I demand.

She shrugs. "I just never thought I'd see the day when the legendary Blake Wilder was all hung up and strung out on a man."

"I am not hung up and strung out."

"Oh, honey, you absolutely are," she says. "This random explosion of crazy? Yeah, that's proof of it."

"Shut up," I tell her with a smile, knowing she's right.

"I won't and you can't make me," she replies and sticks her tongue out at me.

Sitting forward in my seat, I replay the whole morning in my head, silently kicking myself repeatedly for it.

"Okay, so you screwed up. He's not cheating on you," Astra says. "You guys will laugh about this at some point down the line. These things happen in a relationship."

"So, you've gone full psycho on Benjamin?"

"Well, maybe not to the extent you did, but yeah, I've had my moments."

A rueful smile curls a corner of my mouth upward. "I knew this was a bad idea. I knew I never should have gotten back with him in the first place."

"Don't say that. You need to be open to the possibility of love," she says. "Or at least, you need to know that you actually have....feelings. Like a normal person. You need to be reminded that you're not a robot. If nothing else, you need to be reminded that there are more layers to you than your FBI Super Chick persona."

"I happen to like being FBI Super Chick. I love what I do."

"And there's nothing wrong with that, Blake," Astra says. "But you're not just that. And if this morning's Chernobyl-esque neurotic meltdown served any purpose, it's that it reminds you of that. Having normal feelings and emotions is a good thing. And having normal grown-up interactions and relationships is too."

"Yeah well, I didn't feel like a normal grown-up this morning," I tell her. "I don't even remember feeling that crazy when I was a hormone-riddled teenage girl."

"You're beating yourself up too much about this, you know," she says. "He's apparently moving on from it while you sit here and continue flogging yourself. I mean, I know that's your thing and all, but maybe you should take this all as a lesson learned and move on?"

"Yeah, I know. Maybe so."

Astra looks at me closely, doing that thing with her eyes that tells me she's peering into the deep recesses of my soul. I hate it when she does that, because she usually dredges up the emotional crap that I'm trying to hide from everybody, including myself.

"What is it?" she asks. "There's more to it than you've said so far."

"You can't possibly know that."

"And yet, I do, which means I'm either psychic, really good at my job, or know you that well," she replies. "So, spill it."

I frown and try to put my thoughts in order. I know that expressing what's going through my mind is going to make me sound even more insane and insecure than I already feel. But it's a thought that's stuck in my brain and I can't get it out. It's like a song that's just playing on repeat and I can't make it stop.

"It's just... I don't know. This is going to sound nuts," I start.

"Most of what you say sounds nuts. But go ahead anyway."

"It's just that it feels as if there's something he still isn't telling me. That there's something he's still hiding," I say.

Astra frowns. "So, you think this Dr. Frank guy may be a cover for another woman? Like maybe put her number in under this other guy's name to throw you, just in case you asked?"

"Maybe. I don't know."

"I dated a guy once who asked for my number and I happened to glance over when he was putting it in under the name of Aaron. And when I called him on it, he copped to being married. Said he needed to camouflage my name, if you can believe it," she says with a wry laugh. "Suffice it to say, I told him to lose my number – after giving him a swift kick in the junk."

It is not difficult at all to picture Astra doing just that. And given that she was a soccer star back in college, I'm pretty sure the guy wasn't walking right for a few days afterward.

"I'm not sure that's what's going on here. He spends too many nights at my place for him to be married," I say.

"Doesn't mean he doesn't have a side piece," she offers.

"No, I know. Maybe," I reply. "But as I've sat here thinking about it –"

"Brooding."

I cock my head as I look at her. "What?"

"Brooding. The technical name for what you were doing is called brooding."

I laugh. "Fine. While I was sitting here brooding, I just kind of got the idea that it has nothing to do with another woman at all. There's something....else."

"Something like what?"

I shake my head. "That much, I don't know," I admit. "I mean, I don't know anything. This could just be my brain jumping at shadows that aren't even there. It was just a feeling."

"You're the one who always tells me to trust my instincts, Blake. You always say they'll never lead me astray," she parrots words I've said to her about a billion times. "For the good or the ill, your instincts will lead you to the truth of things."

"Even if I don't like where they're going."

"Right. But at least you'll be arriving at the truth of the matter," she nods. "Better to confront a hard truth you don't like that hurts you, than to walk around in bliss because you're being deceived."

"Ain't that the truth," I reply, then look up at her. "What's your take on him? Is Mark the type to keep secrets?"

"Honey, we all keep secrets. The question isn't whether somebody is the type. The question is what secrets does he have, and will they hurt you?"

I can always count on Astra to give me the unvarnished truth of things. She'll always give me a blunt assessment without sugarcoating her words. It's tough to take sometimes. She's brutally honest and there are times it's difficult to hear what she has to say. But it's something I appreciate about her – even if only in retrospect.

"But as far as Mark goes, I can't see him running around behind your back. I want to believe he's a good guy who really cares about you," she goes on. "That being said, any man has the ability to morph into an absolute prick. So, trust your instincts. If they're telling you something's funny, listen to them. Don't just brush them off as craziness on your part."

I give her a soft smile and a nod. Her words are wise and as always, I appreciate her candor. Through the wall of windows behind her, I see the rest of the team filtering into the shop. Though I don't necessarily feel better about the situation, she's given me a kick in the butt I desperately needed.

"Team's here. We should get to work," I say.

She gets to her feet and flashes me a smile before she heads for the door, but I stop her.

"Thanks for listening and talking," I tell her. "You're a good friend, Astra."

"Correction. I'm a great friend," she states with a grin. "And you're welcome. God knows, you've been there to listen to me more times than I can count."

She heads to her station out in the bullpen as I gather up my things and try to push everything that happened this morning out of my mind, along with my lingering suspicions. I don't want to be distracted by any of it.

It's time to get to work.

THREE

Criminal Data Analysis Unit; Seattle Field Office

"Okay, boys and girls –"

"Boy. It's boy and girls," my tech analyst and class clown, Rick Scanlon calls from his station at the back of the room. "Since, you know, I'm the only man in the room, it's –"

Astra turns in her seat and throws a ball of crumpled up paper that bounces off his forehead, cutting off his words.

"Shut up, Rick," Astra says. "Mo is more of a man than you are."

Special Agent Maureen Weissman – Mo to all of us – formerly of the white-collar crime division, turns and gives Rick a small shrug, a mischievous smile on her face.

"Sorry, bud. It's true though," she says.

Rick shoots her an obscene gesture that gets them all laughing. Maureen, a former cop with the Seattle PD, is a solid woman. She's a couple inches shorter than me, but has a good twenty-five pounds of solid muscle on me. Her dirty blonde hair is cut almost military short, and she's got eyes the color of milk chocolate. Mo can be intense and she's a little bit... rigid. To her, there's a right way and a wrong way to do things. She's started to loosen up a little bit, and laughs a bit more than she did on day one, but she's still a work in progress.

Rick is a civilian contractor and is the epitome of a hipster. He's got shaggy light brown hair that looks as though it's never seen a brush, and is about my height, maybe an inch taller. He's a bit stocky, has a bushy beard, and hazel-colored eyes hidden behind his horn-rimmed glasses. He only buys his clothes at second-hand vintage stores and is the kind of guy who will only drink craft beers while listening to his vinyl records. He's actually said they sound better.

Mo and Rick have formed what I consider an unlikely friendship, but there's no questioning the bond between them. Neither of them had any experience with this side of the Bureau before. Neither of them had worked violent criminal investigations, so it's been a bit of a learning curve with them. The biggest obstacle so far has been getting them over their squeamishness and aversion to blood. But they're starting to come around. Or at least, are learning to avoid looking at the particularly gruesome bits.

So, that's my team. They're my new family, dysfunctional as we can be sometimes. But there's no question that for all our quirks and idiosyncrasies, we do good work. We've put some bad people away, saved some lives, and in my humble opinion, have lived up to our billing. As Astra once said, we're small but mighty.

"Alright, settle down, children. We've got a case," I announce, pacing at the front of the bullpen.

"Time to earn our paychecks," Astra says.

"This is one I've been tracking for a long time now," I tell them. "He was quiet for a while and fell off the radar, but he's back."

"How many bodies are we talking?" Mo asks.

"Not bodies. Robberies," I correct her. "This unsub hits payday loan and check cashing stores. Over the past five years, I can connect twelve of them to our unsub. I'm assuming when he went dark, he was knocking over stores in other states. But you know how local PDs are about sharing with us."

"Robberies? I thought we were focused on serial killers," Mo says, a hint of disappointment in her voice.

"We're focused on serial crime in general," I tell her. "I know it's not as sexy as taking down a serial killer, but these are real crimes, and real people are getting hurt."

"How do you know the twelve you've flagged are connected to the same guy?" Astra asks.

"Same basic description of the unsub. Same MO," I reply. "I've seen surveillance footage from all twelve scenes, and I'm satisfied it's the same guy."

I walk over to the tall table where I've got a laptop set up and pull up the file I've put together on this case. Across the four large computer screens mounted to the wall at the front of the bullpen, the surveillance footage from the first four stores he hit starts to play. All four show the perp coming in right around closing time, moving hard and low.

On all four screens, he disables the employees, then turns and hits the camera with spray paint to obscure the view. Once the screens go dark, I play the next set of four. And then the final set of four. I tap a key to end the show-and-tell portion of the briefing, and turn to them.

"What did you guys notice?" I ask.

"The guy is efficient. Moves with purpose," Astra notes.

"I read that as a guy with military or police training," Mo says.

"Could be," I say and nod. "I had the same thought."

"He could also just be one of these militia jagoffs," Rick

adds. "They like to pretend they're hardcore military types. They train like soldiers for – whatever reason. I consider it LARPing for military fetishists."

"LARPing?" Astra asks.

"Live action role play," Mo explains. "People like to dress up and go out into the woods to live out their Dungeons and Dragons fantasies."

"Or their military, super soldier -fantasies," Rick says.

"That, too."

I nod, taking it all in. This is good. This is all really good stuff. To be honest, I hadn't considered the militia angle before, and it's worth keeping in mind.

"Did you guys notice anything else?" I ask.

"You already know the answer, don't you?" Mo says with a grin.

"Of course, she does," Astra says. "She wants to see how observant we are."

I turn to Astra. "So, do you have the answer?"

"Of course, I do," she replies. "I am a genius and an FBI Super Chick too, after all."

"Oh, I know you are," I say and turn to Mo. "Did you pick up on it?"

Mo looks at me blankly. "No, I'm afraid I didn't."

I turn back to Astra and give her a nod. She gets to her feet and goes over to the laptop, then plays the first set of surveillance videos. I lean back against the wall and fold my arms over my chest, letting her take the reins. I knew she'd see it right off. As I said, she's observant and intuitive. The woman misses almost nothing.

"In this set – the early crimes – we see that our unsub is economical and efficient," she starts. "He gets in and gets out with the cash."

Astra turns back to the laptop and pulls up another set of

surveillance videos. "Note the dates," she continues, pointing to the date stamps in the corners of the screens. "About two years ago, our boy started getting violent. Really started to beat on the employees."

"I don't see a change. In all the videos, he beat the employees. It looks as if he knocked them out before stealing all the cash," Mo says.

"That's true. He disabled all the employees we've seen. But in those early videos, he did it quickly and efficiently. One blow to the head and they were down, and then he went about his business," Astra explains, replaying those initial videos again.

She cuts off the early videos, then calls up another set of four. She pushes play and they all start rolling. Both of us are watching Mo to see if she's getting it yet. And when I see her eyes widen slightly, I know she has. Astra pauses the videos.

"Starting about two years ago, our boy started getting off-the-charts violent," Astra continues. "He was really beating on those employees, even after he put them on the ground. He seemed to be enjoying it. He seemed to be getting off on inflicting as much pain and damage on these people as he could."

"So, what changed?" Rick asks.

"That's the question we need to answer. Or at least, one of them. But there is no doubt something changed somewhere along the way," I say. "This guy went from quick, efficient robberies, to taking the time out to bludgeon the people he encountered within an inch of their lives. A couple of them have sustained permanent damage because of him."

"So, I'm assuming that because this is on our plate now, he struck again last night?" Astra asks.

"You have a wisdom beyond your years, dear child."

"So, I guess we're headed out to Bellevue?" she asks.

"We are indeed," I nod, then turn to Rick and Mo. "I need

for you two to start combing through any reports of robberies with similar MOs in the surrounding states. I want to see if we can fill in the gaps in this guy's timeline and trace his movements."

"Could be we get lucky and somebody remembers him," Mo says.

"We're never that lucky," Rick groans.

"There's a first time for everything," I tell him.

Astra and I grab our things and head out. No, it's not as sexy as running down a serial killer, but we're in the business of fighting all crime – not just tracking down the worst of the worst. And knowing that innocent people are being hurt adds a couple of logs to the fires burning inside of me, stoking the flames.

I want to get justice for these people every bit as much as I want to get a violent thug off the streets.

FOUR

"FBI. Huh," Detective Nash says. "Didn't think a simple robbery would warrant a visit from the Feds."

"It's a little more complicated than that," I reply as I slip my credentials back into the pocket of my blazer.

The sky overhead is a deep, azure blue with fat, fluffy clouds lazily drifting across that ocean above. It's in the low sixties, the sort of perfect day people don't think we get in the Pacific Northwest. When you say Seattle, most people immediately conjure up images of a gray wasteland where rain is the only weather. And although we do get our fair share of rain up here, we also get picture-perfect days like this.

I'm standing alone with Detective Donald Nash of the Bellevue PD, and he's looking at me as if I'm Typhoid Mary. Needless to say, like a lot of local law enforcement officers, he's not a big fan of the FBI. I swear to God, some of the cretins who came before me destroyed the Bureau's reputation because they couldn't work and play well together with the locals. Some guys see our Bureau creds as a club to beat the locals into submission. Obviously, that sort of attitude has left a lot of hard feelings in its wake.

"Complicated?" he asks.

I nod. "I believe this is just one in a long series of robberies that I've been investigating for the last five years."

He scoffs. "Five years and you ain't caught this guy yet? I'd say you're not very good at your job, then."

I bristle but bite back the acidic reply that's sitting on the tip of my tongue. Nash looks to be about middle-aged and he's carrying a chip on his shoulder larger than me. He's got iron-gray hair, a Sam Elliot-style bushy mustache, and sharp green eyes. I get the feeling that his slow drawl and laid back, "aw shucks," demeanor is nothing but camouflage for a sharp intelligence and determined intensity. He invites people to underestimate him. Wants them to. But it's a trap that will bite you in the butt every single time if you're dumb enough to fall for it. Fortunately for me, I'm not that dumb.

"If you don't mind, I'd like to tour the crime scene," I say.

"And if I do mind?"

I sigh. "Detective Nash, there's no need for things to be contentious between us. We're on the same team –"

He chuckles. "I'm not even sure we're playin' the same sport, Agent Wilder."

"I assure you that we are. And that we both want the same thing – to catch whoever it is who robbed this place and put two innocent people in the hospital," I growl. "I mean, the last I checked, we were both in the business of protecting people, saving lives, and putting criminals in prison where they belong. Or has something changed with your mission statement?"

There's more heat in my voice than I intended. I'd meant to keep things as civil as possible, but this guy is really pushing my buttons. It has the desired effect, though. He looks down at the ground, an embarrassed expression crossing his face. He finally raises his head and looks at me.

"You're right. And I apologize, Agent Wilder. That was discourteous and unprofessional," he says. "It's just been a long night here."

"Long night?"

He nods. "In addition to dealing with this, we had one of the most savage murders I've ever seen last night," he explains. "We're spread pretty thin and we're all a bit tense. Things like this just don't usually happen here. I mean, we have our fair share of crime here, don't get me wrong. But the way that girl was cut up – it's somethin' I'll never get out of my head."

"I'm sorry, Detective," I say, my curiosity piqued. "Anything connecting the two crimes?"

"Nah. Not that I can see," he frowns. "We're zeroing in on that girl's boyfriend. I expect we'll be pickin' him up today."

I nod, but my mind is working. It seems an unlikely coincidence that this place would be robbed and that a brutal murder would take place on the same night. Especially given that Bellevue historically has a very low rate of homicides. If I recall correctly, Bellevue only gets at most one or two murders per year, which is astonishing for a city of its size. The highest total in any one year was three and that was a decade and a half ago. By all metrics, Bellevue is one of the safest cities in the country.

But, unless there is something that definitively connects these two crimes, I'm chasing shadows. I need to focus on the crime that brought us here. I'll keep an eye on the murder discreetly, just in case it's part of a string.

"If you don't mind, may I have a word with the boyfriend when you do pick him up?" I ask.

He nods. "I think we can arrange that."

"Thank you, Detective," I say. "Now, is there anything you can tell me about the robbery? Anything stand out?"

"Seems pretty straightforward. Perp came in through the back door. Bashed one of the employees to gain entry. Then moved to the front," he said. "Really worked the poor guy over somethin' fierce. Took all the cash from the drawers and the safe, then for whatever reason, stopped to carve a flower into the first guy's face."

"A flower?"

He nods. "That's what it looks like to me. Poor guy's gonna have a daisy-shaped scar on his face for the rest of his life."

"Huh. That's weird."

"What's weird?"

I turn as Astra steps up beside me and fill her in on what Nash has told me. I can't help but notice that as I'm speaking to Astra, Nash is gawking at her. As in, wide-eyed, open-mouthed gawking. It's all I can do to keep speaking and not break into laughter. Astra is much more practiced at ignoring the gawkers than I am and is totally unfazed by it. When I finish the story, she frowns.

"Sadistic," she mutters.

"Very," I reply. "But why take the time to stop and carve a design into the guy's face?"

"Maybe the guy popped off to him," Astra offers. "Maybe it was to teach him a lesson."

"I can say for sure that Robbie Dutch – that's the guy who's gonna be wearin' that scar – is a smartass. It seems likely to me that he said somethin' stupid," Nash confirms.

I nod again, but it still seems like quite a risk to take, time-wise. But I shelve it for the moment. We can return to that later. Right now, I need to see the scene.

"Detective Nash, would you mind if we went in and took a look at the scene?" I ask.

"By all means," he nods.

"Thank you."

Astra and I turn and walk across the parking lot toward the store. She leans closer to me and pitches her voice low, so only I can hear what she's saying.

"That guy is not happy we're here," she says.

"Oh, I'm quite sure he's thrilled *you're* here. I could see it in the way he was drooling on himself," I reply. "The Bureau, though? Not so much."

She laughs and nudges me with her shoulder and laughs. "Shut up."

We walk into the store and all activity stops. A dozen pairs of eyes turn to us, expressions of curiosity, skepticism, and even open hostility. We're used to it. We get looks like this all the time whenever we have to liaise with local PD. I've found the best way to deal with it is to just go about our business. Either they'll go back to ignoring us, or one of these yutzes will get it in his mind to confront us, at which point, I'll humiliate him – and then we'll go about our business anyway.

Astra and I walk behind the front counter and I see the fingerprinting powder all over the different surfaces. At scenes like this, we usually like to divide and conquer – the sooner we get in, the sooner we can get out. I like to think of it as working smarter, not harder. But the truth is, I like to get in and out of the crime scenes quickly, because it seems that the longer we stay, the more chance there is of somebody working up the steam to confront us. Every PD has those hotheads and guys whose disdain for the Bureau trumps their common sense.

Astra stops beside the dark, dried patch of blood on the cheap carpeting to talk with one of the blood-spatter guys. I see one of the crime scene techs, a young Asian woman, dusting the safe in the back. Whenever we invade a crime scene, I usually look for the youngest techs. They're less apt to be cynical and jaded about talking to the Feds, and are most likely to be more forthcoming with the information.

"Hey," I say and flash her my creds. "Blake Wilder."

She gives me a smile. "Lily Park. Good to meet you."

Lily is probably in her mid-twenties, but looks even younger than that. She's diminutive, no more than five-three and ninety-nine pounds soaking wet. She's got long black hair that's tied back into a ponytail, dark, almond shaped eyes, and has fawn-colored skin. She's a pretty girl who looks as if she was usually the smartest one in class.

"You, too," I say. "You guys find anything yet?"

She shakes her head. "So far, nothing. The prints we've found belong to employees," she says. "I'm kind of thinking our guy was smart enough wear gloves."

Based on the past surveillance footage I've seen, she's right. He always wears gloves and a black balaclava so only his eyes can be seen. But I can hope that he'll make a mistake, can't I? His increasing violence could indicate that he's spiraling, which could lead an unsub to screwing up. But as I think about it more, that doesn't jibe with the controlled, efficient movements we see before he blacks out the cameras. When he first storms the store, he's in perfect control. There's no spiraling to be seen. So why is he growing more violent and savage with each robbery?

"Hey, did you hear anything about a murder last night?" I ask.

She nods and her face practically turns white. "Yeah. I helped process that crime scene," she says grimly. "Most horrible thing I've ever seen – and I've seen some things."

"They still working the scene?"

"Yeah, they're going to be there a while," she says. "There's a lot to process and Bellevue PD isn't exactly up on the latest, most efficient methods, if you know what I mean."

Sadly, I do. It's common for towns and cities that have murder rates that hover around zero to not have the latest and greatest, cutting-edge crime scene units. A lot of these departments still do things old school. Really old school. It's disappointing to see, because there's a lot that gets missed. Justice is often delayed, if not outright denied, simply because they don't have a forensics unit that's up to the task.

"Happen to remember the address of that murder?" I ask.

"1208 Bellwood Avenue," she replies instantly. "Apartment 234."

"Sharp memory," I note, impressed.

"Not quite eidetic, but close."

"I've got a friend like you," I tell her. "His recall is downright spooky."

She grins wide. "It's pretty handy, I've found."

"Yeah, I bet. Is there anything else you can tell me about this crime scene? You find any nuggets of information that can help?"

"Unfortunately, I'm only on prints at this scene and so far it's squat," she replies. "What is the Bureau's interest in this anyway?"

"I'm pretty sure this isn't this guy's first rodeo," I tell her. "And his level of violence is increasing with each robbery, which is worrisome. I'd like to stop him before he graduates from assault to murder."

Her eyes widen and her mouth falls open. "Oh, do you think that's possible?"

"I'd say, given his current trajectory, it's not just possible, it's likely."

"Oh, that's bad. I wish I had something for you, Agent Wilder. I really do."

"It's alright. It was a long shot anyway," I say and hand her one of my business cards. "But can you do me a favor? If you hear anything that might help, could you give me a call?"

"You got it."

"Oh, one more thing. Do you think you'd be able to send me a copy of the surveillance footage?" I ask, pointing to the security camera.

"Yeah, sure. I can do that."

"Great. My email address is at the bottom of the card."

She slips it into her pocket and smiles. "Hey, what does it take to get a job in the FBI forensics lab?"

"Putting in an application is a solid first step," I say with a laugh. "Thinking about changing things up?"

"I think my skills would be better used in a... broader setting," she says. "Bellevue PD is great and all, but most days I feel as if I'm rotting on the vine here."

"Tell you what," I say. "You send in your application and I'll put in a good word for you."

"You'd do that?"

I nod. "I would."

"I'd really appreciate that, Agent Wilder."

"No problem, Lily."

"Poaching the local talent?" Astra whispers as I step away back to the crime scene. "No wonder people hate us."

I give her a crooked grin. "Looks as though they're coming up empty here. I figured they would," I say. "But I'm going to want to talk to the two employees."

"Robbie Dutch the smartass, and Chris Tomlinson," Astra says. "Other than the names, there's not much to go on here. Hopefully, they'll be able to give us something more."

"Right. We'll head over to the hospital to ask them some questions," I say. "But before we do, I want to make a stop."

FIVE

"Jesus," Astra mutters. "This is bad, Blake."

"Yeah, that's certainly one word for it."

After we butted heads with Detective Esposito, a loud and abrasive man who's obviously proud of his Italian heritage, he finally let us into the crime scene. We practically had to fill out a form in triplicate and sign it in our own blood for him to believe we aren't here to bigfoot his case away from him. Trying to convince him that this isn't a Fed takeover of his crime scene, but was simply for our own gratification, wasn't easy.

The more I think about it, the more upset I get. I personally couldn't tell whether he was so enraged and insistent on keeping us out of here because we're Feds or because we're women. The odor of chauvinism was coming off him so thick, I'm pretty sure I'm going to have to dry-clean my suit just to get that stench out. In the end, Astra had to talk him down to keep him from deploying the National Guard just to keep us off his crime scene. She had to talk to him Italian to Italian – in Italian. And it was a rather vigorous exchange.

"What did you say to Esposito to get him to back off, anyway?" I ask.

"I threatened to cut off his junk and feed it to his family in a homemade Bolognese sauce," she shrugs. "If there's one thing that can get an Italian man to back off, it's an angry Italian woman threatening to remove his pride and joy – mostly because we don't mess around and will always make good on our threats."

I laugh and shake my head as we move deeper into the room. The techs all backed out to give us a little space, which I appreciate. Though I kind of wish they'd taken the bodies with them. I've seen some terrible things in my time with the Bureau, and this is most definitely in my top-ten list of most horrible.

"I can see why Lily looked ready to lose her lunch," I comment.

"You think?"

I move over to the bed and look down at the body. She was young, no more than twenty-one at most, and when she was alive, she must have been stunning. She had dark brown hair, hazel eyes, and a sandy-colored complexion. The girl had a trim, petite build, and surprisingly long legs for somebody who couldn't have stood more than five-five. There is a hint of something exotic in her features, but it's ambiguous. I can't tell what different ethnicities went into the grab bag to make her, but whatever they were, she was gorgeous.

"Lacey Mansour," Astra reads off the driver's license in her hand. "Twenty-years old. Student at U-Dub."

"Mansour," I say, letting my mind work it out. "That's a common Egyptian surname. So, she was at least part Egyptian."

"It's a shame," Astra mutters, looking down at Lacey. "Just a crying shame. She was so young. So much life to look forward to."

I nod. "This is just evil. Pure evil."

Lacey had been bound by the wrists and ankles to the posters of her bed. She's naked and lying spread eagle, a terrible indignity. It's a position of absolute powerlessness. She's been stripped of any sort of control. Whoever did this obviously had the need to feel in total and absolute control. The killer needed to dominate Lacey in every way possible. The condition of the girl's body further underscores that point.

Lacey has been cut to ribbons. I count at least twenty stab wounds in her torso and extremities, not to mention a huge number of slashes as well. There's a gaping wound in her midsection, and the killer physically reached into her and tore her insides out, leaving them to hang outside of her cavity on the bed. Now I can see why Nash was so rattled by this crime scene. In a place like Bellevue, this sort of sadistic murder really is unheard of.

There is barely an inch of her body that isn't covered in bruises or cut to hell – except for her face. Her face is untouched and pristine. It even looks as if makeup has been applied . And at some point, after she'd been made up, the killer had put a clear plastic bag over her head and cinched it tight.

It's as if the killer, a man who'd inflicted all this misery and brutality upon this poor girl, had wanted to keep her pretty. It almost seems as if her looks are what both turned him on and enraged him at the same time. It's confusing, and the signals it sends are jumbled. This is something that I'm going to need to noodle on later, back at the shop.

"I'm assuming we're going to find she's been sexually assaulted," I say.

"I'd say that's a safe bet," Astra replies. "I'm also going to go out on a limb and say that giant gash through the center of her abdomen is the cause of death, rather than that bag over her head."

I nod. "I agree. I won't say for certain, but I'm pretty sure her face was made up and her head bagged post-mortem," I reply. "But judging by the fact that her sheets and blankets are covered in blood and her insides are now on the outside, I think you're right."

"This is messed up. Really messed up," Astra says.

"Yeah."

"You said that Mansour's a common Egyptian surname. And Egypt is a Muslim country," she notes. "You think we're looking at a hate crime here?"

I screw up my face and shake my head. "Could be the killer wants us to think that. But I don't think so," I reply. "I think her ethnicity and religion were secondary factors, if they factored into our killer's thinking at all."

"Then what do you think it's about?"

"It's about power and domination," I reply. "He wanted to degrade this girl. Humiliate and demean her. That's why she's being displayed like this – naked and spread eagle. Even in death he wants her to be degraded."

"Charming," she notes.

"We need to get the ME's report on this," I tell her. "I'm going to want to keep tabs on this one, because I've got a feeling this isn't an isolated case."

"So, while investigating a serial robber, we stumble onto a serial killer," Astra says brightly. "It's not often we get a two-for-one."

I flash her a grin. "You are one morbid, twisted chick," I reply. "And I'm not saying we've got a serial. But this all feels –"

"Ritualistic," Astra completes my thought. "Practiced."

I nod. "Exactly."

"So, what does this have to do with our robbery?"

I shake my head. "Nothing. But Detective Nash mentioned the murder and he was pretty rattled by it. Said he'd never seen anything like it, so I wanted to check it out," I tell her. "And I'm glad we did. We may have inadvertently stumbled onto a monster."

I walk the perimeter of the room, looking for anything that stands out. The chances are good that the techs who've been through here have already bagged and tagged anything of evidentiary value, but a fresh set of eyes never hurts. Especially eyes that have long since become desensitized to the sort of horrors inflicted upon Lacey Mansour.

The girl was neat and tidy, that's for sure. Everything has a place, and everything's in its place. I don't see a speck of dust anywhere. It's unusual for a college kid and I suspect it has a lot to do with how she was raised. I wouldn't be surprised to find that her parents are fastidious, perhaps even bordering on the obsessively neat. I run across three depressions in the carpeting, though, and squat down to look at them. They haven't been flagged by the techs, which means they've been dismissed as unimportant, but I'm not so sure.

"Astra," I say.

She comes over and squats down beside me. Together, we stare at the divots in the carpet for a long moment in silence.

"Something was sitting here," I say. "Something was taken."

"Looks like the legs of a small table or something," she says. "You sure she didn't just move it somewhere else?"

"Look around the room. It's not just neat and tidy, it's freakishly neat and tidy. I mean, there is not one thing out of place," I reply. "If she'd moved a table or something, she would have run a vacuum or something over this spot to get those divots out. It would've been like a compulsion for her."

"Hmmm... alright, so what was taken then?" she asks. "I can't see our butcher taking a small table as a memento. Not when there's smaller, less obvious stuff that could be carried out."

I frown as I look at the divots. "I don't know for sure. Maybe we can ask her friends –"

"Not our case, Blake. And if you go steppin' on Esposito's toes like that, he very well may have a coronary," she interrupts. "Or he might just shoot you. One of the two."

I grin and chuckle. "Right. Sorry," I say. "We should point it out to Detective Esposito on our way out. Give him some direction to run in."

"That's better. Good girl," she says mockingly. "Jesus. And you have the nerve to call poor Lacey up there the obsessive one."

I laugh grimly. "Yeah. Well, we had our look," I say. "We should probably get down to the hospital to interview our witnesses."

"If you can call them that," she replies. "I'm not sure what they could have witnessed, face down on the floor as they were."

I shrug. "Oh, ye of little faith," I say. "You never know until you ask."

"This is true," she replies.

We both stand up and head for the door. As we go, I cast a look back at Lacey Mansour, feeling a wave of pity for her wash over me. The need to get justice for this girl is threatening to overwhelm me. But Detective Esposito seems firm in his desire to handle this on his own, which is just macho, territorial bull-crap. I think he's more interested in having his name attached to a high-profile case than he is in actually getting justice for that poor girl. So, I'll be watching this case unfold from the sidelines and seeing how it progresses. For now. At some point, I may just have to step in.

Yeah, okay. Maybe I am a little obsessive.

SIX

St. Anne's Community Medical Center; Downtown Bellevue

WE FLASH our credentials to the nurse at the duty station and she gets that "deer in the headlights, ready to bolt out the door," look people tend to get, even if they haven't done anything wrong. I guess something about having law enforcement in your face just puts some people on edge, regardless of whether they've done anything or not.

"We need the room number for Robert Dutch and also for Chris Tomlinson," I tell her, copping a glance at her name badge. "Please, Nurse Wilcox."

I've also found that when you badge somebody, if you use his or her name, he or she tends to get even more nervous. And right on cue, Nurse Wilcox tenses up. She's so nervous, it makes me wonder if she really has done something. But she fumbles with the chart in her hand, looking down at it for a moment, a look of confusion on her face.

"They were both brought in after the robbery at Speedy Check Cashing. Beat up pretty bad," Astra offers helpfully.

"Oh, ummm... right. Yes, of course," she says, a slight tremor in her voice. "I think they're both resting right now."

"That's fine," I tell her. "We can wait. But I'd like the room numbers, please."

"Okay, right. Of course," she says. "Mr. Dutch is in room 304 and Mr. Tomlinson is in room 310. They're located in the recovery ward on the third floor."

"Thank you," I say.

"Yes. You're welcome," she stammers.

We turn away and head for the elevators, and I glance behind me at Nurse Wilcox, who's staring at us. But she quickly turns away when my eyes meet hers. Even from where we are, I can see her face flush red. I have to bite back the laugh.

"You know you're a jerk, right?" Astra asks.

"Why do you say that?"

She chuckles. "You used your FBI-voice on her. You know that freaks people out," she says. "And then dropping her name like that? That was just mean."

"You do realize I learned that from you, right?"

She shrugs. "Yeah, because it amuses me," she replies. "But I'm supposed to be the jerk in this relationship. You should know by now that I'm a very bad example for you."

"Sure, now you tell me."

We take the elevator up to the third floor and step out into the lobby. There's a waiting room to the right, a nurse's duty station to the left, and a long corridor in front of us. The nurse looks up and gives us a quick smile, then turns back to her paperwork. I can't tell if the nurse downstairs called and warned her we were coming, and she doesn't care, or if she just flat doesn't care when new people arrive on her floor. Either way, it doesn't matter to me so long as we get what we came here for.

"Okay, so should we hit Dutch or Tomlinson first?" I ask.

She shrugs. "How about whichever room we come to first?"

"That's fair."

We walk out of the lobby and head down the corridor, pushing through a set of double doors and into the recovery ward. The fact that the nurse didn't stop us tells me she got the heads-up we were on our way and probably figured it wasn't worth it to hassle us.

The tile beneath our feet is worn and cracked in some places and the walls were all the same shade of canary yellow once upon a time. They're all dull now, looking more like urine yellow than canary yellow, though there are still a few spots of that vibrant color hanging on somehow. This place obviously hasn't been refreshed in quite some time. It's kind of depressing, really.

"Room 304," Astra says.

"I guess we hit Dutch first."

She nods. "Lead the way."

We push the door open and go in. The curtains are all drawn tight against the light outside, leaving the room gloomy and dim, making the baby blue walls in here look darker. Whoever decided on the hospital's color scheme should be fired for such an obvious lack of taste. I'm no interior designer, but even I know the colors on the walls here are horrid.

In the bed, though, is Robbie Dutch, a lump beneath the sheet. I can tell that he's a large, stocky man, but other than that, his actual features are indistinct. He's not moving, and it seems likelooks as if he's barely even breathing. He's covered in so many bandages, he could be auditioning for the part of a mummy. The skin we can see is dark purple. Both of his eyes are swollen shut, his nose is crooked, and his lips are cracked and puffy. He obviously went through hell when all he was trying to do was his job. My heart immediately goes out to him.

"Robbie?" I say softly. "I'm Blake Wilder. I'm with Astra Russo. We're both with the FBI and we were hoping we could talk to you."

I was half-sure he wasn't going to answer. To be honest, given his condition, I was half-sure he'd expired already. So, when he speaks, it comes as a surprise. But his voice is hoarse and cracking. It's raspy. Astra glances at me and I can see she feels as bad for him as I do.

"Okay," is all he says.

The bed starts to move, the sound of the electric motor loud and shrill in the otherwise silent room. It moves him into a sitting position, and he looks at us from beneath the bandages that cover his forehead.

"Water. Please," he rasps.

Astra moves quickly and fetches the cup and fills it with water from the plastic pitcher on the table, then puts the lid back on it. She walks to the bed and holds the straw to his lips. He leans forward and grimaces, as if the effort is excruciating, but he manages to suck down some water before flopping back against the pillows. His eyes are both red, thanks to the broken blood vessels he suffered during the beating, but I can see that they're blue.

"Thank you," he says, his voice slightly better – but only slightly.

"Mr. Dutch –"

"Just call me Dutch," he says.

"Alright, Dutch. We want to talk to you about what happened last night," I say. "Did you happen to see the man who attacked you?"

He starts to shake his head then winces and draws in a sharp breath. He slumps back against the pillows.

"No. he wore a mask," he says. "All I could see were his eyes. They were green."

"Did he say anything to you?" Astra asks. "Did he speak at all?"

"Just kept telling me to shut up. Yelling at me to shut up. And he just kept kicking me. Hitting me," he replies. "That's all I remember before I blacked out."

He looks away and I can see the shame on his battered and swollen face. I've seen it in victims before. They always blame themselves for not being able to protect themselves. They think, if only I were stronger, if only I had done this, or done that. Victims always find ways to blame themselves when the truth is that sometimes, there's nothing you can do. Nothing you could have done to prevent what happened to you. Sometimes, bad things just happen.

I reach out and put a hand on his arm. Dutch looks over at me and even though his eyes are swollen shut, fat tears are spilling down his cheeks, but he says nothing.

"This isn't your fault, Dutch," I tell him. "You didn't do anything, and you certainly didn't deserve this. Don't beat yourself up about this. It's not your fault."

"There's a poor choice of words," Astra mutters.

I groan, realizing I just stuck my foot in my mouth. I do that, sometimes. "Sorry," I say. "I didn't mean to say that."

A choked sound that sounds like a laugh escapes him and a ghastly-looking grin crosses his beaten and swollen face. At least he's still in somewhat good spirits. But this is about what I figured it was going to be. I didn't expect to get much of value out of Dutch. When you're getting hammered like that, taking note of somebody's physical description isn't really going to be high on anybody's list of priorities. But it never hurts to check. Doing your due diligence is essential when you're trying to make a case.

"Okay, we're going to go," I tell him. "You get some rest and just focus on healing, Dutch. You get better soon."

He nods slowly and I see his body relax as he gives himself over to sleep. Astra and I back out of the room, closing the door quietly behind us. We stand in the hall, looking at Dutch's door for a long moment, neither of us speaking.

"This guy really did a number on that kid," Astra finally says.

I nod. "Yeah. Which is why we need to catch this guy sooner, rather than later," I say. "He's only going to get worse."

"There's a cheery thought," she replies. "Let's go talk to Tomlinson."

"I doubt we'll get much more out of him," I say. "But we have to do our due diligence."

"Due diligence. That's government-speak for a pointless circle-jerk."

"Pretty much."

We share a laugh and head down the hall, locate room 310, and step inside. Christopher Tomlinson is in far better shape than his coworker. He's sitting up in bed watching TV, and when we walk in, his eyes are immediately drawn to Astra. Tomlinson is a tall, lanky kid with long hair and the look of a habitual stoner. He's got bandages over half of his face, but still manages to greet us with a smile.

"Hey," he says. "Here to give me my sponge bath?"

"Clearly, they've given him the really good drugs," Astra cracks.

We flash him our credentials, which kills his buzz pretty quickly. He slumps back against his pillows and turns off the TV.

"So, what can I do for you, agents?" he asks.

"We just wanted to talk to you about what happened last night," I say.

"It's like I told the detectives, there's not much I can tell you," he replies. "The bell at the employee door rang, I opened it and got blasted in the face by the butt of a gun. I took another blow to the back of the head and I was down and out."

He gestures to the bandage on his face, a look of anger flashing across his features. He picks up the glass of water on his bedside table and takes a long swallow, no doubt giving himself a beat to calm down. I can only imagine how upsetting it would be to wake up and find out that somebody had carved designs into your face while you were out cold.

"And when I woke up, I found that he'd carved a flower into my face for some reason," he growls.

"Pure sadism," Astra says.

"And you didn't say anything to him?" I ask.

"I didn't have time. Like I said, I opened the door and got thumped."

"Why did you open the door, Mr. Tomlinson?"

"Because the bell rang."

"Do you always open the door at night?"

"No, we're not supposed to open the door. But Janice had just left, so I figured she forgot something. I didn't even think about it," he replies.

Astra looks at him closely. "Christopher, did you know the man who did this to you?"

"What? No."

"So, you weren't working with him? This wasn't an inside job?" she presses.

"Dude, no," he says. "I got blasted in the face. What are you even talking about?"

"So, you weren't involved in the robbery in any way whatsoever?" Astra asks.

"Hell, no!" he snaps. "What kind of question is that?"

Astra paces over to the window, drawing his attention that way as I remain focused on him. I'm watching his reaction to her, looking for signs of deception. I'm sure it's not an inside job, but it's still a good line of questioning, calculated to rule out every possibility; due diligence and all that. But as I watch his micro-expressions and body language, I can see that he's telling the truth. He wasn't involved in the robbery.

Astra looks over at me and I shake my head. She nods, then turns to him.

"Didn't mean to upset you, but I had to ask," she said. "You'd be surprised at how many banks and cash businesses are robbed by somebody on the inside."

He seems mollified as he slumps back against his pillows. But this is another dry hole.

"We're sorry to bother you, Mr. Tomlinson," I say, laying a business card down on the bedside table. "If you think of anything else, please give me a call."

"I'll do that," he says, then smiles greasily at us. "So, is there any chance of me getting that sponge bath from you two?"

Without even missing a beat, Astra whips out a notepad and pen and turns to me. "What do you think, Agent Wilder? Two counts of sexual harassment of a federal officer?"

"Hard time," I nod grimly. "That's a felony, isn't it?"

Tomlinson's jaw gapes open and his eyes dart back and forth between us. "W-wait," he stammers. "I, uh, I didn't mean—"

Astra silences him with a glare. The tension holds for a long moment, and then she collapses into a fit of laughter. Despite myself, I join in, clutching my stomach. Tomlinson tries to laugh too, a cold sweat visibly dripping down his back, but he clearly doesn't know what to expect anymore.

Good. Maybe that'll teach him not to be such a pig.

Having struck out on all fronts, we turn and leave the room, and as we head for the elevator, I try to figure out what our next move is going to be.

SEVEN

"WE GOT the surveillance footage from the store," Rick announces as we step into the shop.

"And what did you see?" I ask.

"Well, nothing yet. We thought we'd wait until you guys got back," he replies with a grin. "Movie night just wouldn't be the same without the both of you."

"You're such a sentimental fool," Astra says as she drops down into her seat. "Emphasis on the fool."

"You're such a sweet talker, Agent Russo."

"Did you get anything in Bellevue?" Mo asks.

I grab a bottle of water from the refrigerator we have in our makeshift kitchen area in the corner. I twist the top off and take a long swallow, relishing the feeling of the cool liquid sliding down my throat. I take a moment and drain the rest of the bottle, then toss the empty into the trash can, then grab another bottle from the fridge.

"We got nothing," I say. "The check cashing store was

empty and neither of the victims was able to provide much detail."

"We did get to tour a seriously brutal murder scene," Astra adds.

"Murder scene?" Mo asks.

"It's times like these when I'm glad I don't go out into the field with y'all," Rick says.

"There was a murder last night," Astra tells her. "Twenty-year-old coed named Lacey Mansour. She was just – butchered. The scene was just awful."

"Is the murder connected to the robbery?" Mo asks.

I shake my head. "No. I didn't see a connection between the two," I reply. "But I do want you to keep an eye on that case, Mo. I want to know if anything pops."

"You got it, boss," Mo replies.

"And Rick, I want you to get the murder book from Bellevue PD and do a search in VICAP for any crimes that have the same signature as the Mansour murder," I say.

"I'm on it," he nods.

"Mo, I sent you the file," I say. "Can you play the surveillance footage from last night?"

She turns over to her computer and taps a few keys. "Yep. Coming up now."

I turn and watch as the screens come to life. The scene starts with Tomlinson, Dutch, and a woman I assume is Janice behind the counter. Janice finishes what she was doing and waves to the two guys, apparently leaving for the night. The tape rolls for another ten minutes, and then Tomlinson disappears from view when he goes to the back.

"Is there no tape from the back of the store?" I ask.

Mo shakes her head. "They apparently don't have cameras in the back of the store."

"Well, that's poor planning," Astra remarks.

On the screens, our unsub comes in, moving fast and low, just as in the previous surveillance feeds we watched. Dutch turns around just in time to catch the butt of the unsub's AR-15 in the face. What follows is an act of total savagery, as our unsub lays into Dutch. I'm desensitized to all kinds of violence, but this is disturbing, even to me.

It's over a few minutes later, and on the screen, we see Dutch laying in a bloody heap on the ground. The unsub is moving around, spray painting the lenses of the cameras in the store. When he hits the last one and the screen goes black, Mo cuts the feed off.

"Well, that was brutal," she comments.

"Honestly, the kid is lucky to be alive," Astra says.

"They both are," I nod. "But at the rate this guy's pattern of violence is escalating, it's not going to be long before somebody's luck runs out."

"So, where do we start?" Astra asks.

"Mo, were you guys able to find additional cases?" I ask.

"We think so," she tells me. "We've identified eleven additional possibilities in four different states: Idaho, Oregon, California, and Nevada."

"Twenty-three jobs in the last five years?" Astra raises an eyebrow. "He's been a busy boy."

"Did you get the case files, Mo?" I ask.

"Shockingly enough, I did," she replies. "I did a cursory review, and the description of the perp matches our guy here."

I mentally pump my fist, feeling validated. I was right that the twelve I'd flagged weren't the only ones he was responsible for. I didn't expect such a widespread pattern, but I knew there were others out there. This is one of those cases that's been a hobby of mine for a long time, but I hadn't put the energy into it that I should have. There was always something on my plate that I had to deal with first.

But now that I'm running my own team, my time is my own, and I pick the cases we chase. So, I think it's fortuitous that Speedy Check Cashing got hit last night. Not to sound too ghoulish about it, considering Dutch and Tomlinson were both beaten within an inch of their lives, but at least I now have the time and resources to really go after this guy. About the only solace I can take from this is that at least our perp hasn't killed anybody yet. So with any luck, we can get ahead of this guy before he does.

"Tell me about those cases you've found. Where do they fit into the timeline of these other twelve we've got?" I ask.

"They're scattered throughout, but it's pretty consistent – he hits one of these check cashing places every three months or so," Mo says.

I nod. "So, he hits a check cashing place, lives on the proceeds for a few months, moves around, then hits another to replenish his funds."

"Then lather, rinse, and repeat," Astra says.

"But the extreme violence didn't start until about two years ago," Mo continues. "According to the cases I've found so far, the first case of our perp's beating somebody half to death was about two years ago. Each of the last seven – sorry, eight – cases now, our guy has sent at least one of the employees to the hospital."

I pace in front of the monitors at the front of the bullpen, thinking to myself for a long moment, trying to put some of the pieces together.

"So, for three years, our unsub was content with robbing these stores. He settled for binding the employees and taking the money," I muse. "Two years ago, he gets a taste for violence and now he's beating people near to death. So, what changed?"

"Something seems to have really pissed him off," Astra says.

"The death of a loved one?" Rick chimes in. "A bad breakup?"

"Could be either one of those, or something else entirely," I say, frustrated. "We need to find his trigger."

"So, we're looking for a needle in a stack of needles," Astra says.

"Basically."

"Any pattern you can pick up in the series?" I ask. "Does he have any sort of repeating travel route?"

"Not that I can pick up on," Mo replies.

I've got no doubt that Mo was thorough, and if she says there's no pattern, there probably isn't one. She's as good at picking up on patterns as I am. But I still want to look at the expanded scope of these robberies myself to see if I can find anything. I just need to be sure.

"If this really is random, it's going to make him tough to catch," Astra says, giving voice to my dread.

I nod because she's right. Serial criminals, like most people, have patterns that guide their lives. Most of the time, it's not even something they're conscious of. There are very few I can think of who are truly random. Richard Ramirez, or as he came to be known, the Night Stalker – a serial killer who terrorized Southern California back in the '80s – comes to mind. Not only was he an omnivore, meaning he killed without regard to gender, race, religion, or age, but he really did strike completely at random.

But then you take a guy like Ted Bundy. Many people thought his kills were random, simply because he traversed such a wide area, but a close examination showed that the pattern was there all along. Bundy liked to kill women who fit a certain mold – they all looked a certain way. They were all young, white, pretty, and had dark hair – often parted in the middle. That was his pattern. And a study of the history of other killers would show that they, too, had patterns that they adhered to, whether they were aware of them or not.

I remember reading about the case of a migrant worker in California named Miguel Arredondo who, about twenty years ago or so, was robbing houses and sexually assaulting women. Police up and down the state were baffled. It all seemed to be random until somebody figured out the pattern. The robberies and attacks lined up with the produce picking seasons in various parts of the state. Wherever he was working at the time, there was a spike in robberies and assaults. Figuring out that pattern helped the police nail this guy. He's currently doing life without parole at Folsom.

That's not to say our serial robber is the same as Ramirez or Bundy, or even Arredondo. Not yet. But his escalation of violence is worrisome to me. If we can't figure out who he is and stop him, he very well could start racking up a body count that would rival that of either one of those infamous killers. And I think one of the keys in figuring out his identity is finding his trigger.

What was it that, after three years of simply robbing these stores and largely ignoring the employees, made him start savagely beating people? If we can figure that out, I think it'll give us a boost in trying to figure out who he is and how to stop him.

EIGHT

Marco's Corner Diner; Downtown Seattle

"Mom wanted me to ask when you thought you'd be able to make it over for Sunday dinner," Maisey says the moment I slide into the booth.

"Et tu, Brute?"

"No. Well yes, she did want me to pass that along. But I thought I'd just get it out of the way right up front so we can move on and have a pleasant evening," she says, flashing me a grin. "Honestly, it's kind of nice having dinner together just because, instead of having dinner together because you're leaving the next day and you think you're going die."

I laugh. "Wow, talk about a dramatic interpretation and a terrible oversimplification of the way things were."

"Not really."

"Totally. You know you can't deny it," Maisey crows.

We share a laugh together and I settle back into the booth. After my parents were murdered when I was a kid, I came to live with my Aunt Annie. Maisey is my cousin but we grew up like sisters. Aside from Astra, she's my best friend in the world. We shared everything together growing up, and that bond we have is stronger than the Rock of Gibraltar.

I suppose if I'm looking at patterns, I'd be a hypocrite to not acknowledge my own. Maisey isn't entirely wrong in her assessment, but it was a pattern I wasn't even aware of. For a while there, the only time I made the effort to call her and make plans for dinner or whatnot, was when I was about to leave on a trip for a case. And maybe somewhere deep down, like she said, it was because I feared I wasn't coming back, and I wanted to say goodbye.

She called me on it and ever since then, I've made a concerted effort to see her – and my aunt – more often. It's not that I don't like spending time with Annie, but she can be incredibly taxing. Annie is a bit of a recluse. She's also very down on my job. She thinks a woman shouldn't be doing law enforcement work, and that I take stupid risks. She could be right on the last point, but on the first one, I couldn't disagree more. Annie has mastered the art of the backhanded compliment and never fails to take pot shots at my choice of career – all while making it sound like praise. It would be an impressive skill if it weren't so infuriating.

Annie is a bit of a traditionalist. More than that, ever since I graduated and moved out, she's gotten increasingly bitter. Angry, even. And the worst part of that is that she is rubbing off on Maisey who, like her mother, is generally incredibly shy and withdrawn when it comes to men. She's always down on herself and never sees her own virtues. I've been trying to chip away at that wall for years. Maisey never thought she was a pretty girl or that men would ever have any interest in her, anyway. That was her justification for never taking chances with romance.

Maisey is a couple of inches shorter than I am and has a

killer figure. Her hair is dark and wavy, her eyes sparkle like emeralds, and she has a spattering of freckles across the bridge of her nose that is adorable. Her skin is like alabaster and totally flawless. Seriously, she's got the kind of complexion most women would kill for. Maisey has curves in all the right places and that wholesome All-American, sweet-as-apple-pie appeal that men absolutely love.

She's a knockout, plain and simple. Maisey hasn't ever gotten to the point of being bitter and shutting herself away from the world, thank God. But when I saw her headed down that road, I knew I had to step in and stop her. Since then, I've done all I can to help bring her out of her shell and into the light of day.

I've tried to show her how beautiful life – and the world – can be. Yeah, it's got a lot of darkness and terrible things. The work I do exposes me to the dark side on a daily basis. But there are also a lot of beautiful and wonderful things out there. If you can learn to overcome your heartbreaks and failures, you can really enjoy life – because there are a lot of things to be enjoyed. Or, you can do what Annie does and sit home, angry all the time, and snipe at anybody who is chasing her dream or living her best life.

Don't get me wrong, I love my aunt and I'll always be grateful to her for taking me in after such a horrible start to my life. She's like a second mother to me. But that doesn't mean I have to subject myself to her angry rantings, her potshots at me and my career, or her soapbox speeches about how terrible the world is. I see how terrible it – and people – can be on the daily. But I choose not to dwell on it. I choose to live a good life and soak up the positive and happy things. I'd rather focus on joy than wallow in misery like my aunt.

"And what can I get you ladies this evening?"

I look up to see Marco, the owner of this little diner – and

Maisey's boyfriend – standing at the table. Though he addressed us both, his eyes are locked onto hers. They're sharing one of those kinds of smiles reserved for people in love. He eventually tears his eyes away from Maisey's and looks at me, his smile changing but becoming no less warm or genuine.

Marco is a tall, lean man with thick, dark hair, dark eyes that I swear to God, smolder, and the tawny skin of his Mexican heritage. He's handsome and could probably have a solid career on one of those telenovelas if he wanted. But he's also very down to earth and a genuinely nice man. Even better, he treats Maisey like a queen – as she deserves.

"It's nice to see you again, Blake," he greets me.

"It's good to see you too, Marco," I reply. "And it's even better to see Maisey smile the way she's smiling right now."

"She makes me smile the same way," he says, casting those dreamy eyes at her again.

"It makes me really happy to hear that," I say. "You two are an adorable couple."

Maisey's cheeks flush and she looks away, which makes Marco and me laugh. I do so love embarrassing my cousin sometimes. But it really is nice to see her happy and in love – two things I worried she'd never feel. I didn't want to see her continue morphing into her mom so, to make sure she didn't, before I left for New York, I made sure she and Marco got together. They'd been flirting wildly for months and the connection between them was more than obvious, so I forced the issue.

And I'm happy to see that even after all this time, they're still together – even if Annie knows nothing about it. Maisey has finally, wonderfully come out of her shell. It's a beautiful thing to see, but there are still some things she can't confront Annie about, her relationship with Marco being one of them. It seems ridiculous that a grown woman like Maisey would have to hide something like being in love from her mother, but knowing how volatile Annie can be, I can't say that I blame her. If Maisey told Annie about her relationship, my aunt would hit the roof and things would get very... tense.

Annie's mindset seems to be that if she's not happy, nobody's going to be happy. And that's just no way to go through life. Life is meant to be lived. Enjoyed. And we are meant to be happy. The way Annie goes through life is entirely unnatural. In fact, it's kind of sad, really.

Marco laughs softly. "How's work?"

I shrug. "People still breaking the law and killing each other. Some things never change," I reply. "But then, I suppose if they did, I'd be out of a job."

"Don't worry, you've always got a job here," he replies.

"That's why you're the best."

He chuckles and looks around as the dinner rush starts to pour in. He reaches down and takes Maisey's hand and gives it a squeeze, then looks at us.

"What can I get you two?" he asks.

"We're in your capable hands," Maisey says. "Surprise us."

"I'll do that," he replies, tipping her a wink.

He bustles off to see to his new arrivals and to put our order in motion. I turn to Maisey and see her grinning. The cartoon hearts are practically floating over her head.

"So, things are going good, I take it," I observe.

"Better than good. They're amazing," she replies.

"And things are still serious?"

She nods. "I think they're starting to get even more serious."

"No," I gasp, my eyes widening.

"I don't know for sure, but I think he's going to ask me to marry him soon."

I reach across the table and take her hand, squeezing it excitedly. "Maisey, that's incredible. I am so –"

"And it's also uncertain. I mean, I could be reading the signs wrong. I could be seeing things that aren't there," she says. "But I just have a feeling he's going to ask soon."

I am genuinely thrilled for her, but know that if Marco does propose, it's going to mean Maisey will have to have some difficult conversations with Annie. She looks at me and her smile slips slightly, as if she's reading my mind.

"Yeah, I guess the time's coming to tell Mom," she says.

"Oh, I don't know," I shrug. "You two have managed to hide your relationship for a while now. Who says you can't hide your marriage?"

She squeals with laughter and tosses a sugar packet at me. I love seeing her bloom the way she has. It doesn't seem all that long ago she was a recluse like her mother. And now look at her – possibly getting married. I couldn't be happier for her. But I do worry about how Annie is going to take it all.

I push it all aside, though, as we start gabbing about things. As usual, she wants to know every last detail of the cases I'm working on. Maisey has always been a true-crime junkie and she gets her fix, as well as lives a bit vicariously, through my stories about the job. I'm always happy to tell her all I can – which isn't everything, of course – and she just eats it all up. She can't get enough of the gore.

We talk for a few hours at our table, with Marco treating us to an absolutely wonderful meal, and we catch up on each other's lives. Even though it's only been just over a week since we last saw each other, it feels like longer. Or at least, we have a lot to tell each other, which is satisfying. It's a real pleasure to hear about her life and how she's doing.

Finally, though, it's time to call the evening to an end. And as we're walking out to the parking lot, she turns to me and smiles.

"You know you can't dodge Sunday dinner forever," she says.

"I can sure try."

She laughs. "Hey, if I have to go, so do you."

I sigh dramatically. "I know, I know," I reply. "Tell her I'll be over this Sunday."

"Why don't you call her yourself?"

"Because I'd rather not subject myself to an hour-long conversation – and by conversation, I mean a lecture about how wrong I am for my job, how law enforcement should be left to the men, and how I'll never get a man because I've sacrificed my femininity for the job. Not really how I want to spend an evening."

Maisey laughs, a wry smile crossing her face. "That's fair," she says. "I'll talk to you soon, Blake."

"Definitely."

We give each other a hug and I'm walking back to my car when Maisey calls to me. I turn around and she's still standing where I left her.

"You do know she's proud of you, don't you?" she asks. "Mom. She talks a lot, but when you're not around, she always says how proud she is of you. And also, how proud your parents would have been of you, too."

Her words make me smile and hit a chord deep within me. It's sweet, and knowing that Annie feels that way – if only in private and never around me – touches me. It fills me with a surprisingly overwhelming sense of happiness.

"Thanks, Maisey," I say. "Tell Annie I love her, will you?"

"I'll do that," she says. "But you really should tell her yourself."

I nod. "Fair point."

Without specifically calling me out, Maisey is in fact calling me out on yet another one of my patterns: avoiding the unpleasant things I don't want to deal with. Who knew that shy little wallflower would blossom into the woman in front of me? I like it. I like it a lot. And I'm proud of her, too.

"See you Sunday, Maisey."

"You, too."

NINE

IT'S BEEN a couple of weeks since the Bellevue heist, and we've gotten exactly nowhere. No new leads have surfaced, no witnesses have stepped forward, and sadly, the unsub has not come to the field office and turned himself in. Which is a bummer, to say the least. But we're still working hard, trying to find that needle in a stack of needles that Astra referred to. And it's looking as if she was right about it.

Conversely, things in my personal life are going just swimmingly. Though I still feel the simmering of uncertainty inside of me, things with Mark have improved. I no longer feel crazy – or at least, *as* crazy – about his habits and etiquette on the phone. I don't feel threatened that he's running around behind my back. But I still haven't been able to shake that feeling that he's hiding something. I don't think it's a woman, but I don't know what it is. It's tough to ignore, but I manage it most days and have been able to just enjoy my time with him without any added or undue pressure or strain.

I've had dinner with Annie – twice, now. It's been a little bit tense, but nothing I couldn't handle. She predictably sniped at my job behind a veneer of civility. If she actually said she's proud of me, like Maisey told me she did, I'm seeing no trace of it. But then, Annie's always been incredibly guarded with her emotions. The important thing is that I've spent time with her and made sure she knew that no matter what, she's my family, and I love her. So, yay for me.

Despite all the good things going on in my life at the moment, I'm sitting in my office brooding about the lack of progress on the case. Now that I have the time and resources to devote to this guy, I have nothing to work with. I don't have a single stinking lead to follow and it's really starting to grate on me.

I've studied all the new case files, as well as having gone over all the old ones I've already been through. I know them inside and out. Chapter and verse. By this point, I can probably recite them by memory, and still I have found absolutely nothing. No hints, no clues, no flashing neon signs, and no patterns to speak of. As far as I can tell, everything about these crimes appears completely random, which is more than a small problem. Unless this clown makes a mistake – something he has yet to do thus far – it's going to take a miracle to catch him.

Rosie – the Special Agent in Charge of the Seattle Field office – asked me for a status update yesterday, and I had to go to her and admit that at the moment, we've got absolutely nothing. She, of course, told me not to be too hard on myself. She gave me the usual, "some cases take longer to crack than others, and you're an outstanding agent who will get the job done," pep talk I so loathe. It makes me bristle just thinking about it.

That sort of pep talk is reserved for people like Grant Bryant, my arch-nemesis. Bryant's a churlish, rude, going-nowhere agent who doesn't care enough to do the small things to crack a case. He doesn't pay attention to the details and he sure as hell doesn't do his due diligence. It's one reason I rejected his plea to join this team. I want people who are committed to the job and are willing to roll up their sleeves and do the crap work to get it done. He's not that kind of guy. He simply wanted to join on just for the resume boost it would give him to be part of a high- profile squad. And because of that – and many more reasons – he's not the kind of agent I wanted on my team.

Another reason I rejected him is because he's gone out of his way to make my life a living hell since I was first assigned to the SFO years ago. Admittedly, it did feel good to tell him to take a flying leap. Really, really good. Yeah, I can absolutely do petty and do it well.

Grant is part of that good old boys' club, guys who don't think much of female agents, and think male agents are inherently better just because they can pee standing up. I obviously don't subscribe to that sort of thinking. He would have been a cancer on this team. On my team. So, I got to say not just "no," but "hell. no," with a smile.

Astra glides into my office and drops down into the seat across from me. She sits back and crosses her legs, a frown on her face.

"What is it?" I ask.

"The lack of activity is killing me."

"Join the club."

"How can we not have a single whiff of this guy?" she asks.

"He's good. Really good," I reply. "And more than that, he's completely random. He doesn't follow any sort of pattern I can see, other than hitting low risk targets like check cashing places."

"And there's so many of them in the city, there's no way we can predict which one he's going to hit next."

"For all we know, he could be in Utah right now, scoping out his next job," I offer with a shrug. "He might have already moved on after Bellevue."

"I don't think so. I feel as if he's still here. In the city," she says.

"Could be because we want him to be here so badly, so we can snatch him up."

"That's a possibility, too," she admits.

"This is a tough nut to crack," I say. "It's killing me just as bad as it's killing you."

"I know it is."

She groans dramatically and drums her fingers on her knee. Her frustration is palpable, and I absolutely relate to it. All I need is one hint. One clue. Something to give us a direction to run to. But this guy is so clean and precise. People say there's no such thing as the perfect crime, but this guy is pretty damn close to it. He's a ghost. It's like he knew exactly where all of the camera's were located and how to avoid them.

"Any word on that murder in Bellevue?" she asks, changing the subject.

"Not yet. They're baffled down there," I say. "I saw a report from Esposito that's the paper equivalent of him throwing his hands in the air and shouting, 'I got nothin'.'"

"More good news," she sighs.

"Rick's still running it through VICAP and I'm really hoping he gets a hit," I say. "There is no way that was the killer's first murder. It was too –"

"Clean and precise?"

I laugh ruefully. "Yeah, exactly."

"What are the odds we get two perfect crimes in the same

city on the same night?" she asks. "In Bellevue, of all places. I mean, really, what are the odds?"

"So, you think they're connected."

She shrugs. "I don't know. It just seems like a huge coincidence."

"Yeah, I know. But the differences between the crimes tell me no," I counter. "I mean, our guy's level of violence is skyrocketing, but he still hasn't actually killed anybody. The guy who killed Lacey Mansour though – that is a practiced hand at killing."

"Yeah, I get it," she says. "I just hate coincidences."

"That makes two of us. I just don't see the correlation. Two different MOs. Our guy's attack is utilitarian and mission oriented – he needs the money; he gets the money. In, out, and he's done," I say. "The guy who killed Lacey – that was pure sadism. Gratuitous violence just for the sake of it. The guy enjoyed murdering her. And he took his time doing it."

"Both of these cases really suck," Astra sighs.

"They do. No matter how hard I try, I can't stop thinking about both of them," I say. "I really want to catch our guy, and the guy who murdered Lacey Mansour."

"What do you think about our guy? Have a profile yet?"

I shake my head. "I need more information before I can put together a coherent profile. All I can say at this point is that our guy is good. He's fast and efficient. Moves with purpose," I say. "I agree with Mo's assessment that he moves like somebody with military or police training."

"Or Rick could be right, and this guy is one of those survivalist militia LARPing kind of guys, or whatever he called them," Astra counters.

I sit back in my seat and ponder it a minute. Then an idea occurs to me and I give her a grin. She returns it and I see the mischievous glint in her eyes.

"Feel like a field trip?" I ask.

"Is there a possibility of getting to beat up and/or shoot anybody?"

"Absolutely."

"Then I'm in. Let's go."

TEN

Frank's Automotive; White Center CDP (Census Designated Place)

"THIS PLACE IS CHARMING," Astra notes.

"Oh, it gets better."

"They should gentrify this place quick."

I shrug. "They tried, but the invading yuppies had a habit of walking face first into bullets and baseball bats. Way I heard it, one guy even swallowed an explosive device."

"Oh, it gets better and better."

"At least you're out of the office," I offer. "And there is a very good chance you will get to beat and/or shoot somebody here."

"This is true," she acknowledges.

I pull into the lot that fronts a dingy car repair shop in the run-down White Center neighborhood. Just south of Seattle, White Center is a low-income neighborhood that is basically held by whoever's got the guns and the will to use them. Drugs, gambling, prostitution, murder – it all runs rampant here. And as of now, the power in White Center is held by Frank Metcalf, who heads The Revenants, a survivalist militia group with a sprinkling of white supremacy for flavor. The rumor is he first moved here because of the name – he expected to find a white enclave that would embrace his racist views. Imagine his surprise to find that isn't the case. That story still makes me laugh. Moron.

Astra and I climb out of the car and immediately, all eyes in the parking lot turn to us. The sounds of pneumatic wrenches, country music, and air compressors fill my ears, and the stench of gas and grease saturates the air. We walk into the garage and all the noise suddenly stops. Even the music turns off. It feels like a scene out of a Western movie when the gunslinger walks into a bar to confront the man in the black hat and everybody stops what they're doing, teetering on the edge of drawing their guns or taking flight out of there. There's that sort of tension in the air.

A tall, well-built man walks out of a back room, wiping his hands on a rag, and looks over at us. He's wearing grease-stained coveralls I think used to be blue at one point, and black steel-toed boots. He's got silver hair that's cut military short, a mostly silver goatee, and hard, blue eyes. He's made of tightly corded muscle and looks as though he just stepped out of the prison yard.

"Frank Metcalf," I greet him. "Good to see you again."

"Wish I could say the same about you."

I shrug. "I won't take that personally."

"Boys," he calls out, his deep, gravelly voice echoing around the garage. "Meet Special Agent Blake Wilder. She's the one who sent me up for those two years I was in prison."

There's a scattering of boos mixed in with catcalls around the garage, as well as a plethora of comments about our physical appearances. There seems to be a general consensus among the men that Astra and I would look great bent over the hood of one car or another.

"Oh, these boys are all so delightful," Astra notes.

I look at Frank, narrowing my eyes. "You should have been in prison for a lot longer than two stinking years."

"Probably. But I had a very good lawyer."

"Combine that with a spineless ADA who wouldn't prosecute for the hate crime because he feared he'd lose and tank his conviction rate, and here you are two years later," I fire back.

"Ain't the American justice system grand?"

"For those who can buy it, I suppose."

Frank chuckles and tucks his rag into his pocket. "So, what can I do for you pigs," he says. "Or wait, you're lady pigs. Or would I call you pigettes?"

"There someplace quiet we can talk?" I ask.

"Nah. Out here suits me just fine. I got nothin' to hide from my boys."

"Fine," I say. "The Revenants are a known survivalist militia. We know you have a fortified compound out near Easton and Kachess Lake. And I know you have plenty of unlicensed and illegal guns out there on said compound. You and I both know that's a violation of your parole."

He leans forward, a smile on his face. "Prove it, pig."

"Listen, right now, I don't care about your freakishly racist, anti-government, end-of-the-world, bullcrap agenda. It's not my job to deal with the likes of you. Not right now, anyway," I say ominously.

"So, what do you want?" Frank asks.

"Information. We have a suspect who could possibly be part of your little army playgroup. Or if not yours, somebody else's," Astra jumps in. "And if he's part of yours, you know he'll bring that heat down on you and everybody else in your little... club."

"Playgroup," he mutters and shakes his head. "We train because we know –"

I hold up my hand to stop him. "Like I said, we're not interested in your crap. What we want to know is –"

Frank's eyes are sliding up and down Astra's body as he takes her in from head to toe. The slow, salacious smile that crosses his face, and the suggestive way he licks his lips has me needing a hot shower. With bleach.

"As a rule, I don't really go in for women whose skin is darker than mine," he says. "But I think I'd make an exception in your case. I'm sure you've never had a virile white man like me before and don't know how good it can feel."

Astra rolls her eyes. "I'm flattered," she says, her tone dripping with sarcasm. "But if I were to ever have sex with you, I would immediately have to set myself on fire."

"On account of me ruinin' you for other men, huh?"

"No, it's the only way to be sure to kill all of the bacteria and sexually transmitted diseases I know I'd contract," she says.

Frank's face darkens and twists with rage and he lunges for her. But Astra is ready – she was baiting him after all. She grabs his hand and bends it backward at an awkward angle. And as he throws his head back and screams at that, Astra uses her leg to sweep his feet out from under him. Not even an instant after he hits the ground, she pounces on him, flipping Frank over onto his belly and wrenching his arm up behind his back. He screams in agony, letting out a string of curses so foul, they'd make a sailor blush.

The sound of tools hitting the concrete rings out and I quickly draw my weapon and take aim at the man closest to me. Astra coolly draws hers and places it against the back of Frank's head, a devious grin on her lips.

"Tell them all to back off or I'm going to blow a hole in the back of your skull large enough to fit a spare tire in," she hisses, her voice cold.

He doesn't say anything for a moment, grunting and growling in pain and frustration instead. The men stop where they are and look at each other with uncertainty in their eyes. They're so conditioned to obey Frank that they don't know what to do without his orders, which is good news for me. I'll be able to plug most of them before they even get close to me with whatever weapons they've got in their hands. Unless they have guns, in which case I'm screwed.

Astra taps Frank on the top of his head, hard, with the barrel of her weapon, making him screech.

"I said tell them to back off," she repeats. "Or I swear to God, I'll paint the floor in this dump with your brains."

"You do realize you're not going to be able to paint a very big area then, right?" I ask.

Astra laughs as Frank launches into another string of vulgarities. But I can see his guys growing more agitated by the minute. And unless he tells them to stand down, they're going to make a move. It'll end with most of them dead and me with a super-sized load of paperwork to do and legal hurdles to jump through – all of which, I'd rather avoid.

"Tell them to stand the hell down, Frank," I call out.

To emphasize my point, Astra presses the barrel of her gun flush against his head, forcing his face into the concrete beneath him, and twists his arm even more, making him scream.

"Tell them, Frank," she snaps. "You know we government types can murder you and get away with it, right? Isn't extrajudicial murder one of your idiotic beliefs?"

"Fine. Stand down," he shouts. "Everybody back off. Go on. Get on out of here."

Slowly and uneasily, the men back off, then filter out of the garage altogether, leaving us alone with Frank. Astra climbs off him and stands just out of arm's reach, but with her weapon still trained on him. A sour look on his face, Frank rolls over and sits up, his back against a rolling toolbox. He glares at us with hatred etched into his features.

"So, tell us, Frank. Have you heard of anybody knocking over check cashing stores?" I ask. "Anybody in your club bragging about beating the hell out of innocent employees?"

He looks up at me. "Even if I knew of anybody doin' that, why would I tell you?"

"Because you don't want me to dismantle your group piece by piece, then send you back to prison – for a lot longer this time," I say. "The guns I know you have out there on your compound make this a federal case. You'd be doing federal time, buddy."

He grimaces but continues to glare at me. "I ain't heard nothin' about anybody robbin' check cashing stores."

"Frank."

"What? I swear to God. Nobody in my club is doin' it!" he shouts. "If they were, I'd know about it. Believe me. Nothin' happens in the Revenants that I don't know about."

I frown but nod, knowing that much is true. Frank is a control freak, and he wants to know anything and everything. Knowledge is power and Frank wants it all for himself. And as much as I hate to say it, as I watch him closely, monitoring his micro-expressions, I believe he's telling me the truth. As shocking as that is.

"Have you heard of anybody else in one of these little militia groups doing it?" Astra presses. "It looks as if our unsub has military or police training."

He shakes his head. "No, I ain't heard of anybody doing it. But it ain't like all of our groups get together for mixers or anything."

"Fine. You keep your ears open for me, Frank," I say. "And

if you hear even the slightest whisper, you call me right away. You understand?"

I holster my weapon and pull a business card out of my pocket and toss it into his lap. He sneers at me.

"What's in it for me?" he asks.

"How about I don't let Astra here kick your ass again?" I offer. "I have to imagine it not only hurts your cred to get your ass kicked by a woman, but it has to be doubly humiliating that it's a woman with skin darker than yours."

He shakes his head. "Ain't good enough."

"Alright," I say. "How about this... you tell me if you hear anything and I won't have the Bureau raid your compound. That's the best you're going to get out of me."

"You give me your word on that?" he asks.

"I do. I give you my word I won't have the Bureau raid your compound."

"Fine. If I hear anything, I'll tell you."

"Great. Then we're done here," I say.

Astra and I walk back to our car and get in. Frank's guys are still milling around the parking lot, all of them shooting us dark glares. But we pull out without incident and get on the road, headed back to the shop.

"That was a lot of fun," Astra grins. "Thanks for bringing me along."

I laugh. "Anytime. I'm glad you enjoyed yourself."

"You know he's never going to tell you anything, don't you?" Astra asks.

"I know."

"So why did you promise not to raid his compound?"

"I promised the Bureau wouldn't raid it and I intend to keep my word," I say. "I never said anything about not calling the local PD to do it. It would have been a nice collar for our guys but hey, putting the Revenants out of business is good no matter who gets the glory."

Astra laughs and shakes her head. "You are one cold-hearted, evil woman."

"Yes, I am," I reply.

ELEVEN

Wilder Residence; The Emerald Pines Luxury Apartments, Downtown Seattle

The steam billows around me and I let the hot water rain down on my head. I savor the warmth of the water on my skin and can feel it sluicing the tensions of my day away. After finishing up at the shop, I put in a call to the Kittitas County Sheriff's Office and told them about the Revenants compound and all the guns they had stockpiled there. The Sheriff told me they'd get some help and take the place down.

I'd hoped to build a stronger case against the Revenants. The guns are definitely going to put them away for a while, but not forever, as I'd hoped. But Frank is smart. Cagey. And after our visit today, I know if we don't move on him now, he'll have the guns transported elsewhere and we'll have to start all over again. So, it's better to get something than to walk away completely empty handed. Getting the guns out of the hands of a bunch of white supremacist whackos is good for everybody.

I finish up in the shower and throw on some pajamas after

drying off. I run the brush through my hair, then leave it down so it can dry naturally. I'm sure I'll wake up with a tangled mess of hair, but I couldn't not wash it after standing in that garage today. I swore I could smell the place on me after we left.

I walk out into the living room and smile as I inhale the delectable aroma of garlic. Mark is sitting at a candlelit table set for two with the rest of the lights dimmed, and soft jazz music plays from the Bluetooth soundbar.

"Well, isn't this romantic?"

Mark smiles. "Yes, it is."

"What's the occasion? Did I forget something?"

"Do I need a special occasion to spoil you by treating you to a lovely evening?" he asks.

"Of course not. But most men —"

"I'm not most men," he counters.

"That is true."

He gets up and walks over to me. Mark pulls me to him and wraps his arms around my waist. I lock my hands behind his neck, and we slow dance to the music for a few moments. He kisses me gently, his lips lingering upon mine, making my entire body tingle.

I've never been the overly romantic type. I've never even had a man go to this kind of effort for me. Except for Mark. He seems to routinely make these romantic gestures that make me feel incredibly special.

Mark steps back and takes my hand and leads me over to the table. He holds my chair out for me, then pushes it in as I sit. The perfect gentleman. I look at the vase on the table, see the white roses and smile. I run my fingertips over their smooth, velvety petals and smile. He has never once forgotten my aversion to the color red, and whenever he gets me flowers – which is more often than I care to admit – there is never a single red flower to be seen. It's such a small gesture, but it really is one of the most thoughtful things anybody has ever done for me.

Most people would tell me to get over it already. I've dated a few guys who tried to force me to incorporate the color red back into my life by sending me bouquets of red flowers, or buying me red jewelry, or red clothing. Most guys think my phobia of the color red is immature or just plain silly. I actually had one guy tell me that my parents were killed a long time ago and it's time to move on from it.

He thought my aversion to anything red was only keeping me tied to the past, then surmised that I didn't want to get over it and preferred being held hostage to the past by something as simple as a red flower. I told him to walk in on his parents lying in bright, vivid, almost unnaturally red pools of blood, and see how he reacts to it from then on. Needless to say, that was our last date.

But Mark, as he said, is not like most guys. He actually listens to me. He might think my aversion is silly, but he never says it. And he goes out of his way to ensure he never gets me anything red. It's beyond sweet, and the fact that he takes my feelings into account and doesn't hound me about them means a lot. It's just one of the many things I adore about him.

Mark reaches over and lifts the cover off my plate and the rush of rich aromas wafts up to me, making me smile and make my stomach rumble. My plate is covered with a seafood fettucine that looks absolutely amazing. He hands me a basket filled with cheesy garlic bread, and on a separate plate is a small Caesar salad. It's a feast fit for a king. Or a queen.

"Did you make all this?" I ask.

"Well, I made the call to Il Pescatore to have it delivered," he grins. "Does that count?"

I laugh. "It's good enough for me. Thank you. This is wonderful."

"Of course."

We tuck into our meals and I relish the explosion of flavor in my mouth. It's been a little while since we had Il Pescatore. I didn't realize how much I craved it until now. The moans of pleasure coming out of my mouth sound obscene, but I can't help it. It's just that good.

"So, how was work today?" I ask.

He shrugs and finishes chewing. "Not bad. Nothing too major," he says. "No federal agents to patch up today."

I grin. "Well, that's a good thing," I say. "But that's it? That's all I get?"

"What else do you want?"

I shrug. "You're always so tight-lipped about your job," I say. "I don't know, I guess I just kind of want to know what your day's like."

He smiles. "Honestly, it's just a series of patching up wounds and sending people on their way," he replies. "Once in a while we get the odd gunshot or car wreck victim that needs a little more care. But it's not as if I'm out there kicking in doors and all the exciting stuff you do. I'm an ER doctor, and while it's stressful, it's definitely not as intense or exciting as they make it out to be on TV. We don't have all the drama."

"Only you can make emergency medicine sound so... boring," I chuckle. "It's almost as though you're embarrassed by it or something."

He laughs softly. "I'm definitely not embarrassed by it," he says. "I take pride in what I do, but I'm not changing the world."

"You are for some people," I reply. "Saving somebody's life? Yeah, that's kind of world-changing for that person, and his or her loved ones."

"Fair enough. I'll take that," he says. "How about you? What did you do today?"

"I didn't change the world or save anybody's life, so I suppose it was boring."

He laughs and tosses a small piece of garlic bread at me. "Don't be a brat."

"I am what I am."

"That you are."

I smile and then tell him about my day. About the trip out to White Center and our run-in with Frank Metcalf. After that, I go into my frustration with not being able to get into this case and figure it out. And he listens to me, never interrupting, and looking at me as if my story is the most fascinating thing in the world to him.

"Well, I'd say getting all those guns off the street is changing the world," he says with a laugh. "I'd say you had a good day."

"Yeah, well, we'll see how long Frank and his boys go away."

"I worry about that," he says softly. "When they do get out, I worry that they'll come looking for you."

"Don't worry. I'll just shoot him next time."

Mark laughs and I'm struck by how domestic this whole scene is. Man and woman sitting down to dinner, sharing the stories of their day. I remember dinners around the table with my parents talking just like this; Mark and I are acting like an old married couple. For somebody who's been avoiding serious relationships like the plague, I'm further reminded that I'm kind of in one. It's a thought that makes me laugh to myself.

"What are you laughing at?" he asks with a grin.

Before I can answer, though, the ringing of my phone cuts through the music. I hop up and grab it off the counter, hoping something's popping on my case. I connect the call and hold the phone to my ear.

"Wilder," I answer.

"Is this Blake Wilder? Daughter of Nora and Ryan Wilder?"

I don't recognize the voice but something about it sends a cold chill straight down my spine. That and the use of my parents' names strikes an ominous chord inside of me.

"Yes, that's right," I say.

"My name is Claude Rosen," the man says. "I knew your parents. Was good friends with them, in fact."

I search my memory and the name definitely rings a few bells, but I can't put a face to it. I think, if anything, they may have mentioned him in passing, but that's about all. That tells me he's one of their friends from the NSA. I distinctly remember that my folks kept their two worlds separate – they had their friends at the NSA and would sometimes go out with them, but they never came by the house. I don't recall ever meeting any of their coworkers. Then they had their civilian friends: the 'normal people', as they called them. They were the ones who came over for barbecues, parties, and other social functions.

I recall that my father always quoted Mark Twain whenever I asked him about his work friends. He'd always give me that roguish smile of his and say, *"East is east, and west is west, and never the twain shall meet."* I never understood why they kept east and west completely separate. To be honest, I still don't.

"Wh–what can I do for you, Mr. Rosen?" I ask.

Mark gives me a curious look, wanting to know what's going on, so I hold up a finger, telling him to wait a moment, then turn back to my call.

"I know it's strange for me to be callin' you out of the blue like this, Blake. But I really need to speak with you. It's imperative we meet and talk. It's about your parents. Specifically, about their deaths," he says.

And it feels as if an anchor just dropped on my head.

My stomach is roiling as my heart flutters like the wings of a hummingbird. The past is rising up within me, and those old ghosts are reaching out from the grave, trying to pull me down under the surface once more. Having worked with Dr. Reinhart for so long, I've gotten to a place in my mind where I've accepted my parents' deaths. The memories are no longer controlling me the way they used to. Yeah, there are still some lingering issues that I need to work through, but I'm finally getting into a good headspace regarding their murders.

And now Claude Rosen is threatening to blow everything out of the water. All the hard work I've done on myself, the intensive counseling – it's all circling the drain with those four words: *"Specifically, about their deaths."* Once more, the specter of a conspiracy rises up in my mind. The belief that they were killed for knowing too much. Everything I've worked hard to tamp down is coming to the fore once again.

"I am sorry to drop this on you, Blake. But I wouldn't have called if it wasn't important. Critical, really," Claude says.

"Why now? Why after all these years are you contacting me?"

"Because I've only just learned there are things in motion that must be stopped. Things you must know," he explains. "I cannot say anymore over an open line, but I will be traveling to Seattle soon. I'll make contact once I arrive. Tell no one of this call or our meeting. Please, Blake. I wouldn't have contacted you if I had any other choice."

The line goes dead in my hand and I look down at my phone as if it's a snake, coiled and poised to strike. I start to tremble. I thought I had more or less escaped the shackles of the past that bound me tight.

But one phone call has proven just how wrong I was.

TWELVE

Wilder Residence; The Emerald Pines Luxury Apartments, Downtown Seattle

"Blake? Talk to me. What is it?"

Mark's voice cuts through the chaos in my mind and pulls me back to the present. I come out of my mental fog and find myself standing in my living room, staring down at my phone. Mark has gotten up and is standing beside me, his hand on my arm, his face etched with concern. I look back at him, my heart hammering away inside of me, the amazing food we've just eaten suddenly tasting like ash in my mouth.

"Who was that, Blake? What did he say?"

I shake my head and my vision starts coming back into focus. I still feel lightheaded, as if I'm trapped in a landscape of the surreal, not knowing up from down, what was real and what was false. I let Mark guide me back to the table and I sit down, the remnants of the food on my plate turning my stomach. I push the plate away and grab my glass of wine, draining it in one long swallow. I refill the bottle and am just about to down the second glass when Mark puts his hand over it and gives his head a shake.

"You should go easy on it," he says.

I'm just about to spit a caustic reply at him but bite it back. Mark didn't upset me and doesn't deserve my lashing out at him that way. I take a sip anyway, though, then set the glass down as Mark walks around the table and retakes his seat. He puts his elbows up on the table and rests his chin on his hands, his gaze laser-focused on me, an expression of expectation on his face.

"Who was that, Blake?"

I open my mouth to tell him but then close it again without speaking. Mr. Rosen had warned me not to tell anybody about the call or his identity. And if he's former NSA who has information about my parents' deaths, his request for anonymity is not without good reason.

But this is Mark. Kind, thoughtful, generous, and compassionate Mark. I tell him everything. Or at least, most everything. Don't I? Why would I keep this from him?

Something inside of me tells me to not say a word. To anybody. It's not that it's only Mark I'm hiding it from. Mr. Rosen wanted me to keep his call a secret from everybody, and my curiosity is spiking off the charts.

"Blake?"

"I – uhhh – it was nothing," I say.

"Nothing?" he replies, his eyes wide with disbelief. "You're shaking like a leaf, Blake. I'd really hate to see what would happen if it were something."

"It's just – it's fine," I tell him. "Can we just pretend that didn't happen and enjoy the rest of our evening?"

"Sure. Fine."

Mark frowns and as I push the remaining food around my plate, he stabs his food, angrily scraping the fork against his teeth. The mood is definitely dead in this room and the air is dripping with tension. I don't want to deal with this right now. I don't know what I want, but it's definitely not dealing with Mark's attitude. I take another drink of wine, hoping it will dull my senses enough to let me go to sleep.

"Are you really not going to tell me?" he asks.

"Mark, I don't want to do this."

"Really? Because I didn't want to do it that morning you accused me of sneaking around behind your back," he spits. "But because I care for you, I did it anyway. I talked it out with you and proved I wasn't running around on you."

"This isn't the same, Mark. Please, just leave it alone."

He blows out an exasperated breath and drops his fork. It hits the plate with a loud and sudden crash that makes me jump in my seat. I reach out with a trembling hand and pick up my wine glass, taking another long swallow of it, wishing it would get me drunk quickly. But I have a feeling the amount of adrenaline flowing through my body is counteracting the alcohol. Basically, I'm pretty sure I can drink all night and still be sober as a judge.

"Are you really going to shut me out like this?" Mark asks.

"I'm not shutting you out of anything."

"You most certainly are," he growls. "Whatever that phone call was, it shook you up pretty badly. I'd have to be blind not to see it. And yet, instead of talking to me about it, you're just doing what you always do and bundling it all up inside."

"What I always do?" I snap, my mouth falling open.

"Yes, Blake. It's what you always do," he doubles down. "You expect me to be an open book, but when it comes to sharing your stuff, you just clam up on me. You do this all the damn time."

"Mark, stop."

"Stop? I haven't even gotten started yet."

"I am not doing this. Not tonight."

He scoffs. "And you have the gall to accuse me of keeping secrets from you."

"Please, just leave this alone."

"This isn't fair, Blake. This isn't how relationships work," he says, his voice rising. "Oh, wait, we're not actually having a relationship, because you don't want to commit to me."

"I told you I didn't want anything serious when we started seeing each other," I say. "I was very explicit on that point."

"Yeah, you were," he shoots back. "So why is it that you get so worked up when you think I'm seeing somebody else then, huh?"

I feel my shock wearing off as my anger starts to rise. I've been begging him to leave this alone and stop pushing me, but he won't listen. He just keeps pushing. Keeps picking. And he's driving me toward an explosion. I don't need this tonight.

"Well? Answer me, Blake."

"Mark, not every piece of my life is available for your scrutiny. I'm sorry if that upsets you, but I don't owe you everything! I'm allowed to keep some pieces of myself....for myself!" I raise my voice in agitation. I didn't realize I was yelling until the words were already out of my mouth.

"And yet, you expect to be able to scrutinize every piece of my life!"

"I don't. And I don't press you when you say you don't want to talk about something," I tell him, taking a couple deep breaths to calm myself down. "But when it comes to my thinking you were running around, that's because it impacts me directly. It has to do with respect as well as my own health and safety. Sorry if that upsets you."

He pushes away from the table violently and gets to his feet. I watch him as he paces around the living room, looking like an agitated lion I once saw at a zoo. His face is red, his jaw clenched, and an expression of absolute contempt mars his face. If he thinks that's the way to get me to talk, he couldn't be further from the truth.

"Why can't you just respect me when I say I don't want to talk about something?" I ask, doing my best to keep my voice even. "Why can't you just let it go?"

"It's about basic fairness and equality here, Blake," he replies, less evenly. "You demand my secrets but give me none of your own."

"Is that the way you really see things? That I never open up and share with you? Ever?"

"That's the way it feels right now."

"That's ridiculous and overly dramatic, don't you think?"

"Actually, no. I don't think it is."

"So, you think I should just tell you everything. Give you every last part of me that you demand and keep nothing of myself for myself," I press. "Is that the way you see things? Is that equality in your eyes? Is that fair?"

"It sure as hell is fair," he says through gritted teeth. "That's the way people who care about each other act. They share with each other."

"Healthy people who care each other have boundaries," I respond. "And healthy people respect each other's boundaries."

"Oh, did you get that little pearl of wisdom from your shrink?"

The mocking tone in his voice sets my blood boiling. There are a lot of different ways you can attack me. Some of those ways are even valid. But going after me because I've sought counseling to help me overcome my issues is a low I would never have expected from Mark. It's lower than low.

I narrow my eyes and clench my jaw as I look at him. "I think you need to go now."

"Oh, things getting a little too real for you, Blake?"

"No. You crossed a line," I snap. "And now I think you should go."

He stares at me, confused. "What line? What are you talking about?"

"If you don't know, I'm certainly not going to explain it to you."

He sighs and shakes his head. "That is a really childish game."

"Go, Mark," I demand, my voice ice cold. "I don't want you here right now."

"Are you serious?"

"Get out!" I scream as tears roll down my cheeks.

He gives a start and looks at me with wide eyes and an expression that says he realizes he screwed up. I've never yelled at him like that before, and I've certainly never cried like this in front of him. He takes a step toward me, but the look I give him obviously conveys my message, because he backs off. He opens his mouth to say something, but I cut him off.

"I said go. Now."

Looking absolutely flummoxed, Mark grabs his coat and storms out of my place, slamming the door behind him so hard, it knocks a small, framed picture off the wall beside the door. It hits the floor with a sharp tinkling sound as the frame shatters. I sink back down into my chair and bury my face in my hands, sobbing and heaving for what feels like forever.

I cry until I'm all cried out, and when I'm done, I finish off the rest of the wine, then fall into a deep and troubled sleep.

THIRTEEN

EZ-4U Payday Loans and Check Cashing; Federal Way, WA

THERE WAS a time in my life when I wanted to do great things. I wanted to be a famous chef at one point. A painter at another time. I even used to secretly harbor dreams about being an actor or a model. But then I went and joined the military, and my life went completely off the rails. The things I saw and did over there messed me up but good. I freely admit that.

Well... I admit that now, after spending some years with a VA shrink. Fat lot of good that did me. About the only thing I can say about my time with the shrink is that he finally got me to admit that I'm screwed up in the head. There are only so many people you can kill, or see killed in front of you, before you're good and thoroughly screwed up.

After I gave up on therapy, I just kind of wandered and meandered through life doing odd jobs here and there. I was a line cook at a greasy diner for a while. Then I did some construction and house painting. I even worked security at a local theater for a time. It was as if there was part of me that remembered who I was and those dreams I once had, but the person I am now corrupted those dreams and made a mockery of them.

Life back then was dull and gray. I was simply going through the motions with no real direction or purpose. But then Ricky, a buddy of mine from the service, came to me. Said he was in dire need of money and asked me to help him rob a check cashing place. He assured me it would be easy work. And it was. We each earned a couple grand from that heist. I did a couple more jobs with him before branching out on my own. I found out Ricky was shot and killed on his first job without me. I know I should feel bad about it, but whatever.

It wasn't the money that kept me pulling those jobs in the early days. Don't get me wrong, the cash was nice. It had me living a lot better than those part-time jobs I was slogging through. No, it wasn't the money. It was the thrill of it all.

It's such a rush to pull a job like that and get away scot-free. There's always the danger and the possibility that you end up like Ricky. You never know if the dude behind the counter is going to be waiting to put a hot slug in your chest or not. And that's what makes it so exciting.

But even that excitement dulled after a while. The jobs were too easy. The cashiers were all too willing to give me whatever I wanted and the thrill I got started to fade. Oh, I'd still pull jobs, simply because I had no desire to go work some menial gig somewhere. But after a while, it just wasn't the same anymore.

And then I met Sasha. She is a dangerous kind of crazy, and has me taking risks I never thought I'd take. She's opened me up to so many new ways of doing and seeing things that I never even considered before. Sasha is the one who convinced me to kill. She convinced me the rush of taking another life was an unimaginable high. I told her I took plenty of lives when I was in the service, but she said what she had planned was different.

So that first night, after I pulled my first job with her, we were driving around, and she spotted a girl walking alone on the street. She said she wanted the girl, and that it was her turn. So, we did it. We snatched the girl up, went somewhere private, stripped her down, and tied her up. I was all set to kill her when Sasha told me she wanted to watch me have sex with her. I was taken aback, since Sasha was the only woman I wanted. But she said that was the rush for her – watching me be with the girl, then end her.

So I did it. While Sasha videotaped us, I took the girl and then I killed her. Those first couple of kills were hairy. I was hesitant and made a huge mess of things. Looking back on it now, I see how sloppy those early kills were. I mean, there's a difference between shooting at somebody a way off and actually plunging your knife into warm, living flesh. But Sasha was right. It was a rush of strength and power like I've never felt before. It's better than any drug I've ever taken, and I've taken a lot of them.

After we were done with the girl, Sasha and I had the best sex we've ever had. It was intense and powerful. I felt connected to her in ways I never knew you could be connected to another person. Our bond grew so deep that I can't picture my life without her now. Don't want to, actually. And I know she feels the same way.

For the last two years, we've been robbing and killing and living the high life together. The money we steal allows us to go where we want. Do what we want. And live how we want. But we always come back to the basics: knocking over a check cashing store, then hunting a girl for our pleasure later.

But lately, Sasha seems to need more. We're taking more risks and hitting the stores more often than we should. Doing more robberies and murders means giving the cops more of a chance to find us. It increases the possibility that we leave evidence behind. I'm always exceedingly careful, but living life this way means we're taking chances. And one day, I know we'll make a mistake, and those chances are going to run out. But we vowed if that happens, we're going down together in a blaze of glory. We're going down together.

I know we shouldn't be out here tonight. Not so soon after the Bellevue job. And definitely not so close to it. I mean, hell, Federal Way is less than an hour from Bellevue. But still, I'm hoping that since they're different cities and different jurisdictions, we can scrape by the way we always do. I tried to talk Sasha out of doing it tonight, but she was insistent. Said she really needed it.

And I cannot say no to this girl. Ever. About anything.

"Okay, they're closed up. You ready?" I ask.

"You know I am, baby. I'm already so excited thinkin' about later," Sasha says. "You and me are gonna have some fun tonight."

"I can't wait."

"Me either. I'm hot for it. I'm hot for you, baby."

"Well then, let's get this done."

We get out of the car and walk to the alley that runs behind the strip mall where the check cashing place is located. Aside from the tattoo parlor, the check cashing store is the only place that's open at this hour, so the alleyway is empty. There are two cars parked behind the shop, which lines up with what I saw when I passed by the front windows and saw two cashiers behind the counter earlier.

Sasha throws her arms around me and presses her mouth to mine, giving me a passionate kiss full of fire that gets me all aroused and has me looking forward to later on. I'm anxious just to get this done. She steps back and takes her position beside the door, then pulls her balaclava down. After taking one last look around the parking lot and alleyway, confirming we're alone, I pull mine down as well, then bang on the door, trying to make it sound as authoritative as I can.

A minute later, a voice comes through the speaker Sasha is leaning against. Startled, she jumps away and then does her best to stifle her giggle. I'm grinning at her and shake my head, putting my finger to my lips.

"Yeah?" comes the voice, sounding tinny coming through the speaker.

I step over and press the button and lean close to the square intercom pad. "Hey, I'm with Jiffy Tow and I just needed to let the owner of the..." I turn and look at the two cars parked behind me, "green Toyota, know that it's blocking the alley. I got a call and am supposed to tow it. If you want to move it though, I'll let you do it."

There's no peephole in the door, so he can't look out and see. Not that it would do much good. There's no light in the parking lot, and it's darker than pitch out here.

"What? That's my car. It's not blocking the alley –"

"Looks like it rolled back, man. I dunno if you didn't put it in park or engage your emergency brake or whatever, but it's definitely in the alley. I don't want to tow it, but I will if you don't want to move it."

"Yeah, yeah, hang on," he says.

I turn my AR-15 around and ready myself. I hear the click and clack of multiple locks being disengaged and when the guy opens the door, I drive the butt of my weapon into his face. Just like the guy the other night, he staggers backward, clutching his nose. Blood is dribbling onto the ground as he sways on his feet; I step forward and bring my weapon down on the back of his neck and drop him. He collapses to the ground with a wet, meaty thump. He groans, his head swaying back and forth on the ground as he leaks blood.

"What are you —" he starts, but he doesn't have time to finish before his words slur out into drool on the floor.

I knock him a few more times just to make sure he's out.

I look around and see two cameras in the back area, so I hit them with the spray paint, blinding the security system in the rear of the store.

"We're good," I call.

Sasha saunters in and gives me a wink as she giggles. I smile beneath my balaclava and return her wink, my mind filled with images of what we'll be doing later.

"Get to it, baby. We'll be waiting," Sasha coos.

"No carvin' on this one," I say with a laugh.

Her eyes crinkle up as she smiles beneath her mask and crosses her heart. Still, though, I have a feeling I'm going to come back and find her carving another flower into the guy's face. Sasha's adorable, but she's definitely not entirely right in the head. But it somehow only adds to my attraction to her.

I move to the door that leads out to the front of the house. Moving fast and quick, I burst into the front area and quickly sweep the store. The only person I see is a tall, thin guy in a blue polo and khakis. His eyes widen when he sees me, and he dives for the counter and the silent alarm button that's mounted there.

He's fast, but I'm faster and get to the counter before him. I slam the butt of my weapon down on the side of his head. The guy staggers to the side, blood pouring from a gash in his head, but he quickly rights himself and looks at me with an expression that's equal parts fear and rage. He launches himself at me, his hands balled into fists.

If I had time to shake my head, I would have. The kid's fit

and in good shape, but he doesn't know the first thing about fighting. When he closes on me, I punch out with the butt of my weapon again and jab him hard in the face. The snap of his nose is audible, and despite the blood flowing from his nose now, too, the kid stays on his feet and manages to deliver a punch that rocks my head to the side. My mouth fills with the coppery taste of my blood and points of light burst behind my eyes.

I dance backward, out of his reach, to give myself a second to recover. He's the first one who's ever gotten a hand on me, and it pisses me off. The kid rushes me again and I step to the side, slamming him in the back of the head with the butt of my weapon. His head snaps forward and he staggers, then goes down hard.

I'm on him in a moment, standing over him with the barrel of my weapon pointed right at him. He groans and rolls over, his eyes widening as he sees me standing above him. I could just light him up right now and be done with it. But that wouldn't be as satisfying.

"Get up," I tell him.

"Please," he gasps. "Please don't –"

"I said, get up!" I shout, my voice filled with rage.

Holding his hands up, the kid gets to one knee, and that's when I step forward and drive my boot into his face. He goes down hard again, landing flat on his back with a loud groan. I step forward and deliver a kick to his groin, making the kid cry out. Just the sound of his voice fuels my rage and I stomp on his chest as hard as I can. Something in there snaps, and a wet gurgling sound passes his lips.

The taste of my blood in my mouth is thick. I kick him again. And again. The kid is screaming bloody murder as I kick him, which is only pissing me off even more. He's rolling around on the ground, cupping his injured groin, moaning miserably. So I take the opportunity to hit the security cameras with the spray paint to blind them.

The kid stirs, and it looks as if he's about to get to his feet again, so I step back over to him and drive the butt of my weapon into his head yet again. He slumps back to the ground but doesn't go out. The kid is tough and must have a head harder than stone. So I kick him again.

"Get him, baby," Sasha cries as she steps into the front area. "Get him!"

Sasha's eyes sparkle with excitement and she's bouncing up and down, clapping her hands. Just the sight of her fills me with power and energy and I keep kicking the kid. My leg is getting tired and my breathing is ragged. I've kicked him so many times, it's wearing me out. And since I don't want to be too tired to enjoy the rest of the night, I draw my foot back one final time and deliver a soccer-style kick to the kid's head. I hear a loud snap, and then he's still.

"Baby, you got him good," she squeals. You got him real good."

I pull the black bag out of my pocket and shake it out, then move from station to station, emptying the drawers and putting all the cash in the bag. The safe is open, so I grab that money as well, thinking I must be the luckiest man in the world.

"We should go buy a lottery ticket," I say.

"We can do that after," she replies. "We have a date to keep. And we don't want to keep our girl waiting, now do we?"

I raise the balaclava up to my nose, then pull hers up as well and press my mouth to hers. Our kiss is fiery and hot and stirs my passion to new heights. I can't wait for the rest of our evening.

I step back and pull my mask back down. "No, we don't want to keep our girl waiting," I say. "Anything for you, baby."

"And that's why I love you," she replies. "Now let's get out of here."

"Lead the way."

She tips me a wink. "Don't I always, baby?"

She does. And I'm always happy to follow.

FOURTEEN

"BLAKE, SERIOUSLY? YOU THREW HIM OUT?" Astra asks, her eyes wide with surprise.

"He wouldn't stop pushing me. He just pushed, and pushed, and pushed even though I told him to stop. To leave it all alone," I say.

"So, is that it? I mean, are you done seeing him?"

I shrug and spread my hands out wide. "I really don't know and at this point, I really don't care. I've got a lot bigger things on my mind right now."

She nods. "Right. The phone call."

Of course, I told Astra about the call. Aside from Maisey, she is the one person in this world I have no hesitation about telling everything. My trust in her has never been shaken and I never fear that she'll either judge me or spill my secrets. My trust in Astra – and Maisey – is absolute. Always has been.

"I don't know what to make of it," I tell her. "I mean, the

name rings a bell, but I can't say why. I know for sure I've never met anybody by that name. And I can't say for sure that it's not just a false memory. I mean, my folks were so secretive about their work that I could just be filling in that gap because he said he worked with them. It's entirely possible I've never heard the name before in my life."

"Well, did you look him up?" she asks.

I nod. "I did. After I threw Mark out, I looked through all the files I've collected on my parents' case over the years; – I even did a Google search," I tell her. "But I came up completely empty. The guy is a ghost."

"Did you have Rick take a look around?"

I shake my head. "That's not something I want to get him involved with. If he trips some alert and somebody finds out he's looking, the people who killed my folks could come looking for him next."

Astra sits back in her chair and takes a drink of her coffee, seeming to be processing everything. She cups her hands around the mug of coffee and frowns.

"So, we're back to its being a conspiracy?" she asks.

I shrug. "What else am I supposed to think? This guy I've never met before calls me out of the blue almost twenty years after they were killed and says he's got information about their deaths. Says it's critical he talk to me and that there are things in motion that need to be stopped. If that's not a conspiracy, what is it, Astra?"

She shakes her head. "I really don't know. Is it possible this is just some crank? Could the guy be a tinfoil hatter himself? Maybe he actually was friends with your folks and has had trouble coping with their deaths, too. Maybe he's making up conspiracies to help him do that."

I open my mouth, then close it again and give it a moment. Astra's words sink into my head and I let them rattle around for a few minutes, thinking about them. I take a drink of my coffee and then set the cup down gently, giving myself another second to properly put my words into order before I speak.

"I mean, I suppose it's possible. But it doesn't track for me. A friend of theirs that shaken up by their deaths that he invents this fairy tale in his head two decades later?" I ask. "I mean, I'm their daughter, and I got to the point where I was finally at peace with the past. I would think somebody who was only their friend would have made peace with it long ago."

She shrugs. "You never know. Death hits people weird sometimes. Maybe they were all really tight. Maybe he was kind of walking that fine line between crazy and sane already and their murder pushed him over that edge. Anything is possible."

"But I won't know until I speak with him."

"I would advise you not to do it. I mean, if the guy is crazy, he could try to hurt you, for one thing," she says. "For another, let's say he's right and there are things in motion. What if his job is to take you out because you're a loose end?"

"But I'm not. I don't know anything."

"If there really is a conspiracy though, the people behind it don't know that. Not for sure," she continues. "I mean, you haven't really made it a secret that you were looking into their murders. What if they're afraid you found something?"

"If I had, wouldn't I have exposed them already?"

"Again, they might not know what you know – or don't know. If there really is a conspiracy, they can't afford to take chances. The only way to eliminate the possibility is to eliminate you," she says. "And what better way to do it than to have somebody appear out of the blue with new information you just have to have. Either way you slice it, this thing smells like a setup to me, babe."

"Or the third option is that Claude Rosen really does have

information that can expose my parents' killers. Maybe even a lead on where and how to find Kit," I say.

"I'm not going to say it's impossible, because it's possible. But is it likely? I don't think so," she tells me. "I think the risks outweigh the rewards."

"Not if the reward is finding out who murdered my parents and stole my sister."

"Yeah, but that's a might big 'if'."

I nod, knowing that she's right, but not truly wanting to admit it. I can always count on Astra to give me the unvarnished truth of things and provide me with some much-needed perspective. If not for her, I'd probably be going off half-cocked most of the time. Okay, some of the time. I'm not impulsive by nature, but there are certain things that will always get a rise out of me and make me go blindly charging in. My family is one of those things.

"This is all kind of spooky," she comments. "I mean, why now?"

"And what things does he think are in motion?"

She frowns and shakes her head and we both sit in silence for a minute, both of us consumed by our thoughts. I know she's right about things. I probably shouldn't go meet with Claude Rosen. There really are too many risks. But there's still a piece of me that thinks finding out who killed my parents and took my sister is a reward that completely outstrips the risks.

"So, not to beat a dead horse or anything, but what are you going to do about Mark?"

I shake my head. "I have no idea. I really think he crossed the line last night when he made fun of me for seeing Dr. Reinhart."

"Why is it that men always find a wonderful relationship with a gorgeous, kick-ass Super Chick like yourself and insist on shooting themselves in the foot like that?"

"Beats me," I reply. "You'd think being a doctor, he'd be more clued in on the importance of mental health."

"Look, I like Mark and all but both as a doctor and as a general human being, he knew better than to play that card with you. If you think that's the line crossed, that's the line crossed, babe."

"I don't know. Haven't we all said stupid, insensitive things when we were angry?"

"Like the time you told me when we had a spat that I should stop with the Botox?" she chirps.

I groan and cover my face with my hands, feeling that familiar burn of shame in my face. Yeah, I told her that once long ago. Lucky for me she remembers it and is able to trot that thing out just to remind me. What would I do without her?

"Are you ever going to forget that?" I sigh.

"Not bloody likely," she replies. "But I guess you're right. People say stupid things when they're upset. And I mean, really stupid."

She stands up and spins around, displaying herself like a commodity. I bury my face in a hand and laugh despite the maelstrom of negative emotions swirling around inside of me.

"This is all natural, baby," she says, then retakes her seat.

Thank God for Astra. If not for her, I'd be wallowing in misery most of the time. I would also have probably gotten myself beat up or shot a time or twelve because my mouth sometimes gets the better of me. It's not the side of my personality that is normally on display, but I'd be lying if I said it didn't exist. I have been known to shoot my mouth off and make bad decisions from time to time – something I'm not particularly proud of, but something I won't deny either. It all goes into making me who I am.

"I'm getting such mixed messages from you," I tell her. "Should I drop him like a rock or give him another chance?"

Astra shifts back and forth in her seat as if considering the options, then lets out a big sigh. "Other than this... whatever the hell this is, Mark is a great guy. He's kind. Thoughtful. And he obviously adores the hell out of you. And you guys have been on and off for, what? A few years now, right?"

"Yeah," I nod. "But I stand by what I said – not every single facet of my life is open for his scrutiny. I'm allowed to have some things I keep to and for myself."

"And you deserve that," she states. "It's clear he has some issues with boundaries, so maybe before you put him in a rocket and shoot him directly into the sun, talk to him about that. See if you can't both set some healthy boundaries with each other."

"We'll see how he reacts to that," I say.

"Well, if he reacts badly, then feel free to throw him out to the curb. We can even TP his place together if you want."

That draws a laugh from me, and I sit back in my seat. Maybe it's foolish, but I don't think I'm ready to let Mark go just yet. I care for him. Quite a lot. And this was our first real fight. I know better than most that when you're caught up in the heat of the moment, you do sometimes say stupid things. I've certainly had to remove my foot from my mouth more than once. So maybe I can forgive him, and we can put this behind us.

If he wants to, that is. But part of our being able to put this behind us requires that he accept the fact that I do have boundaries. That every single facet of my life isn't open to him. There are and will be things I don't want to share with him. And he needs to be okay with that. Even as a couple, people need to have those parts of themselves they keep only for themselves. It shouldn't be a controversial thing.

So I guess we'll have to see how it goes. I figure I'll give it a few days before I call him so we both have a chance to cool down and get our heads on straight.

"Thanks, Astra."

"Hey, you know I've got you," she winks.

There's a knock on my office door and when I look up, I see Rick with his nose practically on the glass. He's excited about something – I can tell because he's breathing heavily on the glass door and leaving a round steamy spot. Astra and I share a laugh as I wave him in.

"What's got you so worked up, Rick?" I ask.

"There was another one last night," he announces. "Our guy hit a check cashing place in Federal Way."

I cut a glance at Astra, who grins. "I told you he was still in the area."

"Well, let's go see what we see then."

"Road trip," Astra squeals.

FIFTEEN

A LITTLE LESS THAN an hour south of Seattle is Federal Way. With a population near a hundred thousand, it's the fifth-largest city in King County, the tenth largest in all of Washington. It's not quite as peaceful as Bellevue, but with just four murders reported in the last year or so, it's not exactly the Wild West. It's also not as wealthy as Bellevue, with a considerably lower median income, but it's not a slum, either. By most accounts, Federal Way is kind of... average.

Astra parks the car, then we get out and head for the crime scene. Once we get to the tape, we flash our creds for the patrol cop, Officer Moore by his name tag, manning the line. He holds it up for us to duck under. After we cross the line, I turn back to the patrol cop.

"Sorry, Officer Moore, but who's in charge of the crime scene?" I ask.

"That'd be Detective Ralston," he says, pointing to a man

standing just outside the front door of the store. "That's him over there."

"Terrific. Thank you."

"Yep."

We head for the man Officer Moore pointed out. He's engaged with one of the crime scene techs, and the conversation appears to be pretty animated. Ralston's face is red and he's gesturing wildly.

"He seems stressed out already," Astra observes.

"Great. Because I really wanted to deal with a high-strung detective today."

Astra laughs quietly, then looks over at me. "Are you ever going to let Mo come out to the crime scenes? Or is she permanently parked on the bench?"

"I'll eventually let her come out with us," I reply. "I want her to get a little more seasoned before we get her out here. She's a good agent. I just want her to be able to handle whatever comes our way."

"Are you still holding it against her that she puked at a murder scene?"

"Well, forgive me for not wanting to hire a cleanup crew to come with us every time we want to hit up a crime scene."

"You know, the best way to get her over it is through immersion."

I shrug. "Maybe we should send her out to the Body Farm in Quantico."

"Now, that would be cruel."

"It'd be very immersive."

She laughs. "That it would."

The tech leaves as we get there, and when Ralston sees us, a look of pure exasperation crosses his face. Ralston is a tall, lanky man with dark hair in a crew cut and dark eyes. He's clean shaven and looks to be somewhere in his mid-forties. He's thin but looks fit. He's probably a runner or a swimmer.

"How did you get past the tape?" he snaps. "This is an active crime scene. There is no press allowed in here."

We flash our badges, and he rolls his eyes, looking even more exasperated than when he thought we were reporters.

"SSA Blake Wilder," I introduce myself, using my title to impress him. "Special Agent Astra Russo."

"Great. Feds. This day just keeps getting better and better," he groans, not sounding the least bit impressed. "What do you guys want?"

"We only want to look at your crime scene," I tell him.

"Why?"

"We're relatively certain this is part of a string of assaults and robberies," I say.

He shakes his head. "This ain't one of your string, then."

"Why do you say that, Detective?"

"Because this is a robbery and a homicide. Not a simple assault."

"Homicide?"

"That's what I said," he replies.

Astra and I exchange a look as we realize our biggest fear has come to pass. I take a breath and let it out, then look up at Ralston.

"Was there black spray paint on the cameras?" I ask.

He nods. "Yep."

"And was the victim beaten to death?"

He nods again. "Sure was."

"Then I'm pretty sure this is our guy. His pattern of violence has been steadily escalating," I tell him. "His attacks have gotten more and more vicious."

"And now he's apparently graduated to murder," Astra adds.

Ralston sighs and runs a hand through his dark hair. Originally, I thought he was just a high-strung guy prone to irritability. But as I watch him react to what's going on, I see it's not that. He's upset. This crime is hitting him personally.

"You knew the victim," I say.

He nods and turns away, but not before I see his eyes shimmer with unshed tears. We give him a moment to gather himself, and when he's ready, he turns back to us. His face is ashen, his expression grave.

"His name is..." his voice trails off and he chokes back a tear. "His name was Peter Huffman. He was a friend of my son's. He was a good kid."

"I'm sorry," I tell him.

He grits his teeth and nods. "You can go ahead and go on in."

"Thank you, Detective."

Astra gives him a nod, and we turn and step through the front door. The interior of EZ-4U looks roughly the same as the last place. There's a large waiting area with a long counter across the room from us. Thick, bulletproof glass sits atop the counter with small pass-through trays at the four stations. A door to the right of the counter stands open and the police department's techs are coming and going through it. They give us strange looks as they pass by.

We go through the door and step into the work area. Fingerprint powder dust covers almost every surface, but it's the body on the ground that draws our attention. He was tall and lean in life, but I can't tell you what he might have looked like. His face is absolutely pulped. Our unsub really went to town on this kid and left his face bloody, broken, and battered beyond all recognition.

"Jesus," I whisper.

"Okay, this is beyond the pale. The violence... Christ, Blake. I might just pull a Mo right here," Astra says.

The moment is solemn and it's completely inappropriate, but I have to bite back the laughter that's bubbling up in my throat. I nudge her with my elbow to make her stop. But she gives me a wink, a grin curling a corner of her mouth upward. We glove up and squat down next to the body and do a cursory examination of it, but nothing stands out to me. It looks like a vicious bludgeoning.

"Look at this," Astra says, pointing to the kid's cheek.

"Is that...?"

Astra nods. "The guy stomped this kid hard enough to leave an imprint of his boot."

I shake my head. "Unbelievable," I say. "The level of violence is off the charts."

"Pure savagery," Astra adds.

"This guy is an animal. We need to get him off the streets."

"Agreed."

We get to our feet and walk the perimeter of the scene, noting the different spots of blood, overturned tables, knocked over chairs, and stacks of paper strewn all over the place. All around us are the signs of a tremendous struggle.

"The kid put up one hell of a fight," Astra notes.

"That might have been the trigger that set this animal off," I say. "Our unsub doesn't like people who fight back. It turns him up to eleven."

"Looks more like it turned him up to fifteen," she quips.

"So, the kid fights back. Maybe got a good shot in on our guy.

"And then he goes ballistic. Stomps this poor kid so hard, he left boot prints in his face."

"That tells us he's got anger control issues. And his control has been slipping. This put him over the edge," I say. "My fear is now that he's gotten a taste for the kill that this is going to become standard at every store he knocks over."

"Based on what I'm seeing here, I think that fear's justified."

"We need to get the surveillance footage, but I have a feeling we already know what we're going to see on the tapes," I say, pointing to one of the blacked-out cameras.

We walk out of the store and into the bright afternoon sunlight. A cool wind blows down the street and I watch a tin can rolling along the pavement for a moment for no other reason than I want something else in my head than that bloodied and battered corpse inside.

"That help any? Give you any clues to follow?"

I turn to Detective Ralston, who's still standing where he left us. He's managed to regain his composure, but his eyes are still carrying a hard edge to them. He's angry. Wants to do to the killer what the killer did to his son's friend in there.

"It gives us another couple of pieces to build a profile with," I tell him. "And we are certain the man who did this is the same man we've been looking for. He's now committed thirty-two robberies over the last five years, and nineteen assaults."

"He done this in all of 'em?"

I shake my head. "No. It's as I said though, over the past couple of years, his pattern of violence has been escalating."

"This is the first time he's actually killed somebody," Astra tells him.

Ralston sighs and runs a hand through his hair again, his pained expression only deepening, and my heart goes out to him. There's really not much more I can say and not much more to be done here. We've gotten all we can out of the scene, which, sadly, isn't very much. Other than getting a couple of new bullet points for my profile, we're no closer to finding him than we were before we arrived. But this is me doing my due diligence, as usual.

"There is one survivor," Ralston says. "Jeffrey Searles. He's at Federal General."

"Thank you, Detective Ralston," I say. "And again, I'm sorry for your loss."

"Keep me in the loop?" he asks.

I nod. "Absolutely."

We turn and are walking back to the car when I hear a couple of patrol cops talking. Something I overhear catches my attention and I stop and turn. I step over to the two patrol cops who were talking.

"I'm sorry to interrupt, but what did you just say?" I ask. "To your friend just now."

The cop, a kid whose face is covered with peach fuzz and looks fresh out of the academy, turns to me, and then his eyes slide over to Astra. He stands up a little straighter and puffs himself up a bit. It's adorable.

"And who are you?" he asks.

We flash him our badges. "I'm SSA Wilder and this is Special Agent Russo."

"Very Special Agent Russo," he says.

We both roll our eyes, and his face grows red and looks away from us. He clears his throat and turns back to us, doing his level best to hold onto a shred of his dignity.

I give him a smile. "So, you were saying?"

"Yeah, I was just saying that between this murder and the other one last night, things are getting crazy around here," he says.

"There was another murder last night?"

He nods. "Yeah. From what I heard it was particularly nasty. She was found butchered in her apartment this morning."

Astra and I exchange a look and I feel that familiar churn in my belly when pieces of the puzzle start falling into place. I silently tell myself to throttle back for a minute. I don't want to jump to conclusions or make connections that don't exist. But the fact that we now have two murders in the same town, on the same night our unsub knocked over a check cashing place, seems like a massive coincidence. One that can't be ignored.

"Do you have the address for the murder, Officer Reyes?" I ask.

"Yeah, it's at the Evergreen Apartments over on Sage Avenue," he replies. "Apartment 103. You won't be able to miss the mass of cops out there."

"Thanks, Officer Reyes."

"Sure thing, Agent Wilder," he says. "And thank you, Agent Russo."

Astra laughs as we turn and head for the car. I look over at her and smile.

"I can take the murder scene if you want to go spend some time with Officer Reyes, Very Special Agent Russo," I say.

She laughs. "You can stuff it. I think I'm old enough to be that kid's mother."

"Go get him, cougar."

"I hate you so much right now."

Laughing, we get into the car and head for the Evergreen Apartments.

SIXTEEN

Evergreen Apartments; Federal Way, WA

"Who's in charge of the scene?" I ask.

"Detective Clarkson," the burly cop on the tap replies.

We flash him our badges, but he's unmoved, and doesn't offer to allow us under the tape. Astra and I exchange a look. This is a first. Usually, our badges get us onto any crime scene without question.

"We're federal agents and we'd like to tour the crime scene," I tell him.

The man, Officer Foster, folds his beefy forearms over his even beefier chest, his face as expressive as a stone. The man would look right at home on any football field and be just as effective at blocking people from getting where they want to go, I'm sure.

"Are you serious right now?" Astra asks. "We're federal agents."

"I saw your badges and I can read," he says, his voice a deep, rumbling baritone.

"Then, why are you denying us entry to the crime scene?" she presses.

"Detective Clarkson said nobody gets in."

"I'm sure she was talking about all the rubberneckers and media," Astra says, gesturing to the crowd jockeying for position at the tape. "I don't think she meant keeping federal agents off the crime scene."

"She said nobody."

I sigh. "Please go and get Detective Clarkson, then. I'd like to speak with her," I say. "We will wait right here for you."

A woman steps up beside the lineman-slash-cop and looks at us. "And you two are?"

"Agents Wilder and Russo, FBI," I say. "Detective Clarkson?"

"I am. Can I see your credentials?"

We flash her our badges and she looks them over, then nods. "You can let them through, Foster. They're alright."

"Yes ma'am," he says and holds up the tape.

We step under it and walk with Clarkson. She leads us over to the side of the entryway. Uniform cops and crime scene techs are coming and going. The complex is a hive of activity. Clarkson is about five-four, with honey-blonde hair that falls to her shoulders, brown eyes, and a petite build. She looks at us through icy eyes and she has a noticeably cool demeanor. The way she carries herself tells me she's got a no-nonsense attitude. And the way she holds herself makes me think she's tough.

I like her already.

"So, what can I do for you, agents?" she asks.

"We wanted to take a peek at your crime scene," I say.

"Any particular reason?"

"We have reason to believe this crime is connected to at least one other case we're investigating," I tell her. "We just wanted verify that they are, in fact, connected."

Clarkson frowns. "You tellin' me we've got a serial killer?"

"I didn't say anything of the sort," I say. "I'm simply saying there are some crimes that are potentially connected. I just wanted to –"

"You have to give me something, Agent Wilder," she says.

"You have to understand, Detective, we don't want to cause any undue stress or spread misinformation," Astra says. "We're just gathering facts right now."

"Off the record," she says. "What are you thinking?"

I know I need to give her something to get something in return. And though she hasn't outright said it, I'm getting the feeling Detective Clarkson isn't going to let us into the crime scene if we don't tell her what it is we're looking for. I look over at Astra and she gives me a subtle nod, obviously on the same wavelength that I am.

"We're completely off the record?" I ask.

Clarkson nods. "Off the record."

"Okay, listen, you heard about the robbery at the check cashing place in town?" I start.

"Yeah, one of the clerks was killed. Rough night all the way around," she says, then her eyes widen. "Wait, you think they're connected?"

"We won't know for sure until we check out the crime scene," Astra says. "But there are some fairly large coincidences that can't be overlooked."

"Such as?"

"Look, if we can see the crime scene, we'll be better able to tell you whether this is all smoke and no fire," I say. "Or if we actually have something here."

She sighs and frowns, drawing out the moment. Detective Clarkson is a woman who obviously likes to be in charge. This is her show, and she wants us to know it. I mean, there really is no reason for her to keep us off the crime scene other than she simply wants to flex her muscle. I have a feeling she smells something big in the air and is calculating the possibilities for her career if she's part of the takedown of a serial killer. It's garbage politics and it annoys me.

"Alright," she says. "But I want to be kept in the loop on this."

"Thank you, Detective."

"Sure thing. But like I said –"

"We'll keep you in the loop," Astra says.

"Give me a minute and I'll clear out the techs. Let you ladies have the room to yourselves."

"Thank you, Detective," I say. "Oh, is the body still in there?"

She nods. "Yeah. It's still being processed with the rest of the scene," she says. "She was only found a few hours ago."

"Great, thank you."

She strides off, leaving Astra and me outside to wait until she calls for us. This is just another one of her power play moves. If she were a man, I'd ask her if she wanted to whip them out and measure them.

"Agents," she finally calls to us. "The scene is yours."

"Excellent. Thank you, Detective."

Astra and I enter the apartment and I'm immediately assaulted by the scent of death. It's a faint metallic tinge in the air. It's acrid and unpleasant. And that's before we ever get to the body. We walk down the short hallway to the back bedroom and stop at the doorway. The silence surrounding a corpse always seems to be unnatural to me. The air around death always seems heavier. Denser. It's cloying and uncomfortable.

This scene is no different. If anything, it seems even more ominous, simply because it's so familiar.

"I guess there's no doubt now, is there?" Astra asks.

I shake my head. "Nope. None."

On the bed is a brunette. She's young and pretty, her dark hair framing a round face and large, doe eyes that are blue. In life, she had a curvy hourglass figure and rich, russet colored skin. She, too, had a vaguely exotic look, her ethnicity ambiguous.

"Tanya Abbas," Astra reads from the girl's driver's license. "Twenty-three years old."

"Abbas – that makes her..."

My words taper off as I try to recall the origin of her last name. I'm usually really good with them, but I'm having trouble with this one.

"Iranian. Her surname is Iranian," Astra says. "Which keeps the racial or religious motivation for these murders intact."

Tanya didn't have the posters on her bed like Lacey, so the killer had to make do. Her wrists and ankles had been bound to the legs of the bed instead. But she was still naked, bound spread eagle, and she had been worked over horribly – all except for her face. Like Lacey's, her face had been made up and then a plastic bag had been secured around her head. And also, like Lacey, Tanya had been split down the middle and her insides pulled out.

"I don't think animal is the right word for this guy," Astra says.

I shake my head. "He's a demon. A devil."

I tear my eyes away from the ravaged body of the girl and walk around the room, not sure what I'm looking for, but figuring I'll know it when I see it. And when I spot the three divots in the carpet, I stop, my heart fluttering and my stomach clenching.

"Astra."

She steps up beside me and looks down at the impressions in the carpeting. "What do you think it's from?"

"What about a tripod?" I ask. "Do people even use tripods anymore?"

"I didn't think so. Most people just hold their phones to film anymore."

"It's another of those coincidences," I say.

"Oh, I think we're well past the point of coincidences."

"Yeah. I think you're right," I say. "I think we should get back to the shop. We have some homework to do."

"We really need to nail this animal."

"We will. We absolutely will."

SEVENTEEN

"So you're saying we've got a serial killer on our hands," Mo says. "And here you said this case wasn't going to be sexy."

I chuckle. "To be honest, I'm not entirely sure what we've got on our hands. Other than one of the most sadistic monsters I've ever seen."

"Worse than the guy who was cutting the hearts out of women?" Rick asks. "Because that's pretty friggin' morbid."

"Okay, we need to look back through all of the old cases – all twenty-three of them," I say. "I want to look at the city and see if there was a corresponding murder on the same night. And if so, I need to know if that murder has the same signature as Lacey's and Tanya's."

"Right, boss," Mo nods.

"Rick, did you find anything in VICAP?"

He shakes his head. "No ma'am. But you know that database relies on local PDs updating it. And we know how well that goes."

"Yeah, don't remind me."

"Well, sounds as if we roll up our sleeves and do this the old-fashioned way," Astra says. "You should be able to appreciate that, hipster boy."

"I'm a hipster, not a luddite," Rick cracks. "I prefer to let tech do all the work."

"Doesn't sound like that's in the cards for us this time," she replies.

"Okay, let's get to it," I say. "Everybody tag your files and start reading."

"What exactly are we looking for?" Rick asks.

"Take a look at the Lacey Mansour crime scene photos," I say. "That should give you an idea what it is we're looking for."

I grab a workstation and get to it. I start with the early cases and check the corresponding crime logs in the cities. I strike out with my first case file in Boise. But I'm not discouraged, since it was one of the early cases. My operating theory is that we aren't going to find any murders in the first three years of this guy's run. I believe he didn't make his first kill until about two years ago. That would correspond with his spike in violence. To me, it goes hand in hand. But the case files will bear that out, one way or the other.

"Got one," Mo calls out. "Henderson, Nevada. This was about eight months ago. Our unsub hit a check cashing place and roughed up the clerk a bit, although it wasn't too serious. That same night Henderson PD responded to a murder."

"What do we know about the murder?" Astra asks.

"Shelby Morton, twenty years old," Mo recites.

She punches a few keys on her computer and the driver's license picture of a beautiful brunette pops up on the screens. She's young, has a creamy complexion, dark eyes, and dark hair. While not exactly the spitting image of either Lacey or Tanya, she resembles them in some ways. But she's Caucasian.

I look over at Astra. "I guess we can put the racial and religious motivation to bed now."

She nods. "It would appear so."

"You can go ahead and say it," I tell her, a grin crossing my lips.

Astra rolls her eyes. "I'm so not giving you the satisfaction."

I laugh and turn to Mo. "Go on."

Mo, not getting the joke, shrugs and goes on. "She worked as a barista and was a student at UNLV. Majored in psychology."

"Do we have the crime scene photos?" I ask.

"Unfortunately, yes," Mo replies.

She taps on her keyboard and the images of Shelby Morton looking very different from her driver's license photo come up on the screens. Like Tanya and Laccy, she's been stripped naked and tied spread eagle on her bed. She has the same gash down the center of her as the other two, has plenty of stab wounds and slices, and her face has been made up and bagged, just like Tanya and Lacey.

"That is disturbing as hell," Rick says. "What's up with the creepy-ass doll makeup?"

I get to my feet and walk to the screen on the far right, looking closely at the photo of Shelby's made-up face.

"He's preserving her beauty. He's telling us that's what makes her special and desirable," I say. "That's what drew him to her – her physical beauty. And he's telling us that's all she's worth to him. So he doesn't mar the face and keeps it as intact as he can."

"Why gut her like that?" Mo asks.

"It's because the rest of her is disposable. The rest of her is garbage. She's displayed like this to humiliate her," I explain. "He's telling us that her body is to be used and discarded. Like trash. To our unsub, her physical beauty is the only thing that matters about her."

"That is just wrong on so many levels," Astra says.

A moment of tense silence hangs over the room as they absorb my words. I'm profiling on the fly, which I'm usually loath to do, but this entire situation is fluid right now, so I need to be flexible. Also, I don't think I'm wrong. As I talk it out, letting it all unfold in my mind, the words ring true in my ears.

"I've got the next one. This was about two years ago," Rick calls out. "This one is from Sacramento, California. Same thing – check cashing store hit, grisly murder the same night."

"What's the information on the victim?" Astra asks.

"Sandy Davis, twenty-four, of Bakersfield, California," Rick says. "Graduate student at Sacramento State. She was working toward her Masters in mechanical engineering."

Rick's fingers fly over the keyboard and we get a DMV photo of Sandy Davis. Young, brunette, very pretty. She's got blue eyes, dark hair, and warm, golden skin.

"That's the before photo," Rick says. "Now, prepare yourself for the after photos."

His keyboard clicks as he works and then on the screens the pictures change. Sandy Davis was naked and bound to her bed, although in these photos, she's not spread eagle. In fact, it's only her hands tied above her head. She didn't suffer the same stab and slice wounds as the others. She wasn't worked over as hard. But like the others, she's been gashed down the middle and had her insides pulled out and put on display for the world to see.

But her face, like all the others we've seen so far, has been made up, although she wasn't bagged. And as a result, some of her makeup has been smeared. The mascara around her eyes has run, her tears leaving black streaks through the foundation on her face, and her lipstick was smeared across one cheek. Her beauty and perfection were marred.

We work through the remaining case files and find all his murder victims, a total of nine, –including Lacey and Tanya. I have Rick put all of the photos up side by side on the computer screens in chronological order. And once they're all up, I cross my arms over my chest and pace in front of the monitors, taking it all in and soaking in all the details.

"These photos tell quite the story," I say. "This is the evolution of a killer."

In all the early photos, the restraint of the bodies is less complicated. They aren't tied down quite as elaborately, and in the first three photos, the heads aren't bagged. The makeup is smeared and worn, and I can't help but wonder if that lack of physical perfection was a turn-off to our unsub. If it angered him.

"The beauty of these women is so important to him. It's vital. You can see that in the care he's put into their make-up," I say. "The first three victims were done up antemortem. And you can see the effect the assault they suffered had on their make-up. After the third victim, it looks to me as if our unsub started making them up postmortem and then bagged them to preserve their perfection. That's how critical it is to him."

"Something isn't jiving for me," Astra pipes up.

"What is it?" I ask.

"The violence he inflicts on the clerks at the check cashing stores has increased to the point that he's obliterating their faces. His attacks are so savage, he's leaving boot prints on them," she says. "And yet, he's so concerned with the beauty of the women he murders, he takes the time to preserve it so carefully. Of course, he savages their bodies, but he puts real care into keeping their faces pristine. It's almost as though we're dealing with two different people."

I nod. It's a good observation, and one I'll have to give some thought to. On the surface, it does look as if we're dealing with separate people. But I know that inside everybody, different facets of our beings exist. We can be different people. We can present as different people. This variation is why I don't like profiling on the fly the way we're doing. It makes it easier to miss things. I don't think that's the case here, but I also know I don't have all the pieces of the puzzle just yet.

"In a case like this, you have two totally different sets of victims. The clerks at the check cashing stores are irrelevant to him. His purpose there is practical – he needs money. So he has no problem obliterating the impediments to his getting what he needs. They serve no purpose to him," I muse. "But with these women, he is drawn to their beauty. But he seems to have some internalized hatred for them as well. It presents as confused or conflicted, but it's really not. His treatment of the bodies is what tells us he sees them as receptacles for him to use and throw away. As I said, they're garbage to him. And his careful preservation of the faces is his way of highlighting the only real thing he likes about them."

"But I don't understand why he'd start ramping up his violence at the check cashing stores, then assaulting and murdering women on the same night," Mo says.

I shake my head. "Something triggered that. Something happened to him two years ago that changed his trajectory. It's almost as though he's getting off on the violence he inflicts on the clerks. It's such a rush that leaves him so excited, he has to find a way to vent that excitement, so he finds himself a woman. It's classic anger excitation behavior."

"But he went three years without getting off on this stuff," Mo points out. "Why now? Or rather, why start two years ago?"

"Because of that trigger."

There is so much we still need to figure out, but the picture is getting a little less opaque. Slightly. We need to find those pieces. I'm sure that if we do, we can find our man.

EIGHTEEN

Java Therapy Coffee House; Downtown Seattle

"Things are starting to come together," Astra says.

"Yes and no," I sigh. "We still need to find the trigger. And there are some things that I'm still trying to figure out. Some things still aren't exactly lining up for me."

"Yeah, I was thinking that, too."

I take a sip of my mochaccino and sit back in my seat, thanking God that when Astra asked me to go have a drink with her after work, we ended up here and not the house of horrors that is Barnaby's Social House. Ever since Astra got together with Benjamin, we've been going there less often, and I couldn't possibly be happier about that. There is just something foul and slimy about that place that I'm so not into.

As for work, though, there are a bunch of things bouncing around in my head that I'm still trying to work out. This case is like a Gordian knot, and the deeper we get into this, the more tangled up it seems to be getting. While some aspects are becoming less opaque, there are other elements that seem to be getting even murkier in my mind.

I let out an exasperated breath and take another drink. I'm tired and frustrated. With a lot of things. It's been a couple days now and I still haven't spoken to Mark. I've thought about calling him, but I just haven't worked up the nerve. By the same token, though, he hasn't bothered to call me, either, so maybe it's all for the best.

"You're thinking about Mark, aren't you?"

I look up to see Astra staring back at me, an amused smile touching her lips. I cover my surprise by taking another drink.

"You always get that look on your face when you're thinking about him," she says.

"What look?"

"That lovesick puppy look."

I laugh. "You're so full of it."

She shrugs. "If you say so. But if you didn't get that look on your face, how would I have known you were just thinking about him?"

"Lucky guess."

"Yeah, that must be it."

I grin and tear strips from the napkin in front of me. I can feel her eyes boring holes into me, though. I look up and give her a crooked grin.

"Could you stop trying to dissect me? It's kind of uncomfortable."

"Well, maybe you should talk to me, then," she offers. "Tell me what's going on in that head of yours."

"How much time do you have?"

"As much time as you need."

I look down at the table and smile, knowing she means it. Astra is always there for me and would listen to me talk for a week straight if I needed it. She's just that good a friend.

"How long has it been since you talked to him?" she asks.

"A few days. We haven't spoken since the blowout the other night."

"And why haven't you called him?"

I shrug. "Why hasn't he called me?"

"Because he's a man, and he's dumb. I was about ready to tell you to kick him to the curb, but you were the one who wanted to save this in the first place. If you really want this to work out, you're gonna have to give him at least an olive branch."

"I don't feel I should have to. I shouldn't have to apologize for wanting to keep some things to myself," I say.

"Oh, yeah, you can use that olive branch to hang him if you want to. I don't care how great he is ninety-nine percent of the time, he owes you the biggest and best apology ever."

I chuckle and shake my head. "Right? I don't feel as if I did anything wrong here."

"You didn't. And as you said, he crossed a line. You have the right to your own privacy, and if he tries to counter that by saying you blew up on him a few weeks ago with the phone call thing, that's totally unfair. This is such a different situation."

"Shouldn't we be allowed to have our own thoughts and feelings? Or are we supposed to lay ourselves completely and totally bare?"

"I mean, some people would say yes. Two lives becoming one," Astra grins cheekily.

"But see, I don't think that's healthy. I think healthy is having those boundaries. And having the ability to keep things to ourselves without having to feel guilty about it."

"Yeah, but you know that men are insecure. They see us keeping things to ourselves and think it's all about them," she says.

"Do you tell Benjamin everything? Are you totally and completely transparent with him?"

"Oh, God, no," she says with a laugh. "I've got my own secrets because like you, I think it's healthy for us to have boundaries and keep some things to ourselves. I personally think those people who say they share everything are either lying, or they're horribly co-dependent."

"Right?" I reply.

I take a drink then set the coffee cup down again and think about it. Astra and I are on the same page with this, which makes me feel somewhat better. But I also know that sometimes, secrets can be poison. They sometimes have the power to destroy everything they touch. I've heard Mark say as much before. He likes to tell me he's totally transparent with me. But I don't know if that's entirely true.

And anyway, I don't think this is one of those things. The deaths of my parents is such a personal thing that I don't like sharing that part of my life with anybody. It's my burden to bear. It's not as if I'm hiding a secret love child, or a secret fling with another guy. All I'm "hiding" from him is something that's intensely personal to me. Something I don't think I should feel guilty about for keeping it to myself.

And then there's the possibility that by including him in this, I'm exposing him to danger. If there really is a conspiracy and my parents were murdered for what they knew, then by dipping my toes back into those waters, I'm putting myself in danger, as well as anybody close to me. If the assassins who killed my parents get wind that I'm poking around in their case again, it's entirely possible, if not likely, that they'll come for me. And I don't want Mark to end up becoming collateral damage because of my crusade.

"Tell me this: why do you feel comfortable telling me, but not him?" Astra asks.

"Because I tell you everything. I always have," I say.

"But you're on a different level of intimacy with Mark."

"Am I? I agree that it's different, but I don't know that it's a different level," I shrug. "You're closer to me than a sister, so it makes me feel more comfortable with you. I trust you."

"Do you not trust him?"

I purse my lips and tear another couple of strips off the napkin. There's not much left of it at this point. But then I raise my eyes.

"It's not that I don't trust him, it's just that –"

"You don't trust him."

"I just can't shake the feeling that he's hiding something from me," I admit. "I mean, the phone call thing aside, I just feel as if there's something more he's not telling me."

"You have any idea what it is?"

I shake my head. "I don't know. It's just a gut feeling."

"Do you think your relationship with Mark could get to the point where you could eventually trust him with something like this?"

"It's possible, I suppose," I admit.

"Has he ever given you reason not to trust him?"

"No, but my instincts tell me to hold onto this. To keep this all to myself," I say.

"Well, there's nothing wrong with that, as far as I can see," she says. "As far as I'm concerned, just because you're with somebody, it doesn't mean you owe them those things you don't want to share. And you've said a million times that you don't know how serious you want this relationship to be. So the question is really more about how far do you want to let him into your life? All of your life?"

That's a question I don't know if I'm ready to answer.

"Thanks, Astra."

She reaches across the table and takes my hand, giving it a

gentle squeeze. "Anytime, babe," she says. "But if he means enough to you that you want to salvage this thing, you're going to have to call him. Men pout. It's one of their things."

"I'm not apologizing," I say stubbornly. "This is all on him."

"And if he doesn't, I have ways of *making* him apologize," she says, cracking her knuckles.

I laugh softly, but my mind is still spinning. I wonder if I would have shared what Claude told me if I didn't have a strange feeling about Mark. If I didn't think he was hiding something from me. Is that what's giving me pause and making me hesitate? Probably.

Secrets can be poison in the veins of any relationship that will rot it from the inside out. But from my perspective, it's Mark who needs to start sucking that poison out. But will he? That's the question that's rattling around in my mind.

Mark either will try to patch things up or he won't. I can't control that. But whether he does or not, I'm going to focus on finding out whether my parents were murdered in a robbery or for some other reason.

NINETEEN

AFTER ASTRA WENT HOME, I hung around the coffee house for a little while longer. I wasn't ready to go home yet, so I had another cup of coffee, then headed back to the office. I think knowing that Mark wasn't going to be there waiting for me kept me from going home. Rattling around my empty apartment would have been depressing, so I figured I'd dive back into some work to keep my mind busy.

At the moment, I'm staring at my computer screen. I've run the name Claude Rosen through a number of different databases and come up empty. I've Googled him. I've run a search for this man in different ways and haven't found a trace of him anywhere. I would have thought if he was ex-NSA, I would have found him in the government databases. But there was nothing. The guy is still a ghost.

That doesn't make me feel very confident. If there really is a conspiracy and I go out to meet this guy I don't know, it's very possible I could end up just like my parents. That thought sends a chill down my spine. But if I don't meet this guy and he actually does have information to pass on, I'm missing out on a chance to find out who killed my parents and abducted my sister.

I'm at a loss about what to do. But there's one card I haven't played yet. I hesitate for a moment but then pick up my phone and punch the speed dial button, then slip my Bluetooth earbud into my ear as the call goes through and begins to ring.

"Blake Wilder, as I live and breathe," he answers. "And here I thought you forgot all about me. You really fed into my abandonment issues."

I laugh. "Oh, you have plenty of issues, Pax. Just not abandonment issues."

"Yeah, alright, that's true. Sounded good, though."

"Not nearly as good as you think it did."

We laugh together for a moment as I lean back in my chair. Paxton Arrington has been a good friend of mine for a while now. We met at an anti-terrorism conference back when he was with the Seattle PD, clicked right away, and we've been great friends since then. We've bonded over our experiences with loss and grief, as well as our passion for justice. Our bond runs deep. I consider him to be family, rather than just a friend.

Paxton comes from one of the country's wealthiest and most powerful families. The Arringtons founded what has become one of the largest media conglomerates in the world. Suffice it to say, he's a child of privilege, with all the snark and arrogance that implies. But after meeting the woman who would become his wife, he dedicated his life to serving others. First with the SPD, and now with his own private investigative firm, a firm that has quickly grown into one of Seattle's most respected.

For somebody who came from such wealth and privilege,

he's become incredibly down to earth. That's his wife's influence at work. Unfortunately, Veronica died in a car wreck some time ago now, and though he remains grief stricken, he is still doing good work. Even beyond the grave, she continues to influence him.

"How are you, Pax?"

"I'm good. Busy chasing down cheating spouses and finding lost children, but doing well," he replies. "How about you? Busy running down Seattle's worst monsters?"

"Always. It's the life," I reply. "You know how it is."

"I do. So, what's up?"

"I need some advice."

"I'm not sure how good my advice is, but I'll offer it up anyway."

"I'll take it."

I lay out the situation with Claude Rosen, telling him everything about the conversation I had, and relaying that I haven't been able to find Rosen in any of the searches I've run. He listens to my story and when I'm done, he's silent for a long moment as he processes it all.

"This sounds dangerous," he finally says. "If he's not coming up in any search, not even in the NSA database, something's not right."

"I know, and I get that. But is it possible they purged him from their files?"

"Not likely. You know how the government works," he says. "They keep everything and purge nothing, just in case they need to cover their butts."

"Unless they're trying to cover something up."

"Even then," he replies. "Why do you think cover-ups are always exposed? Why do you think we know about as much of the garbage they pull as we do? Because a covered-up paper trail will have been a paper trail in the first place. Frankly, the way the government leaks these days, I'm surprised they even bother covering it things up at all."

I laugh softly. "Yeah, that's true. You're not wrong."

"So, if he's not anywhere in the NSA database – or any other government database – his name's obviously not Claude Rosen," Pax says. "And I would really think about what you'd be walking into if you meet with this guy."

"My fear is that if I pass on this, I'll be passing on some information that can help me solve my parents' murders."

"I get that, Blake," he replies. "But you need to be smart about it."

"Yeah, I know," I tell him. "I'm just at a loss right now."

"Well, if you're determined to do this and meet with this guy, then take me along as back-up," he tells me. "I'll watch your back."

"I know you will, and I appreciate that," I say. "And if I end up meeting with him, I may take you up on that."

"There's no 'may' about it. I'm going with you."

"Not sure he'd like that."

"He doesn't get a vote," Pax asserts. "I'm not going to let somebody I care about walk into what seems like an obvious trap alone and undefended."

I sigh. He's right. If I do this, I'll need back-up. I don't want to end up like the proverbial fish in a barrel.

"Thanks, Pax."

"Anytime," he replies. "I'm going to have Brodie look into this Claude Rosen. If there's anything to be found, he'll find it."

"I don't know about that, Pax. I don't want Brodie getting caught up in this anymore than I want you to," I say. "If he goes searching and trips an alarm or something that lets somebody know he's looking, they could be coming after him next. I don't want him to get hurt."

"Brodie's the best at what he does. If there's an alarm, he'll see it long before he triggers it," Paxton says. "He'll be fine. And he'd be upset if you didn't let him help you."

"Even if I say no, you're going to tell him to do it, aren't you?"

He laughs softly. "Yeah, I sure am."

I sigh. "Please tell him to be careful. Really careful."

"I will. Don't worry, Blake," he says. "We'll get you some answers."

"Thanks, Pax."

We make small talk for about an hour, catching each other up on our lives. He has me laughing as he tells me about some of his cases. Some of the cases he gets are just hilarious. I kind of wish we got silly cases the way he does. It'd be a nice palate cleanser to wash away the misery we deal with daily.

After hanging up with Pax, I pull out the copies of the various murder scene photos. I don't know what I'm looking for specifically, but I'm hoping something pops for me. I go through them all several times, starting with the first murder scene. I study them closely, taking in every last detail. I look and look, but nothing is standing out for me. I'm just about to put everything away and call it a night when something finally catches my eye.

It's from crime scene number three, and it's incredibly subtle. It's barely visible, sitting at the edge of the frame. The techs wouldn't have known to look for it, let alone photograph it. But it's there all the same. I feel that familiar fire ignite inside of me as more pieces of the puzzle start falling into place.

I can't see the final picture yet – it's not even really all that close – but I'm starting to feel optimistic that we're getting closer.

TWENTY

"WELL, LOOK WHO DECIDED TO GRACE US WITH HER presence this morning," Astra grins.

"You're lucky I did. I'd much rather be in bed still," I reply as I walk to the front of the bullpen and set the package down on the table.

"Wouldn't we all?" she quips.

"Not me. I feel as if I sleep past six, I'm wasting the day. I like to be up and get my day started early," Mo says.

"That does not surprise anybody here in the least," Astra says. "I'm sure you're in bed by nine every night too."

"What's that supposed to mean?" Mo asks.

"Nothing, dear. Don't worry about it."

"It means she thinks you're a stick in the mud, Mo."

"Hey, hipster boy, nobody asked you," Astra cracks.

Mo turns to Astra. "You know, there are countless scientific studies that link sleep to overall health –"

"I prefer the studies that link red wine and dark chocolate to overall health," Astra interrupts.

She gives her a wide smile and Mo just shakes her head and turns back to her work. I unbox what I picked up this morning and pull it out of all the packaging.

"What's that?" Astra asks.

"You know those three divots we keep finding in the carpet?" I ask.

Astra nods. "Yeah. I remember we saw them at the Mansour and Abbas crime scenes, sure."

"Yeah, well, I came back here after coffee, and took a close look at the photos from the other crime scenes last night and –"

"I have a question about that," Rick calls out as he raises his hand.

"What is it?" I ask.

"Yeah, do you have any sort of a social life?" Rick says and grins.

"Don't you have work to do, Scanlon?"

"Well, yeah."

"Then I suggest you do it, or I'll give the janitors the day off and have you fill in."

He grins and turns back to his monitors. "On it, boss."

I turn back to Mo and Astra. "Anyway, as I was saying, I looked at the other crime scene photos and found those divots in several of the others. Not all of them, but some," I continue. "I'm sure if the crime scene techs had known to look for them, they would have found and photographed them."

I walk over to the laptop and call up the appropriate images and point out the divots where I found them. Mo and Astra nod. I set up the tripod and stand it on the table in front of me.

"This is what made those divots," I say. "This, or something like it, made those divots. It's a tripod that holds a phone."

I snap my phone into the holder to demonstrate. Astra sits

back in her seat and smiles. Mo is late to the party but finally seems to get it.

"So, our unsub is videotaping himself while he's doing his thing," Mo says.

"That's what I think," I confirm.

"That makes sense," Astra says. "Which adds a whole new layer of disgust and sickness to this whole thing."

"Tell me about it," I agree.

"So, these murders are all performative," Astra says.

I nod. "Looks that way. But the question is, who is he performing for?"

"Could it just be that he's taping himself for his own gratification later?" Mo asks.

"It's certainly possible," I nod. "But it's also possible that he's performing for somebody else."

"Like who?" Astra asks.

"Hey, Rick, how are your porn hunting skills?"

"Top notch," he says. "My girlfriend likes to –"

"You really shouldn't finish that sentence," Astra says. "I really don't want or need to hear the end of that thought."

"Don't worry, Astra, I'll send you a video."

"Do that and I'll send it in a mass email to the whole field office."

He chuckles. "You wouldn't do it."

"Test me, hipster boy. Test me."

"Okay, settle down," I say. "Rick, I need you to search every nook and cranny of the web. I need you to find out if this girl's death video is anywhere out there."

"Do you really think somebody would post that online?" Mo asks.

"Oh, yeah," Rick says. "There's a whole subculture of people who like snuff films. The fake snuff film industry is a whole thing. Very popular stuff, actually."

"Okay, that's disgusting," Mo says.

"For once, I agree with the stick in the mud."

That draws a laugh from Mo.

"I'm not going to ask how you know that," I say. "But poke around and see if you can find those videos."

"You got it, boss."

Astra turns to me. "Something's been bothering me about the crime scenes."

"What is it?" I ask.

"The make-up. Have you noticed that the make-up on the bodies is flawless?" she asks. "I mean, it's absolutely perfect. Do you think a guy can do that?"

"So, are you thinking our unsub is a woman?" I ask.

"I'd just like to point out how sexist that is," Rick calls out.

"Can you apply make-up properly, hipster boy?" Astra shoots back.

"No," he admits. "But there are some guys who can."

"He's right," I say. "There are plenty of guys who can apply make-up well."

Astra frowns. "Yeah, I get that. But it just stands out to me."

"Here's a better question for you," I say. "Do you think a woman is capable of committing murders like that?"

"Also sexist," Rick calls.

"And also backed by statistics," I counter. "Historically speaking, women don't commit murders that savage. And before you say 'Aileen Wuornos,' she murdered her victims by shooting them, not tearing their insides out."

Rick nods, ceding the point. Astra still looks troubled, though, and I can see she's not convinced. Or at least, her thoughts are taking her in a different direction.

"We also have the surveillance videos from the check cashing places," I say. "That is definitely a man."

Astra looks up at me. "I get that. But is it possible he's got an accomplice? Is it possible there's a woman in the mix here?"

"It's possible," I say, simply because I can't deny it outright. "But serial killer teams are exceedingly rare."

"But not unprecedented," Astra presses.

"That's true. I don't disagree with that."

"I'm not saying I'm right. But you said something about these murders being performative. What if it's all performative? The violence in those check cashing stores and these murders – what if he's performing, but for her?"

It's an interesting thought. One I hadn't considered before. We have no evidence that points us in that direction, but that's not definitive. It's definitely a train of thought that bears some consideration. It would certainly change a lot of things. And as Astra's words rattle through my mind, I'm struck by a thought.

"What if that's what changed?" I hypothesize. "What if two years ago he met somebody whose crazy matched his crazy and she unleashed the beast in him?"

"That would be like a total Natural Born Killers thing," Rick comments.

The more I think about it, the more intrigued I become. The idea that two people meet, and they bring out the worst in each other – and by worst, I mean homicidal tendencies – isn't unprecedented either. What if our unsub met this woman and she encouraged him to give in to his homicidal urges? I mean, they would have had to have existed prior to his meeting her, but she could have helped bring them out in him.

Two people who share this passion for violence and murder is a scary thought. It's a toxic personality stew, but we've seen it before. And that could account for the perfect make-up application to the corpses, because even though I know there are men who can expertly apply make-up, it's relatively rare.

"If we accept that this is real," I say. "It turns my profile upside down."

"What do you mean?" Astra asks.

"I mean that I've been profiling that our unsub is an alpha male type," I say. "But the murders didn't start until he hooked up with this theoretical woman. She changed him. Which means that he started killing on her orders. At least in theory. But if this pans out, that would put him in the subordinate position and her in the dominant role."

"That would be interesting," Astra notes. "That would be even more rare in a subset that's already rare."

"Or it could be that we have one lone whacko out there slicing women up after knocking over these easy cash places," Mo says.

"That's a possibility as well," I nod. "And right now, I don't think we can discount any possibility."

Astra has my mind working, though, and the more I think about a female partner for our robber-slash-murderer, the more the idea intrigues me. It's something definitely worth giving more thought to. Something worth exploring.

TWENTY-ONE

Residence of Jeffrey Searles; Federal Way, WA

WE GOT a call informing us that the survivor of our unsub's latest attack is finally able to talk. His wounds weren't that serious – especially in comparison with those of some of the other victims – but he remained catatonic for a few days after the attack. So, when we got the call that he was up and around again, and had been discharged from the hospital, Astra and I boogied down to Federal Way on the double.

We pull to stop in front of a small Craftsman-style house in a quiet neighborhood. Astra and I get out of the car and knock on the front door. A couple of moments later, our victim, Jeffrey Searles, opens the door. He looks at the both of us and frowns, obviously recognizing us as cops. We flash him our badges to confirm it for him.

"Jeffrey Searles?" I ask, as if his black eyes and the bandage wrapped around his head didn't already give his identity away.

"Yes?"

"Agents Wilder and Russo," I start. "We'd like to speak with you –"

"I already told the cops everything I know."

"That's fine, and we apologize for the inconvenience, but we'd like to hear it for ourselves, if you don't mind," Astra says.

He sighs as if we're putting him out. "That's fine."

He opens the door, and we step inside. The house is cluttered. Well, not entirely true. It's clean and neat, but cluttered with penguin figurines on every conceivable surface. There must be hundreds of them. Searles is an average-looking guy. He's not tall, not short, not thin, not heavy. He's got limp brown hair and brown eyes. He's unremarkable in most every physical way. He's twenty years old and lives with his mother – and her penguin horde.

Searles leads us into the living room and offers us the loveseat while he stretches out on the couch, pulling his blanket up over him. He's obviously been sleeping out here while he convalesces. Searles isn't beat up as badly as some of the other victims, which surprises me, given the condition of some of those others. Our unsub, caught up in this frenzy of violence, spared Searles the worst of it for some reason.

"How are you feeling, Jeffrey?" I ask.

He shrugs. "Got a pretty bad headache."

"I'm sorry about your coworker," I say.

"Yeah, it really sucks. But we weren't super close anyway."

I'm taken aback by how cold and insensitive that answer is. But everybody processes trauma differently, so it's possible Searles is just putting up a front and trying to play the tough guy for our benefit. Or maybe he really is just that cold.

"Can you tell us what you remember from that night?" Astra asks.

"I don't remember much," he says. "I opened the door and some dude hit me in the face with something. I went down pretty hard. He got my head a couple more times as I was on the ground. Everything after that's kind of a blur."

That jives with the scenario of the last robbery. Our unsub starts with a blitz attack to gain entry and puts the unfortunate person who opened the door on the ground as quickly as possible. Maybe the fact that he was already down and offered no resistance is the reason he's alive today.

"Before he hit you in the face, did you happen to get a look at him?" Astra asks.

He shakes his head. "No, he had a mask or something on. All I could see were his eyes," he says. "I'm still not sure what he hit me with."

"It was the butt of his weapon," I tell him. "An AR-15."

Searles visibly shudders, as if he's just now realizing how close he came to death. I give him a minute to let it fully sink in.

"Jeffrey, you're the victim of a serial offender," I tell him. "This particular unsub has hit over thirty other stores like yours over the last five years."

"Whoa. Seriously?"

I nod. "Seriously."

"So, anything you can tell us will be a great help," Astra says. "We really need to stop this guy before he hurts anybody else."

He shakes his head. "Everything is just a blur," he says. "I got cracked, I dropped, and I wasn't totally out for a little bit, but then I was pretty much out. I don't remember anything right now."

I frown and can't help but feel a bit discouraged. But then Jeffrey offers me an encouraging smile, wavering though it is.

"My doctor says my memories might come back, though. I might still remember things that happened," he says.

"Well, we certainly hope that's the case. We hope you get

back to one hundred percent very soon, Jeffrey," Astra tells him.

He screws up his face and looks as if he's trying to access some memory. But the frustration on his face tells me it remains tantalizingly out of reach.

"You know, as I said, I wasn't exactly out cold, but my memories are really scrambled. I can't say that what I remember right now is actually the truth," he says.

"Did you remember something?" I ask, an ember of hope smoldering within me.

"Maybe. But I don't know if it's real or just something my mind is making up."

"What is it you remember, Jeffrey?" Astra asks.

"I remember seeing two people," he says.

"Two?" I ask, a lightning bolt of excitement piercing me.

"Maybe. But it could've been that my brain is all scrambled and making me misremember things. Or maybe I was just seeing double."

"That's alright," I say. "Anything you recall might be helpful. It might give us a break we really need."

"Well, all I remember is seeing the guy who'd clocked me and after that, I could have sworn somebody else came in."

"Good, Jeffrey. That's good," Astra encourages. "Do you remember anything about this second person?"

He shakes his head. "Same as the first. Dressed in black. Wore a mask that only showed the eyes."

"Was there anything distinctive about this second person? Anything that stood out to you?"

"No, I'm sorry. As I said, I can't even be sure that memory is real," he says. "My doctor told me that as my brain starts to heal that it might make things up to fill in those blanks. But as it heals, those false memories might fade and be replaced by real memories again."

"We certainly hope so, Jeffrey."

"You want to hear something weird?" he asks.

I nod. "Sure."

"While I was lying there on the ground, for just a second, I thought that second person was a woman."

Astra and I exchange a look and I feel my heart start to pick up steam again. This could be the break we've been looking for – if it's a real memory.

"A woman?"

He nods. "I don't know for sure. Again, it could be my mind filling in blanks with false memories."

"What made you think it was a woman, Jeffrey?"

"The eyes. They just looked feminine to me," he replies. "They were kind of narrow and almond shaped. I don't even know if it's real. For all I know, I was imagining my fantasy woman or something."

"I understand," I say. "And that's alright."

I'm sitting here trying to tamp down that feeling of excitement coursing through me. The fact that Astra might be right about our unsub's having a female accomplice is charging me up. I get that familiar sensation in the pit of my stomach when I feel a case start to pick up momentum. Granted, everything is still nebulous right now, and there are no certainties, least of all Searles' memories. But it's got the same ring of truth I felt when Astra first proposed the idea of a female accomplice.

Searles looks at us and frowns. "I lied to you guys earlier."

"About what, Jeffrey?"

"When I told you I didn't care that Peter was dead," he says quietly. "He was my friend and..."

His voice trails off, but he doesn't need, to finish because I know where he's going with it. His tough guy posture was just a façade, maybe even to himself, and it's cracking. His eyes are shimmering with tears and I can see he's doing all he can to keep from breaking down in front of us.

"I really don't know anything else," he says, which is our cue to leave.

"That's alright. Thank you, Jeffrey. You've been a great help," I tell him.

Astra puts a card down on the coffee table. "But if you can think of anything else or you remember anything new, please call us right away."

"I will," he says, his voice quavering.

"Don't get up, Jeffrey. We'll see ourselves out," I tell him. "You just rest and get well."

He gives us a tight smile as we get to our feet and make our way out of the house. As we walk toward the car, from the corner of my eye, I can see Astra looking at me. I glance at her and see the cat-that-ate-the-canary expression on her face.

"You can go ahead and say it," she says.

"Say what?"

"You know what I want to hear."

"I want ten million bucks and a chocolate chip cookie," I say. "So, I'd suggest you get used to being disappointed."

She laughs. "I'm right. And you know I'm right. There's a woman involved."

"It's possible," I tell her. "But we need some independent verification first. Sorry, but I'm not going to rely on the word of somebody who just got his brains knocked in."

She laughs. "You just can't say it."

"If it turns out you're right, I'll say it," I reply. "But it's only an *if* at this point."

"You should start practicing now. There's a woman in the mix here," she says. "No man can put make-up on that well."

"Sexist."

"Realist," she shoots back. "Most guys can't even hit the

toilet bowl. You think they know how to contour cheekbones or properly apply mascara?"

She's not entirely wrong, but it is a sexist stereotype. It's also very limiting. If we lock ourselves into thinking it's this person or that person, man or woman, we risk putting blinders on. And when we put blinders on, we miss things and make mistakes.

That's not the way I do things. I'm not perfect, though I strive for perfection. I believe in doing a thorough job. I believe in turning over every rock and exhausting literally every avenue of investigation. When we do that, when we can say that there is nothing more we can do, only then will I be satisfied with an investigation.

And right now, we don't have one single shred of hard evidence that our unsub has an accomplice, man or woman. But I think we're closing in. I can feel it. Despite our obstacles, I sense we're drawing closer.

We'll figure it out sooner, rather than later, and we'll find him – or them.

TWENTY-TWO

Criminal Data Analysis Unit; Seattle Field Office

We walk into the CDAU after getting back from Federal Way. Mo is sifting through a pile of case files on her desk. She looks up when we walk in and gives us both a nod. Rick, on the other hand, is practically bouncing up and down in his seat, looking ready to burst with excitement. He looks like a kid on Christmas, and I'm tempted to go into my office and ignore him for a little while. But despite what Astra says, I'm not actually that cruel.

"What's up, Rick?" I call out. "Why are you acting like a toddler hopped up on sugar?"

"Boss, you are either going to want to kiss me or give me a raise. Possibly both," Rick says.

"Is that so?"

He nods. "Most definitely."

"And why is that?"

"Take a seat and I'll show you."

Astra and I glance at one another, both of us wearing

amused smiles on our faces. Rick is nothing if not a showman. Astra drops down at her station and I sit at the station I normally use. We both turn to Rick and wait for him to start the show.

"So, I did some digging," he starts. "I looked for all of the illicit websites that host the more extreme pornography."

"Oh, so you just pulled up your bookmarked sites?" Astra cracks.

"Man cannot live by lights out-missionary-only, alone," Rick fires back. "At least, that's what all of your exes tell me, anyway."

Astra looks away but I can see the smile curling her lips. She just doesn't want to let Rick see that he got her good. I turn back to Rick to let him play out his little presentation.

"Anyway, I went through all of the usual searches using the DMV photos of all of the girls. It took some time. You'd be surprised how many hardcore porn sites exist on the web," he says.

"I'm sure it's old hat to you by now," Astra tries again.

He shrugs. "I'm actually more of the soft lighting, arty and airbrushed, girl-next-door type of porn connoisseur, if you really must know."

"I really didn't need to know," Astra groans.

"And I'd like to thank you for subjecting me to that, Astra," I say.

"Hey, we're ride or die," she says. "That means when I suffer, you suffer."

I roll my eyes and shake my head. "The both of you are killing me."

"I'd like to point out that I'm the only one sitting here not saying anything offensive. Just in case you were wondering," Mo points out.

Rick and Astra groan in unison. I just laugh and shake my

head. These guys are seriously too much. I love this team. It's so quirky and everybody's got their idiosyncrasies, but we all work together really well. Even Mo, although she's benched right now, contributes in a host of other ways. She's incredibly sharp and doesn't miss much of anything. Those are traits that will serve her well as a field agent. All she needs is some experience and training. And she most definitely needs to learn to not puke on a crime scene.

"Anyway," I say. "Show us what you found, Rick."

"I thought you'd never ask."

"He's just excited to get the chance to watch porn and get paid for it."

"That is true," Rick chirps. "It's quite the perk of this job."

"Astra, let him get on with it," I say.

"Yes ma'am."

"Anyway, I used the DMV photos of our murder victims to run a search on the illicit sites and it turns out the videos of those girls you were looking for are actually posted online. All nine of them. It was a great insight, boss."

"Are you sure it's our girls?"

He nods. "About as sure as I can be based on the photos I have," he says. "But you'll probably want to verify for yourselves," he says.

"Unfortunately for us, we're going to have to," I say.

Astra looks at me with a frown of disgust on her face. "Due diligence."

"Exactly."

"Alright, Rick. Lay it on us," I say. "What did you find?"

"I found the videos on a site called www.StuffandSnuff.com," he says.

"That's charming," Astra says.

"So it seems the majority of the videos on this site are cleverly executed fakes. There's a whole market for that. Fake blood, gore, the works. People like the idea and aesthetic of it, but it's all above-board and legal and it's obvious that it's not really a murder scene. But..."

"But?" I ask.

"I found a series of videos uploaded by one particular user-name – bloodandsex21," he explains.

"Lovely," Astra comments.

"And these videos seem to line up with the victims we've found so far. But you guys already know, these are not fake."

"Jesus," whispers Mo.

"I make light of it, but this is pretty hardcore stuff, so if you guys have delicate sensibilities, now would be the time to walk out of here. Once I press play, it's going to get... disturbing," he continues. "Mo, hold your cookies. This is not going to be pleasant."

I look around, but nobody is walking out. Honestly, I would have expected Mo to leave the room, but she's gutting it out. I'm proud of her.

"Okay, hold onto your butts, guys," Rick says.

The four monitors at the front of the bullpen blink to life and a YouTube-like video comes up. I hear Rick sigh as he clicks play. The screen starts off black, and white letters that spell out Lacey's name fade in, then slowly turn red. The sound of her muffled groans and screams plays over the blood-red letters of her name, and then the video fades in with our unsub already in action.

Lacey is as we found her – naked and tied spread eagle to her bed. The unsub is on top of her, straddling her waist. He's naked as well, but his face is blurred out. Whoever edited this video is good, because no matter how the unsub moves, the blurry spot follows him. His face is totally obscured, as is a tattoo on his upper arm.

But Lacey's face, eyes wide with terror, the gag muffling her screams, is in perfect focus. We watch as the unsub, with a long, razor sharp knife in his hand, leans forward and drags the edge of the blade along her skin, drawing a line of blood across her flesh. Lacey screams as he stabs fleshy parts of her, all the wounds located in non-fatal areas. And as he stabs her, the unsub's arousal is more than obvious.

"He's a piquerist," I note.

"A what?" Mo asks.

"He's aroused by and derives sexual pleasure by the act of stabbing," I explain.

Blood is flowing from the multitude of wounds on Lacey's body and tears are spilling from the corners of her eyes. The unsub unleashes a stream of vulgarities, calling her every degrading name he can think of, and some I'd never heard of before. His speech is being altered by a voice synthesizer, making him sound robotic.

"He's also a power rapist," I say. "Usually, power rapists behave this way to compensate for their own feelings of inadequacy. They assert their power over their victims."

"He's also got shades of sadism in him as well," Astra offers.

I nod. "Agreed. He's a bit of a hybrid. But underneath it all, are his insecurities. He feels inadequate and feels that he's lacking."

"That could be why a dominant female was able to get him to start killing. Perhaps she's as excited by the violence as he is," Astra says. "In theory, of course."

"Where are we with that?" Mo asks. "Does the theory of a dominant female partner have legs?"

I shrug. "The kid who survived this last attack thinks maybe, possibly, there was a woman there in the shop," I say. "But he got his brains scrambled, so it's unreliable at best."

"But yes, it has legs," Astra says. "As much as anything else, anyway."

On the screen, the unsub moves from inflicting pain with his knife to sexually assaulting Lacey, and I look away.

"Cut it off, Rick," I say. "We've seen enough. That's Lacey."

"Okay, so you were right that his attacks are performative," Astra notes. "And he obviously wants the widest audience possible. Or his evil girlfriend does."

I nod. "Or it could be that uploading these videos is his final act of domination and degradation," I say. "This could be his final act of humiliation – putting their last moments out there for the world to see."

"But do you think somebody who is that insecure would upload videos of himself?" Mo asks. "I never post pictures of myself precisely because I'm insecure about them."

"It's a lot of good food for thought," I say. "And I think we're getting a really good picture of who this guy is now."

"Now all we need to do is put a name to that blurred-out face," Astra says.

"Rick, I want you to play the rest of the videos he uploaded. Just long enough to confirm the identities of the victims, please," I say.

"Yes, ma'am."

We go through the rest of the videos, playing about five minutes of each of them – long enough to confirm that they are indeed, the remaining victims. When Rick cuts the last of the videos, my stomach is churning, and I feel nauseated. And as I look around the room, I see that everybody else looks exactly the same way. Mo's face is several shades paler than normal, Astra's hand is clapped to her mouth, and Rick is taking deep breaths as if he's barely holding back a wave of bile.

"Rick, can you find out anything about this user?" I ask.

I don't have much hope of getting an ID this way, though. The unsub has been operating for five years, and is obviously savvy enough to protect himself. As much as I hope for it, I doubt he's going to trip himself up by carelessly uploading his real identity to a site like www.StuffandSnuff.com.

"Already did a deep dive. I can't even get an IP address on him."

"That's lovely," I say.

"Do you need to register with the site to upload these videos?" Astra asks.

"You do," Rick says. "But it looks like all you need is an email address," he says. "But, if you're lucky, he'll have a credit card on file to purchase the premium content."

"We're never that lucky," Astra says.

"I'd say that means we're due for a bit of luck."

She scoffs. "Believe it when I see it."

"What do you say?" I ask. "Should we go squeeze the webmaster? He could potentially give us a name of our unsub. Or maybe an address. And if the rest of this site is of any indication, we could throw the book at this dude."

"Shake that tree good and hard, and see what falls out?"

I nod. "Absolutely."

"Fun stuff. Let's do it."

TWENTY-THREE

Sticky Hands Web Hosting; Downtown Seattle

WE PULL INTO THE DINGY, somewhat run-down strip mall parking lot and climb out of the car. In between a massage parlor and an adult bookstore-slash-toy shop is the corporate office of Sticky Hands Web Hosting. All I can do is shake my head.

"If nothing else, the name's catchy," Astra offers.

"We're going to be swinging by the hospital for a penicillin shot when we're done here," I say. "We may need two."

"You ain't lyin'."

We walk to the door and I hold it open for Astra. I follow her in and let the door swing closed behind me. The walls are all industrial gray, with the company's logo, a giant red hand with the name in the palm, emblazoned upon the wall behind the front desk, which is unoccupied at the moment. There are a couple of potted plants that are turning brown and dying, chairs along one wall, the seat fabric worn and stained badly.

"I wouldn't sit in those chairs if you paid me," I mutter.

"There isn't a penicillin strong enough to knock out what you'd catch."

An early-twenty-something girl with blue hair and enough facial piercings that she'd set off any metal detector comes out through a door behind the counter. She looks startled to see us, but quickly recovers.

"Good afternoon, ladies," she says, her voice low and smoky. "What can we do for you?"

"We'd like to talk to Curtis Jones, please," I say.

"Do you have an appointment?"

Astra and I both pull out our credentials and the girl's eyes widen, but she keeps her cool. She looks up at us and smiles.

"I'm sorry, but Mr. Jones is tied up in meetings today –"

"I suggest he get untied," I growl. "And I suggest he does it now."

"I'm sorry, but if you don't have an appointment –"

"You really don't want to irritate us," Astra interrupts. "Go get your boss. Now."

The girl hesitates but turns and disappears through the door behind the counter. Astra and I exchange looks and she shrugs.

"Think he might run out the back door?" she asks.

"It'd give us a reason to beat him," I reply. "And after watching those videos, I'd really like to do that."

"Me, too."

I lead Astra through the door behind the front counter and we turn and follow a walkway positioned above a sunken floor below us. On the floor are a couple dozen computer workstations. Four or five people are down there at the moment, each of them working away. Sticky Hands is a popular web hosting company that handles dozens upon dozens of websites. Most of them are legit, but then you have sites like StuffandSnuff.com.

The sound of a man yelling draws our attention, so Astra

and I walk toward the commotion. There's an open door in front of us and the man's voice is booming from there. He lets out a string of curses that's both creative and impressive. I get the gist of his diatribe, that the girl needs to find a way to get rid of us. The girl from the front counter rushes out of the office and pulls up short when she sees us. Her eyes are wide, and her mouth's fallen open as she looks at us.

But then she steps aside with a small grin flickering across her lips. I give her a smile and a quiet word of thanks. She scurries off, leaving Astra and me free to enter the office of Curtis Jones, founder and CEO of Sticky Hands Web Hosting, Inc. And he's so totally not what I expected to find.

I have no idea why, but I'd been expecting to find a rotund, greasy, sweaty man with thinning hair, wearing a food-stained Hawaiian shirt. Instead, there's a skinny kid who looks like he can't be more than a year out of college. He's wearing a red polo, black slacks, and black wingtips. He looks like a Wall Street trader, not a guy who owns a company that hosts hardcore porn and snuff films.

He's sitting behind his desk, his head buried in his laptop, his fingers flying, when we walk in. He sighs as if he senses us.

"Cassy, I told you to just get rid of them, I'm –"

He looks up and his words die on his lips. He looks rattled but quickly recovers and puts on his best professional face. We flash him our credentials just to rattle him a little bit more. He swallows hard, though does his best to look calm and in control. Even pleased to see us.

"Mr. Jones, I'm SSA Wilder and this is Special Agent Russo," I say. "We apologize for dropping in on you like this, but we have a problem."

"Actually, you have a problem, Mr. Jones," Astra adds.

He gestures to the seats before his desk and gives us a wide, greasy smile. "Please, have a seat, Agents."

We sit down across from him and I look around his office. It's modern and sleek with abstract art on the walls, no doubt meant to lend him an air of refinement. Behind him is his vanity wall, where he displays his diplomas from Syracuse and MIT. He's obviously very smart and he likes people to know it.

"What can I do for you, ladies?"

"It's 'Agents,'" Astra corrects him.

"Okay, what can I do for you, Agents?"

"Your company has come up in the course of one of our investigations, Mr. Jones," I start. "And we need to speak with you about it."

"Oh?" he asks, licking his lips nervously. "What about?"

"You host the website StuffandSnuff.com, correct?"

He shrugs, adopting an air of innocence that doesn't quite suit him. "We host hundreds of websites. It's difficult for me to keep track of them all. I don't usually handle the onboarding, so if it's a question of –"

"Yeah, it must be hard to differentiate one porn site from another, huh?" Astra says.

A wry smile crosses his face. "Our adult entertainment section accounts for just twenty-three percent of our total clientele."

"Well, regarding the site in question, StuffandSnuff.com, did you know that snuff films are being uploaded?"

"Well, of course," he replies. "The site is called Stuff And Snuff, after all. That's about what I'd expect. Fake snuff films like that are the hot new –"

"I mean *real* snuff films, Curtis. Actual filmed evidence of murder."

His face blanches and he looks at us with real fear in his eyes for the first time. He clears his throat and takes a beat to compose himself and then that smile comes back.

"That particular site is a fetish site –"

"Oh, so you do recognize the name out of the hundreds you host," I say.

His cheeks flare with color and he gives me a weak, watery smile, knowing I just scored a direct hit. He leans back in his seat and tries to adopt an air of casual indifference – and misses the mark. He's worried. I can see it in his eyes.

"As I was saying, that is a fetish site. It caters to all sorts of....diverse fantasies," he says.

"BDSM, forced intercourse, torture and humiliation –"

"Yes, all of that. But be assured that the performers in those videos are all over eighteen and everything is consensual –"

"That site allows community uploading, so how do you moderate that?" I ask.

"Oh, well, we have strict protocols. We have professional moderators who review the community uploads. And any borderline or questionable material is removed right away."

"Looks as if your professional moderators missed some, then," Astra says.

"What do you mean?" he asks, shifting in his seat.

"There is a series of videos uploaded by somebody going by the username bloodandsex21. They're all rapes and murders, Mr. Jones," I say. "Not consensual performers."

He laughs nervously. "Agents, I assure you, if that was actually happening on this site, I'd personally shut it down. I know they may look real – as they're supposed to. Some people have very disturbing tastes, I admit. But I can assure you that it is all acting. Performance art, if you will."

"Actually, would you pull up that site, please?" Astra asks.

"Agents, I really do have things I need to attend do and –"

"Pull it up now, Mr. Jones," I bark.

He jumps and quickly pulls up the site on his laptop, then looks to me for instruction.

"Pull up the videos from bloodandsex21 and play the one titled 'Lacey.' Please," I growl.

He does as I say and a moment later, I hear the muffled screams and cries of Lacey Mansour issuing from his laptop. Jones watches it and somehow doesn't look the least bit disturbed by what he's seeing. He stops the video and looks up.

"I admit, the realism is unbelievable. The production quality of the video is incredible. It's so vivid and lifelike. But what –"

"It *is* real, Mr. Jones," I cut him off. "We were at that crime scene not long ago and saw her body for ourselves. That video is the genuine article. It's a snuff film."

If he goes any whiter, he'll be invisible. He doesn't even try to hide it. Not that I blame him. I'm sure all of this is quite the shock to his system.

"Th–that's not possible," he says.

"I thought you might say that." I open the folder in my lap and withdraw the crime scene photo of Lacey's body, and then drop the shot from the autopsy on top of it. "How is the production quality on those photos, Mr. Jones?"

He looks at the two photos side by side, his face a mask of fear and disbelief. What I don't see, though, is compassion for Lacey. His concern is strictly for himself and what this could do to his business.

"I–I'm stunned," he says. "I don't know what to say."

"I do," Astra says. "A murderer has been using your site to promote his work."

"And because this is your company, you are responsible for the content posted," I add. "Which, in the hands of an ambitious ADA, could make you an accessory to murder."

"Nine murders, actually," Astra says.

Jones scrubs his face with his hands and leans back in his chair again. He sits silently, and I give him a minute to wrap his mind around what's happening. But only a minute because then I lean forward and press my advantage.

"That's actually not necessarily true," he counters, stammering to get his breath under him. "Under the Communications Decency Act of 1996, web hosters of films, including snuff films, are exempt from liability. You have no jurisdiction–"

"How convenient that you can rattle that law off like that, Mr. Jones."

"Well, technically, I'm correct."

"Care to try that in court? I'm sure a jury would be much more sympathetic to how 'technically correct' your argument is. Or maybe you'd like us to keep digging into your business dealings with some of these sites?"

"What do you want?" he asks with a heavy sigh.

"I want any personal information you have on that user," I say.

"And we also want that particular site and any others like it taken down and deactivated."

"You can't be serious. This is federal intimidation. That's a healthy revenue stream –"

"We're very serious, Mr. Jones."

"As for giving you the personal information, you know I can't do that. Anonymity is guaranteed with us."

"That's your problem," Astra snaps.

"You know, Astra, maybe we're going about this the wrong way. Maybe we should take this straight to the press and tell them all about how our friend Curtis Jones here is making a pretty penny off the murders of innocent women. I think that would be important for the community to know." I turn back to Jones. "What do you think that will do to your revenue stream?"

"This can't be happening," he says, mostly to himself. "This cannot be happening."

"Oh, it's happening," I tell him. "Now, give us the name and information we want and take down the sites we'll list out for you, and we'll go."

"This is extortion."

"Call it what you want," I snap. "But give our tech analyst remote access to find the information we want now, or come this time tomorrow, I'll call up the cyber-crimes unit and see what else you're covering up."

"What's your answer, Mr. Jones?" Astra presses.

"Fine. I'll give you remote access for that one purpose alone. You aren't to do anything else in –"

"You're in no place to be dictating terms to us, Mr. Jones."

Astra calls the office and puts it on speaker. The call goes through and as it rings, Jones' face falls. He looks away, his face still colored with disbelief that this is happening to him. And still, without one ounce of sympathy for the victims.

The call is picked up and Rick greets us. "Scanlon," he says.

"Rick, we're in," Astra says. "Do your nerd thing with Mr. Jones here and he'll give you remote access to the site. I want you to pull down all the videos and find the name of the man who uploaded them."

"Copy that."

I watch Jones as he stares at his computer screen, no doubt watching as Rick powers through his system. His expression darkens and he looks angry.

"Bad news, kids," Rick says through the speaker phone. "The username is a dead end. The credit card he had on file was stolen and deactivated. It's a dry hole."

I curse under my breath, frustrated. This case has been

nothing but a seemingly never-ending series of wrong turns and dry holes.

"Thanks Rick," I say. "And while you're in there, blow up that website."

"My pleasure."

Astra cuts off the call and drops the phone back into her bag. I turn to Jones, who's glowering at us.

"All of that for nothing," he says.

"Not for nothing," I reply. "Rick is currently dismantling that site and others like it. And you will not replace them under new names. We will be watching you, Mr. Jones. If you are a party to murder like this again, you can expect to face the consequences."

"How many times do I have to tell you? I didn't know they were real. I don't usually pay attention to the minutiae," he snaps.

"This is your company, Mr. Jones. Your reputation is on the line with everything you do," I reply. "I'd suggest you pay attention to what your business is doing, because the consequences of not doing so can be dire. As we hope you've learned here today."

"This Gestapo crap is really tiresome. Who do you think you are?" he spits, growing more agitated. "I'm sick of you government types thinking you can jackboot your way in here and tell us what we can and can't do."

"So you approve of murder, then?" I raise an eyebrow.

"That's not what I mean. Stop playing word games with me," he replies. "All of this, even the murder videos, is technically legal."

"Just pay attention to your clients, Mr. Jones," I say. "If we have to come back out here, we will be taking you into custody. Do you understand?"

"You can see yourselves out, right? I have to get on a conference call," Jones snaps and picks up the phone to emphasize his point.

Astra and I walk out of his office, through the lobby, and back out into the overcast gloom of the afternoon. We climb in and get on the road, headed back to the shop.

TWENTY-FOUR

"WELL, THAT WAS A WASTE OF TIME," Astra mutters.

I shrug. "At least we got the site and those videos removed. It's a small win, but I'll take it. Any win is a good win as far as I'm concerned."

"I was hoping for something a little grander."

"Yeah, so was I," I admit.

We're sitting in the bullpen later that day, commiserating with each other. After getting permission from Detective Nash, I sent Mo to gather the evidence from Bellevue. I'd like to have a look through what they've collected to see if we can make any sense of it.

Restless, I get to my feet and go to my white board and pick up the blue marker. It took some time, but the janitors have finally stopped replacing the red ones I keep throwing away. I uncap the marker and start to jot down some notes.

"He's a sexual sadist," I start and write it down. "But he's also an anger excitation and power rapist."

"Other than that, he's a great guy," Astra says.

I grin and look at my notes on the board and frown. Serial killer teams are so rare, but I can't deny the possibility that he is taking his orders from a dominant woman. Mo was right in that a man who feels insecure probably wouldn't post his own sex videos online for the world to see – and judge. I'm starting to think this mysterious woman made him do it. I write 'Alpha' on the board, followed by a question mark.

"This woman must have total power and control over him," Astra says. "It's strange to think, simply when he's in the check cashing places, he presents as an alpha. He's dominant and in control. He's calm and efficient. That speaks to a man with confidence."

"And yet, when he's in a sexual situation, that confidence must bleed away. He does what this mystery woman tells him to. He's performing for her."

"So, this chick wants him to bang other women while she watches?" Rick asks. "Some dudes would be a-okay with that, and not kill anybody, you know."

A small grin crosses my face as I think about it. The idea forms in my head, and as I turn it over, it starts to make sense to me and has that ring of truth I'm always looking for when I'm profiling somebody.

"It's foreplay. These murders – it's about power and control. Dominance. At least for him," I say. "For her, it's the violence and blood that excites her. She gets off on it. I would be willing to bet that when we catch them – and we will – that after our unsub finished killing these women, he and his mystery women had sex. As in, earth-shattering sex."

"Yeah, but it's not enough. Not anymore. They used to go what, three or four months between kills? Now it's a few weeks," Astra notes. "Those first three years, our unsub was disciplined and kept to his timeline. But now, it's accelerating.

She needs that high more often. It doesn't last as long, so they need to hunt more regularly."

I nod. "That sounds right. That shine is definitely dulling."

"So, what happens when that shine is gone?" she asks.

"Good question," I say. "If I had to guess, I'd say it would be an act of extreme violence – one guaranteed to get him killed. And then she'd move on to somebody else."

"Damn, this chick sounds like a puppet master."

"She is," I nod. "Our unsub likely would have gone his whole life without killing anybody, maybe even without escalating violence like this, if he hadn't met her."

"But when their paths crossed, it was as if the planets all aligned just right," Astra adds. "Her crazy matched his crazy, and voila, a murderous duo was born."

"I'm telling you, it's just like Natural Born Killers," Rick says.

We all fall silent, sinking into our own thoughts for a few minutes. I think about the differences in our lives meeting one person can make. It's strange to think that meeting one person can change the trajectory of our entire existence. What if our unsub had met somebody good, somebody who was a positive influence? Would he have stopped robbing check cashing stores? Would he have given up that life of crime entirely and maybe started to walk the straight and narrow? Could he have become a productive member of society?

We'll never know, because his path crossed with that of a predator. A woman who thrives on chaos. Murder. A woman with exactly what our unsub needed at just the right time. And now look at him. A trail of broken, bloody bodies in his wake. His life has been forever altered by one person, and it changed him for the worse. She helped let that beast inside of him out of its cage and groomed him to be a cold-blooded murderer.

And what about me? What changes can one person

wreak in my life? What about this man, Claude Rosen? What is his goal? What is his endgame? What does he hope to accomplish by entering my life at this moment? What does he want from me? But more importantly, how am I going to change because of him? How is my life going to be altered by his presence?

I'm not going to become a killer, that's for certain. But what will I become? What changes will be wrought in me after meeting this man? After listening to whatever information he's bringing me? I don't know, and that scares me. I like to think I know myself. My capabilities. What I can and won't do.

But put into a situation like our unsub's, when the right person comes into your life at the right time – or wrong time, depending upon your point of view – who can say for certain what you will become? Or rather, what that you'll let yourself become? As well as I know myself, I know that deep down, there is a desire for vengeance. A desire to hurt and kill the people responsible for the murders of my parents and the disappearance of my sister.

I can't deny it, because I refuse to lie to myself. If the man who killed my folks were put right in front of me and I was free to kill him without consequence, would I do it? As much as I want to say no, the truth of the matter is...I don't know. I don't know what I'd do.

And nobody can say for sure what he or she would do until put in that situation. That's what frightens me. I don't know what sort of monster I could become if somebody let the beast inside me out of its cage.

"Blake."

Astra's voice cuts through my thoughts and I turn to look at her. "What?"

"You here on Earth with us?"

"I am now," I say, shaking my head.

She grins and points to Rick. "He wants to show us something."

I look over and see that Rick's got his excited face on again. Something's got him amped up and he's dying to share it. And I thought I always had an infamously bad poker face. Mine may be bad, but Rick's downright sucks.

"Let's have it," I tell him.

"Gladly," he nods. "I found something, so please observe the screens."

I turn and the screens blink to life and we see a still frame shot from Lacey's snuff film. I frown and turn to him.

"I don't want to see this," I tell him. "I've seen enough of it already."

"Keep looking. I'm going to enhance the picture and enlarge the section I want you to see," he says.

"Please do," Astra says.

The frame of the picture zooms in, and in the background, draped over a chair, is a jacket that looks to be US Army issued. It's a dull, faded green. Rick zooms in even more.

"That patch," he points. "That's the First Armored Infantry Division," he crows triumphantly. "Our unsub was based in Fort Bliss, Texas."

"Yeah, but when?" Astra asks. "You made the stack a little smaller, but we're still looking for a needle in a stack of needles. How does this help us?"

I grin, knowing where Rick is going with this. "He was in the Army, so he is going to be in the Army database," I say. "That's excellent, Rick. Great spot."

"How do we even know it's his?" Astra asks.

I turn to her. "Did you see this jacket at Lacey's place when we were there?" I ask. "Specifically, did you see it hanging on the back of that chair?"

Astra grins ruefully. "No. I didn't," she says "But what if he bought that jacket at a thrift store? What if it belonged to somebody else first?"

I shrug. "We have to start somewhere. And narrowing it down to Fort Bliss, Texas between a certain number of years – the unsub can't be that old – has got to reduce the suspect list. Once we filter everything else out, we should have a relatively manageable list to tackle."

Astra nods, seeming to be warming to the idea. "Great job, hipster boy. That's a really good spot. Nicely done."

"Thank you, thank you," he replies, taking a bow.

"Can you set up the filters on the search?" I ask.

"Is fire hot? Is water wet? Do bears defecate in sylvan environments?" he asks. "What kind of silly, borderline offensive question is that?"

I laugh. "Fair enough. My bad," I say. "We'll get together in the morning and sketch out the parameters of the search fields."

"Sounds good to me."

"In the meantime, you guys go home. Get some rest. Relax," I tell them. "Astra, go be with your man."

"Don't have to tell me twice," she says and jumps to her feet.

"Rick, can you text Mo and tell her we'll see her in the morning?"

He snaps me a salute. "Aye aye, Cap'n."

"Okay guys, I'll see you in the morning."

TWENTY-FIVE

Wilder Residence; The Emerald Pines Luxury Apartments, Downtown Seattle

I STEP off the elevator and walk down the corridor to my door. Slipping the key into the lock, I push it inward, then go inside, shutting and locking it behind me. The sound of John Coltrane's music fills my ears. I turn around and drop my bag and keys on the small table in the entryway, then walk through the arched doorway and into my apartment.

I stare in disbelief for a long moment at the masses of white roses that fill the living room. There are at least four dozen that I can count. I hear the oven door close and I inhale deeply, the aroma of garlic filling the air. My stomach rumbling suddenly, I head toward the kitchen and see that the table is set for two – complete with candles and all the romantic accoutrements.

I round the corner and step into the kitchen to find Mark standing with his back to me. He's wearing an apron and is swaying with the music. My heart flutters and I feel a rush of warmth flowing from the crown of my head to the tips of my toes.

"What's all this?" I ask.

He turns the flame on the stove off and moves the pot to a cold burner, then spins around. Without a word, he walks over and pulls me into a tight embrace. I wrap my arms around him and relish the feel of his taut body pressed to mine. It feels as if it's been forever since I've been in his arms, and the happiness I feel is so thick, I can't speak for a moment.

Mark leads me back to the dining room table and sits me down. He pours me a glass of wine, then fills his own glass and sits down across from me, his gaze fixed to mine. He raises his glass silently, so I pick mine up and tap it against his, the high-pitched ping the only sound between us. We both take a drink of our wine, then I set the glass back down.

"So... this is a surprise," I start.

He sets his own glass down and looks at me. "I figured after I ruined our last romantic meal that I owed you one."

"That's putting it lightly."

"Look, I have no excuse for how I acted. I was being – stupid. A complete jerk. And I'm sorry."

I get to my feet and come around to his side of the table. Sitting down in his lap, I lock my hands behind his neck and lean forward, pressing my mouth to his. Our kiss is slow, languid, and filled with all the emotion I feel for him. His apology means the world to me.

I pull back and kiss the tip of his nose, then walk back around to my chair and sit down again. We stare into each other's eyes silently for a long moment, and in his eyes, I see the depth of his feeling for me. It's overwhelming, to be honest. But at the same time, it fills me with emotions I've never allowed myself to feel before. Emotions that terrify me. But emotions that also feel completely amazing at the same time.

"I've had some time to think about things," Mark breaks the silence, "And I came to realize that you were right."

"Oh, say that again – I never get tired of hearing that," I say.

He laughs softly. "You were right," he repeated. "You don't have to tell me everything. Not every part of your life is subject to my scrutiny. And I'm sorry that I made you feel likeas though it should be. I let my own insecurity take over and I have no excuse for it. And I should never have belittled you for trying to deal with your mental health. You don't have to forgive me, but I'm sorry."

"And I'm sorry for being so inflexible and hostile," I say. "You didn't deserve that. You didn't deserve my lashing out at you the way I did. I never want you to feel that I'm hiding things from you –"

"As you said, there are some things you need to keep to yourself, for yourself," he says. "I understand that now. I'm sorry I didn't before."

"How about we just hit the reset button on everything?" I offer.

His smile is so warm and genuine, it makes my heart turn somersaults inside of me.

"I think that sounds wonderful," he replies. "I'd like that."

"Done deal," I tell him. "Reset button pressed."

"Excellent. I feel like a new man."

"So... cooking, huh?" I ask.

"I watched a couple of YouTube videos. I figure that makes me about as good as Gordon Ramsay, right?"

I laugh as he gets to his feet and heads back into the kitchen. I watch him bustle around as he finishes getting dinner ready.

"It smells amazing. What are you making?"

"My world-famous chicken parmigiana," he replies.

"World-famous, huh?"

"Oh yeah. World-famous," he grins, turning his head back and tipping me a wink. "Giada De Laurentis keeps pestering me to give her my recipe. But it's a family thing, so I have to keep saying no."

I laugh, then take a drink of my wine. As I watch him finishing up with dinner, a stray thought bounces around in my head. I wonder how our unsub's life would have turned out had he met somebody like Mark – the female version, of course. But it makes me wonder what his life would be like if he'd met somebody good and pure, somebody who inspired genuine happiness and warm emotions instead of his mystery woman who seems to inspire nothing but rage and violence.

"What is it?" Mark asks.

"Oh... I was just thinking about what our unsub's life could have been if he'd met somebody as warm and wonderful as you."

Mark smiles and brings our plates in, setting one down in front of me and one down in front of his place. He returns to the kitchen, then brings back the garlic bread. He takes his seat and looks at me.

"Tough case, huh?" he asks.

I nod. "It really is. But it might not be, had he not hooked up with this woman he's running around with. Before her, he wasn't violent," I say. "Now, he's got ten bodies on him over the last two years."

"Wow. Sounds as if somebody found a bad influence."

"To put it mildly," I nod. "Anyway, enough shop talk. I don't want to spoil another amazing meal with those sorts of details."

He laughs. "I've seen some really terrible things in the ER then went out for lunch an hour later," he says. "I've got a cast iron stomach. Fear not."

"Well, how about I don't want to ruin an amazing evening

with you by dredging up those sorts of gory details," I tell him. "You're like my palate cleanser. Being with you helps wash away the horrors of the world. And I'd rather not spoil that."

"I can accept that," he says with a smile.

"This smells incredible and I am starving."

"Well, let's eat then."

We tuck into our meals, and the food is every bit as good as it smells. I take several big bites, savoring the flavor. I take a sip of my wine to wash it down and dab my lips with the napkin.

"This is outstanding," I tell him. "I had no idea you were so talented in the kitchen. How come you've been holding out on me?"

He smiles at me. "I wouldn't say I'm talented in the kitchen," he demurs. "There's a couple of things I've learned how to do and can do them relatively well."

"I'd say this is better than relatively well. I'm pretty sure Gordon Ramsay couldn't have done it better."

Mark's laughter is a sound I really enjoy hearing. It's just such an open and joyful sound that it's hard to not be happy when I hear it.

"Well, thank you," he says. "Maybe I'll have to learn how to do a few more things, since you seem so impressed."

"I am very impressed."

We continue eating and chatting. The conversation is light and free flowing, with lots of laughter and fun. Maybe I'm reading too much into things, but it seems to me that some wall between us has been removed. A wall I wasn't entirely conscious of, but a wall, nonetheless. Things between us just seem a lot freer and more open than they did before, and I'm at a loss to explain why. But then, maybe this is one of those things I shouldn't overthink. Maybe this is just one of those things I should sit back and enjoy.

Later, after dinner, we're cuddled up on the couch.

Wynton Marsalis is playing softly from the soundbar, and I'm lying with my head on Mark's chest. He's running his fingers through my hair, sending tingling sensations crawling across my skin. I close my eyes and soak in all the emotion and feeling coursing through me.

In all the time I've been seeing Mark, I've never felt closer to him than I do right now. That connection and bond between us is growing and strengthening. I'm not sure where that's going to lead us, but right here, right now, the feeling is perfect. This little bubble we're floating in, shutting the world out, is like heaven.

"That call I got," I start, "it was from a man who's calling himself Claude Rosen. He said he's a friend of my parents."

I feel Mark's body tighten up and I sit up. Mark does, too, and pulls me to him. I lay my head on his shoulder and he keeps stroking my hair, and plants a gentle kiss on my forehead.

"What did he want?" Mark asks.

"He's coming into town and wants to meet," I say. "He said he has information about their murders he wants to give me."

"Why now?"

I shake my head. "He said there were things in motion that needed to be stopped."

"What does that have to do with your parents?"

I shrug. "I have no idea," I say. "But the thing is, there is no Claude Rosen. He doesn't exist. He is a ghost."

"Doesn't exist? Everybody leaves a trail."

"Not him. There's no Claude Rosen in any government database. And if he's ex-NSA, he should have been," I say.

"Maybe he wasn't NSA?"

"If he really was a friend of my folks, he had to be," I say.

"So what are you going to do?"

"I don't know."

Mark looks down at me. "I don't want to tell you what to

do, but I'd feel better if you didn't meet up with this guy," he says. "It just seems really weird. And what if he does have some connection to what happened to your folks? Is he here to kill you too?"

"I really don't know. I have no answers," I reply. "But my fear is that if I don't meet with this man, I'll miss out on my only chance to find out what happened to my parents."

He frowns. "At this point, nearly what? twenty years later almost, does it matter?"

"It still matters to me."

"I know. And I get that," he goes on. "But you'd been doing a great job of moving past it. Do you really want to undo all the progress you've made?"

"I've thought about that, too. And right now, I don't have an answer for that."

"I just worry about your meeting with somebody you don't know. For reasons that are vague and ambiguous," he says. "I'm always going to feel paranoid about that because I care about you."

I give him a smile and a light peck on the cheek. "We could be getting worked up over nothing. For all I know, I'm never going to hear from him again."

"Well, just in case you do, can you do me a favor?"

"Sure."

"Really think about it before you go to meet him?"

"I will. I promise."

He kisses my forehead. "Thank you."

"Thank you for caring."

"Always."

TWENTY-SIX

SSA Wilder's Office, Criminal Data Analysis Unit: Seattle Field Office

"So? Things are good?"

I nod. "They are."

"Back to normal?"

"Better than normal," I confirm. "At least, it felt that way last night."

Astra squeals and claps her hands together, her smile wide, her eyes glinting with excitement.

"Oh, I'm so happy for you, babe."

"Thanks, Astra. Suffice it to say I'm in a much better mood today."

"Yeah, I wonder why?" she asks, giving me a very pointed wink.

My cheeks flush with color. "Stop it."

"Nah. I like that shade of red you turn when I embarrass you. It's adorable."

I sit back in my seat and let out a long breath, letting the joyful feelings I woke up with flow through me. I don't remember the last time I woke up feeling this good. I know the feelings won't last, simply because it's hard to keep it going all day in this line of work. Most days, the horrors we see take a toll on us. They can turn a good mood sour in the blink of an eye. But I'm going to hold onto this for every single second that I can.

"I'm happy for you, babe. I really am."

"Thanks, Astra. And thank you for being such a great friend,"

"Hey, right back at you."

We make small talk for a little while, and she tells me about her evening with Benjamin. This is yet another case of meeting the right person at the right time. Before Benjamin came into her life, Astra was a wild child. She partied all the time, went through lovers like water through a sieve, and drank far too much, in my opinion. But she said she was living her best life and she was able to hold it down well enough, so what did I know?

But when Benjamin came into her life, all the partying stopped. And obviously, so did the lovers. She drinks very little anymore and seems to have settled happily into a life and a monogamous relationship with Benjamin. They're so happy together and seem to be genuinely in love. In all the years I've known Astra, I've never seen her as happy as she is at this moment. I can say now that she is definitely living her best life.

But what if Benjamin hadn't come into her life? What would Astra be doing right now if she hadn't met him? Would she still be hitting Barnaby's after work every night? Would she still be going home with a different guy nearly every night? Would she ever have found happiness – true happiness – if she hadn't met Benjamin?

I don't know. I really don't. But it makes me wonder why some people meet those right and good partners who make their lives better, more joyful existences. Why some people meet those mates who bring out the best in them. And why other people meet those wrong and bad mis-matches who always bring out the worst in them. Why some people meet those who make their lives unhappy and angry.

A knock on my office door draws my attention and I see Mo standing on the other side of it, so I wave her in. She pulls the door open and steps in.

"I've got the box of evidence from the Mansour murder," she announces. "It's out here in the bullpen."

"Box? Singular?"

Mo shrugs. "Seems that way. The killer sure didn't leave much evidence behind."

"Well, that's unfortunate," I frown.

"Can't these guys just make it easy on us for once? I mean, c'mon."

"It'd be nice," I say. "But it wouldn't be reality."

"Well, it should be."

I laugh. "Thanks, Mo. We'll be out in just a minute."

She snaps me a salute. "Yes ma'am."

The door closes behind her and I lean forward over my desk. "He doesn't think I should meet with Claude Rose, either."

"Well, I agree with him," she shrugs. "You don't know who this guy is or what he really wants."

Astra takes a beat and then seems to realize what I'd just said. Her eyes widen and her mouth falls open. "You told him. Babe, you opened up and told him. I'm so proud of you!"

I give her a smile. "It just felt right, I guess. We were just lying there on the couch and the words just started coming out."

"That is awesome, Blake," she grins. "And how did it make you feel?"

"I've never felt closer to him. I really haven't," I reply.

She squeals and claps her hands. "Are those wedding bells I hear?"

"Uh, no. We're not there yet. We're not even close to being there yet," I reply, setting her off into a chortle. "But the fact that I've been able to lose the suspicion and unease I used to have is a good step."

"It's a great step. And I'm so happy for you, Blake."

"Thanks, hon," I reply with a smile. "Well, we should probably get out there and see what Mo's brought us."

"We need to solve this case if for no other reason than that you'll be able to spend more time with your man," she teases.

I laugh as I get up and cross to the door. She follows me out of my office and into the bullpen. I find the box Mo brought back from Bellevue sitting on top of my usual workstation. I sign the log sheet on top, then cut the sealing tape. I take the top off and set it aside, then peer into the mostly empty box.

"Anything interesting?" Astra asks.

"There's hardly anything at all."

"Well, that's encouraging," she frowns. "That'll really help us make the case."

I reach in and take the evidence bags out, look at the contents, then pass them around. There's really not much in the box. Nothing really useful that I can see. But then I pick up a smaller evidence bag and hold it up. I look at the small rectangular piece of dark blue plastic with a gold arrow pointing in one direction. A slow smile crosses my face and I feel my first legitimate shot of excitement.

"Hey, Astra, what does this look like to you?"

I hand her the plastic bag and she looks at it, then at me, as a small smile stretches across her face.

"Looks like a hotel keycard," she says.

"That was my thought."

"Now, *that* could come in handy," Mo chimes in.

"Agree. But it looks as if we're going to have to go back to Bellevue and figure out which hotel this belongs to," I say.

"Why would they not put a name or a logo on this thing?" Astra asks.

"Probably a generic one bought in bulk. The printing costs too much for something that's totally disposable," Mo offers. "Businesses are looking for ways to cut down on cost. They're cutting every corner. Especially these days."

"Makes sense," Astra acknowledges. "Doesn't help us, though."

"Pretty sure helping us isn't in their budget," I add.

"Should be," she says with a smile.

"Shouldn't be too hard to figure it out, though," I say. "I'm sure Detective Nash will be more than happy to help us out."

She laughs. "This is the same Detective Nash who couldn't help us get out of town fast enough."

"Yeah, but all we need him to do is ID the keycard," I say. "If we promise to get out of town right away, he might just give us the info we want. Never underestimate the motivation of a man who wants you out of his face."

"That is an excellent point," she acknowledges.

"Rick, how is the database search going so far?" I ask.

He looks over at me and chuckles. "Slow and painful," he says. "Turns out, there are a ton of Caucasian men between the ages of twenty-five and forty who served in the First Armored Division over the last fifteen years."

A crooked grin crosses my face. "It sounded so simple at the time."

"I blame it on your boundless optimism."

"That's fair," I say. "Well, hopefully we can make this easier."

"Easier is better," he says. "Easier is always better."

TWENTY-SEVEN

Bellevue Police Department – South Sector; Bellevue, WA

A LIGHT DRIZZLE starts to fall as we pull into the police station parking lot. We get out of the car and head across the asphalt to the squat, single-story red brick building that houses the South Sector of the Bellevue Police Department. This is Detective Nash's home sector, so I'm hoping he's in.

"We probably should have called ahead," I say.

"There's almost no crime in this city," Astra says. "I'm sure he'll be here."

I was so anxious to get up here, I went against my instincts and just came up without calling. When we're dropping in on local PDs, I usually like to call ahead. It's a sign of respect, which is something I always want to project when dealing with locals. The downside of calling ahead, of course, is that it gives them time to hide from you. Given the usual tension between the Bureau and the locals, they'll usually find a way to ghost you if you give them half a chance. But still, I try. I'm a firm believer in keeping my side of the street clean.

I pull the door open then follow Astra in. We do our best to discreetly shake the drizzle off us, but there really is no graceful way to do it, and the Desk Sergeant – a tall, fit woman with cappuccino-colored skin, dark hair that's flecked with gray, and darker eyes – is watching us. Under her scrutiny, I feel like a dog that's just shaking my coat off without care.

I clear my throat and approach the desk, giving Sergeant Carter, according to her name plate, a wide smile.

"Good afternoon, Sergeant," I say. "It's a little damp out there."

"Wow. Nothing gets by you, does it. You Feebs are really good."

I laugh softly. "They train us well."

"Clearly," she says. "What can I do for you, Special Agents?"

Astra and I exchange a look, confused as to how she knew. Carter laughs as she sees the surprise on both of our faces. I turn back to her, the question no doubt in my eyes.

"Been doing this job a long time now. The federal aroma just wafts off the two of you like women who put on too much perfume," she says. "It's also your shoes. Most women wear heels. But not you two. Your shoes are all business."

"You're good, Sergeant," I say. "You've got the makings of a good profiler."

"Pass. But thanks. I like what I'm doin' here just fine," she says.

"We have better health plans."

"I'm sure. But I'm good. Thank you, though," she says with a chuckle, the ice between us starting to thaw, if only a little bit.

"Smooth," Astra whispers so only I can hear.

"So, what can I do for you, Agents?" she asks.

"I was hoping Detective Nash was in."

A wry smile touches her lips. "If you really knew him, you

wouldn't be saying that," she says. "But, to answer your question, no, he's out in the field somewhere."

"Well, maybe you can help us," I say, producing the small evidence bag. "You wouldn't be able to tell us which hotel this is from, would you?"

Carter takes the bag and looks hard at the key. I glance over at Astra, but she's looking off into the distance, totally unengaged in what's going on, apparently content to let me handle this. Carter screws up her face, thinking hard about it, then hands the bag back to me.

"That could be from either the Olympia Inn or the Pacific Cove," she tells me. "Don't quote me on it, but I think it's from one of those two."

"That's fantastic. Thanks so much, Sergeant Carter."

"No sweat," she replies. "Who are you two hunting?"

Knowing the historical tension between local and federal law enforcement, if I cop to looking for Lacey Mansour's killer, somebody – probably Nash himself – is going to see it as I'm stepping on his toes. I don't want to cause any problems and would like to keep things cool with the locals. But I also think Carter has a very high functioning BS meter and she'll probably be able to sniff out a lie. I have to tell her something, though.

"We're looking into the robbery at the Speedy Check Cashing place," I tell her.

I'm opting for a partial truth and hoping for the best. But I don't think the locals have put the robbery and the murder together yet, so it's walking a fine line between truth and untruth. I don't like deceiving Sergeant Carter, or anybody, really, but with our investigation building momentum, I think a dust-up with the locals will only slow us down. And I want to keep sprinting.

"Yeah, that was a bad scene," Carter says.

I nod. "We believe this unsub is responsible for over thirty robberies across five states over the past five years," I say, repeating the story I told Nash.

Carter whistles low. "That's a lot of robberies."

I nod. "Yeah, and I'd kind of like to put him away."

"I hope you get him," she says. "Good luck and happy hunting out there."

"Thanks, Sergeant."

Astra and I walk out of the station and get back into the car. The drizzle is light but persistent, and the thunder rolling in seems to be promising something heavier coming in later.

"You were awfully quiet in there," I say.

"I know people like Carter. She can smell BS from ten miles off," she replies with a grin. "The minute I opened my mouth, I'm sure she would've known I was full of it."

"We didn't lie to her," I point out. "Technically."

"Technically? Who are you, that Jones creep? We didn't exactly tell her the truth either."

I laugh. "This is true. But hey, we got what we needed, so let's get to it and put an end to this guy."

"Sounds good to me."

I start the car and we pull away from the station.

As it turned out, the key didn't belong to either the Olympia Inn or the Pacific Cove Motel. Thankfully, the guy manning the desk at the Olympia knew where the key came from. We pull into the lot of the Stargazer Motel and park the car. We get out and I look around. I'm pretty disgusted by the place. This hotel is the definition of seedy.

The Stargazer looks as if it's been around for a century and hasn't been updated since it was built. The three-story, horseshoe-shaped building is coral pink with white trim. As we walk to the office, I see the pool in the center of the horseshoe and note that it's green with algae. The sign on the door says the Stargazer offers daily, weekly, and monthly rates. And I'm pretty sure there's an unspoken hourly rate, too. To say this place is a pit would be a kindness.

"I wonder how many Michelin stars this place has?" Astra muses.

"Is there a negative scale?"

She laughs as I open the door for her. We step into the office and the interior is just as gross as the exterior. The carpet beneath us is filthy and threadbare in some places. The wood paneling covering the walls is cracked in spots, has odd stains in others, and the office is saturated with the odor of rotting meat.

"Just take shallow breaths through your mouth," Astra advises.

The plastic blotter on the top of the counter is scratched and scarred and covers pamphlets and brochures for places that closed years ago. A door behind the counter opens; an older, squat and overweight man with thinning white hair and dull brown eyes steps into the office. He's wearing an unbuttoned flannel, and his formerly white wife beater under it is a dingy gray color with greasy spots on it.

"You ladies looking for a room, are ya?" he asks, his voice dry and raspy. "Don't worry, we cater to all kinds here. No judgment from me."

I look at Astra and have to physically keep myself from bursting into laughter. But Astra, being the nut she is, gives me a seductive and salacious look, sliding her hand up my arm. I choke back the laugh and turn back to the man at the counter. His eyes are fixed on Astra, and I don't have to be a psychic to know what sort of foul thoughts are going through his mind.

I pull my creds and hold them out. It takes the man a

moment to tear his eyes away from Astra. But when he does and his gaze falls on my creds, his eyes widen.

"FBI, huh?" he asks. "So is it a don't ask, don't tell kinda thing there, or can y'all be together in the open?"

I roll my eyes but hear Astra snickering behind me. I turn and glare at her, at which point, she turns around to hide her mirth.

"Take your mind out of the gutter, please," I snap. "We're here on official business."

"Official business? What is it you think I did?" he asks.

"What is your name, sir?"

"Les. Les Bloom," he says. "Owner of this fine establishment."

Clearly Les and I have very different definitions of the word "fine", but I'm not going to argue it with him.

"Thank you, Mr. Bloom. We're Agents Wilder and Russo," I say, holding up the key in the bag. "Is this one of your keycards?"

Bloom takes the bag and holds the bag close to his eyes and studies the plastic card for a moment. Then he hands the bag back to me and nods.

"Yep. That's one of mine," he confirms.

"Great. Do you know what room this belongs to?"

Bloom takes the bag back and looks closely at it again.

He opens his mouth to reply but then closes it again, as if he can't remember. But then he turns to a computer that was old twenty years ago and starts banging away on the keys. The wait is interminable, made all the worse by the stench in this office.

"Looks like Room 243."

An electric charge of excitement shoots through me and my stomach tightens up. It feels as if we're closing in, but still have a way to go. But we're closer than we've been to this point. I'm sure our unsub stayed here while he was preparing for the Speedy job and the murder of Lacey Mansour, but has moved on since then. I already knew that, but it still doesn't mean this is going to be a dry hole.

"Is room 243 occupied right now, Mr. Bloom?" I ask.

He shakes his head. "Nope."

"What was the name of the last occupant?" I ask.

"Says here his name was Bruce Wayne."

I roll my eyes. No, I didn't expect him to use his real name, but I hoped to catch a break. This is what I get for hoping.

"Don't you check IDs at check-in?" Astra asks.

He shrugs. "When I remember."

Frustrated, I turn around and try to calm myself down a bit. Then I spy the cameras in the corner of the room. Unlike most everything around here, the cameras look pretty new and state of the art. In fact, I'm familiar with the security system and know they store the footage digitally, then archive it after a time. But the point is that the footage doesn't get deleted. It gets stored.

I turn back to Bloom and point to the cameras. "That's a nice security system you have."

"I think that system is worth more than this whole hotel," Astra mutters.

"It's for the insurance. Plus, it's nice havin' cameras that actually record the faces of those little punks who rob me."

"What were the dates that Bruce Wayne stayed here?" I ask.

Bloom turns back to the computer screen and leans close to it. "Says here it was the sixteen through the eighteenth."

"Fantastic," I say. "Then I'm going to need a copy of your footage from the office interior from the sixteen through the eighteenth. Start thirty minutes before he checked in, please."

"What am I, your secretary?"

"No, you're a concerned citizen doing the right thing and helping two federal agents with an investigation," I say. "Unless you'd like to be charged with obstruction."

Bloom mutters to himself as he goes into the back again, shutting the door behind him harder than is necessary. I look over at Astra and grin.

"I think he was smitten with you," I tell her.

"Stop it," she replies with a laugh.

"I'm just sayin', if things don't work out with Benjamin, you could have Les all to yourself," I say. "I mean, he's a resort mogul here."

"Don't make me shoot you."

The door opens and Bloom comes back out, still muttering to himself. He hands me a CD in a case.

"Here you go. Just like you asked," he grumbles.

"Thank you, Mr. Bloom," I say. "You've done your part to make the world a safer place. We appreciate your help."

He waves me off. "Bah. What's the world ever done for me?"

"Thank you, sir," Astra says.

"Hey, you come on back anytime, sweetheart. I'll give you a good rate," Bloom calls after her.

The drizzle lightens as we walk across the parking lot, but the thunder in the distance growls ominously. We get into the car and I look at the plastic case in my hand, feeling a rush of excitement and the thrill of anticipation. I hold it up for Astra to see, a wide grin on my face.

"We're almost home," I say. "This is all going to be over soon."

TWENTY-EIGHT

THE MONITORS at the front of the bullpen are all on and playing the same four-way camera split feed on a loop that shows the interior of the motel's office. The swirl of anticipation in my stomach is rising and I'm silently willing our unsub – Bruce Wayne – to show up. I'm dying to get a look at this monster.

"Rick, can you speed it up?" Astra asks. "It's been twenty minutes and I'm getting tired of looking at that empty rat hole."

"You got it."

He hits the fast forward and the tape speeds up. He runs it until somebody walks into the office, then pauses. On the screen is a man. He's middle aged, has a paunch around his middle, graying hair, and a red, puffy, drinker's nose. He's accompanied by a tall woman with long dark hair, obviously fake breasts, dressed in a shirt so tight, there is little left to the imagination, and a skirt so short, she might as well not be wearing one. Obviously, a businessman and a prostitute checking in for a little afternoon delight.

"I'm guessing that's not our well-oiled killing machine?" Rick wonders.

"Definitely not," Astra says.

The tape speeds up again and we go through a long section where nothing's happening. Other than the odd nooners now and then, the Stargazer doesn't get a lot of traffic. But then a large man comes steps to the counter. The man turns and Rick freezes the frame to give us our first look at our unsub. He's massive. Everything about "Bruce Wayne" is large. He's a little over six feet tall, his head is clean shaven, and he's got broad shoulders, a thick chest, and biceps that are large and well defined. He's got blue eyes and a strong jawline.

"Can you save a copy of that picture, Rick?" I ask.

"Already did it."

"Where is our Juliet to this Romeo?" Mo asks.

"Move the tape forward a bit," Astra says, leaning forward.

The tape rolls and then I see her. At the edge of the frame. All we get is an image of blonde hair – the top of her head. The tape continues to roll, and she doesn't move. She doesn't step into the frame and gives us no view other than the top of her head.

"She's smart," I say.

"Scoped out the cameras and knows how to stay out of frame," Astra adds.

"Doesn't matter. As long as we find him, we're going to find her," I say.

"Rick, keep the recording rolling for a while. Let's see if she makes a mistake and steps into the frame.

"She won't," I say. "She's smart. Very smart."

The recording continues to roll, but our unsub walks out of

the office without the woman's having ever set foot into the frame. We don't get a single look at her. The feed cuts off and the screens go dark again, leaving us all sitting there looking at each other. But then I give them all a smile.

"We got him," I say.

"Not yet," Astra replies. "We've got his picture. Not him."

"We're getting there, though. We're getting close," I respond. "Rick, can you –"

"Run this picture through facial rec and then cross check it against the First Armored Division database at Fort Bliss? Why, yes. Yes, I can," Rick cuts me off.

"You're good, Rick."

"I'm not just good, boss. I'm amazing," he says. "It's okay for you to say it."

Astra and I both throw crumpled pieces of paper at him, both of us jeering him. I know I shouldn't jinx it, and I shouldn't get too excited yet, but I'm starting to feel almost giddy. The momentum of the case is moving at breakneck speed. We're closing in on him. I know that nothing is ever certain, and the situation could change in an instant. But getting this guy is going to feel really good.

"It's going to take a while for this to run through the full database. I'm going to set it to run and set an alert then go home. I need some sleep," Rick announces. "It'll flag me when a match has been found. I've already seen database searches take all night and into the next day, so there's no reason to sit here and watch it scroll."

"Sounds good to me," I say, then look over at Astra. "Drink?"

"I'm in," she says, then looks over at Mo. "Drink?"

"Thanks for the invite, but I've got to get home," she says. "Rain check?"

"Definitely."

We all pack up our things and head out the door. Astra and I turn left and head for the elevator that'll take us up to the parking garage. We both get into our cars and I follow her. We drive for about ten minutes before we pull into the parking lot of a small jazz club called Birdie's. We've only been here a few times, but I really enjoy it, especially on live music night. And it's lightyears better than that pit, Barnaby's.

The interior of the club is done in dark wood and black. On the wall opposite the front door is a small stage, just big enough for a four-piece band and a singer. Against the wall to our right is a long oak bar polished to a glossy sheen, and on the wall to our left are spacious and comfortable booths. Round-top tables fill the middle of the floor, save for the space right in front of the stage where people can get up and dance, if they're so moved. Birdie's is small, intimate, and hearkens back to the old smoke-filled jazz club days. I like to think my dad would have really enjoyed this place.

As it's a school night, the club is only half filled at the moment, so Astra and I find a booth in a quiet corner and take a seat. Our waitress is there in a flash and takes our order, then scampers away to fill it. She's back a couple of minutes later with our drinks, and then she's off again. I pick up my martini and raise my glass. Astra clinks her vodka sour against mine and we take a drink.

I settle back in my seat and let Nina Simone's beautiful voice wash over me. I close my eyes and lose myself in the music for a moment.

"So, what are you going to do about this Claude Rosen guy?" Astra asks.

I open my eyes and frown. "I'm not sure yet," I admit. "A lot of it will depend on what Pax comes back to me with."

"What do you have Paxton doing?"

"I'm not having him do anything," I tell her. "I went to him for some advice and the next thing I know, he's telling me he's going to have Brodie run the background and figure out who this guy is."

"I thought you said it was too dangerous to go digging too deep."

"I did. But he insisted that Brodie would see the traps well before they were sprung," I reply. "And you know how Paxton is. Once he gets his mind set on something –"

"There's no stopping him. You'd have a better chance of reasoning with an enraged buffalo."

"You've got that right."

"If you do decide to meet this guy, you will be taking me for back-up, right?"

I laugh. "Paxton has already decided he's going."

"Good, then we'll both go with you."

"This guy Rosen – or whatever his name really is – seems to be the type who spooks easily. I don't know how he'd feel about my rolling in with an army at my back."

"We can be subtle, you know."

I level her with a raised eyebrow.

"I mean it!" she protests.

"I'll be alright. Really."

"Unless you're not," she says. "I don't like the idea of your going out to meet a guy whose real name you don't even know. Especially if this is connected to your parents somehow."

"You sound like Paxton," I reply. "You and he are a lot alike."

"That's why we get on so well, I'd imagine."

"I'd imagine."

We both fall silent and listen to the music issuing from the speakers as we share a drink. I keep hoping to get a message from Rick, telling me we've got a match. I'm dying to get a name on our unsub and start the process of shaking the trees to see which one he falls out of. Because when he falls out, we'll be there to snatch him right up.

TWENTY-NINE

SSA Wilder's Office, Criminal Data Analysis Unit; Seattle Field Office

I'M SITTING at my desk and have been looking at the same sheet of paper for nearly thirty minutes now. I sigh and try to focus on the page in my hand. It's hard to stay focused, though, when I'm sitting on pins and needles, waiting for that match to be made.

I take a drink of my coffee then lean back in my seat, trying to wipe my mind and calm down. But then the anticipation and excitement of finally bringing this boogieman down rises up again and blows my concentration all over again. I sigh and lean back in my chair, trying to focus on something else, and have no more success than before.

I give up and turn my attention to our unsub. I think about what it is we know about him, and try to figure out some of the things we don't know about him. His alias at the hotel intrigues me. Most people would say it's just a name he pulled out of thin air and nothing more. I don't think so. Because even our smallest gestures have meaning. We may not be consciously aware of it, but they do.

Take his pseudonym, for example. The fact that he used Bruce Wayne tells me how he sees himself: angry, disassociated from the world, alone, vengeful. I don't think he associates with the heroic aspects of Bruce's alter ego. No, I think he associates with the darker aspects of the man who watched his parents get killed. I think he associates with those dark, tortured aspects of the character. I think he aligns with them closely.

I can't see Rick's workstation from my office, so I get up and go to my door and lean out. Rick catches sight of me and shakes his head. Again. I've been getting up from my desk and checking every fifteen minutes or so. I'm sure he's tired of seeing my face. With a sigh I turn around and start pacing my office, feeling restless.

My phone buzzes with an incoming call, so I go and pick it up and connect the call, then press the phone to my ear.

"Wilder."

"Blake, it's me. Claude Rosen," he says.

My blood instantly runs cold, and I feel the flutter of butterfly wings in my belly. I swallow hard and try to control myself.

"Mr. Rosen," is all I reply with.

"I wanted to let you know I will be in Seattle next Wednesday. I'll let you know where I'll be staying –"

"Who are you? I ask.

"I told you. Claude Rosen. I was a friend of your mother and father."

"I don't know you. I don't know your name. They never mentioned you."

"Because they compartmentalized. They had work life and home life – east is east, west is west, and never the twain shall meet."

My eyes widen and my mouth falls open, and I feel ice flowing through my veins. If he wasn't a friend of my folks, how would he know that? How would he know my father used to say that exact thing to me? My throat is suddenly dry, and my heart is beating a drunken rhythm in my chest. If somebody were trying to get to me, would they be able to do a dive deep enough to know that? How could this man know that? It's not possible. Not unless he truly knew them.

"Blake? Are you there?"

"Yeah – yes," I say.

"Are you alright?"

"I'm not sure."

"I know you must have a million questions. And I want to answer them all," he says. "But I need you to trust me. I need you to meet with me. There are things happening that must be stopped, and I need you to help me do that, Blake."

"I don't even know who you are," I say. "What I do know is that your name isn't Claude Rosen. I know that's an alias."

There's nothing but silence on the other end of the line for a long moment. But then he laughs softly.

"You are your parents' daughter," he says.

"Who are you?"

"I will tell you everything in due time, Blake. All you must know right now is that I am your friend, and I am no danger to you," he says. "I need you to meet me next Wednesday."

"What is your name?"

"Patience, Blake. There is only so much I'm willing to say on an open line," he says. "But I will meet you face to face and tell you everything."

"You expect me to just meet a man I don't know?" I ask, incredulously. "A man who's already lied to me about his name?"

"Yes. I do," he says simply. "And I will explain my reasons

for the deception. I swear it. I do apologize that it has to be this way."

I don't say anything, because I don't know what to say. Of course, I'm curious. I don't think this is some elaborate plot to kill me. Why go through with this whole charade?

"I will contact you when I'm in town. And I implore you to meet with me," he says. "I'll be in touch, Blake."

The line goes dead in my hand and I set my phone down on my desk. My mind is spinning, and my heart is only now just slowing down. I take a deep breath and let it out slowly, calming myself down.

Next Wednesday. I still have a little time to decide what to do next. I just hope Pax comes through with something soon.

Through the wall of glass, I see Astra get to her feet. She's looking over at Rick's workstation, and I feel a surge of adrenaline. I move to the door and lean out again. Rick is looking back at me, a wild smile on his face.

"We got it, boss!" he crows.

I hustle into the bullpen and he puts the photo from the motel up on a split screen, and on the other side of the screen is a photo of our unsub in his Army uniform.

"Everybody, meet Gary Suban," he says. "Formerly of the US Army, where he did three tours in Afghanistan, achieved the rank of Second Lieutenant, earned two meritorious service commendations, and then narrowly avoided a court martial, but was given a dishonorable discharge from the service after he beat a superior officer nearly to death."

"Sounds like some things never change," Astra remarks.

I step closer to the screen, studying his features, letting them really sink into my mind. So this is him. This is the boogieman we've been hunting.

"Do we have anything on the woman yet?" I ask.

"No boss. Nothing in Suban's files about her. And because we can't get her on film, facial rec is out," Rick says.

"What do we know about Suban's family?" Astra asks. "About his personal life?"

"After being discharged, he came home and did a number of low skill jobs – line cook, janitor, a few others. Then he just kind of dropped off the grid," Rick says.

"Let me guess, that was about five years ago?" I ask.

"That would be correct," he nods.

"I guess we know what he's been doing all that time," Astra says.

"Family?" I ask.

"His mother lives in First Hill," Rick says. "He's got one younger sister, but she lives in Florida. He's got no other family."

"That's how we'll get him," I say, then turn to Astra. "Tomorrow morning, we're going to pay a visit to his mother."

"Oh, this is going to be fun."

THIRTY

"I'M HALF afraid that when we come back out, our car is going to be stripped down and up on blocks," Astra notes dryly.

"That's a distinct possibility, I'm afraid," I reply. "Thank God it came out of the Bureau motor pool."

We share a laugh as we get out of the car. I look around at the neighborhood and frown. It's dirty and dingy. Most all the houses have bars on the windows – if they have windows at all. The yards are brown and dry, which is a real feat in the Pacific Northwest where we get more than our fair share of rain.

We walk up the cracked and chipped walkway, then mount the three rickety steps that creak and groan beneath us. The exterior of the house was once white with dark green shutters and trim. Now it seems to be a dirty gray, with light green shutters that are cracked, broken, and hanging on by a lone screw here and there.

I knock on the door and take a step back. I cast a glance at

Astra and she looks around as well, an expression of pure disdain.

"Charming," she mutters.

The locks open with loud clunks and the door swings wide. Standing in the doorway is a woman who's no more than five-three, but she probably weighs close to two hundred pounds. She's got limp, greasy gray hair that falls to her shoulders, brown eyes, sallow skin, and, judging by the way she's sneering at us, a bad attitude.

"What do you want?" she snaps.

We flash our badges and she couldn't look more unimpressed if she tried.

"Agents Wilder and Russo," I say. "You're Agnes Suban?"

"You know I am, or you wouldn't be standin' on my doorstep right now."

"Fair enough," I say. "May we come in?"

She sighs loudly and I think she's on the verge of telling us to stuff it, but she surprisingly opens the door and steps aside, letting us in. The inside of the house is as torn up and dirty as the outside. There are stacks of newspapers lined up against the wall, bags of trash lined up and waiting to go outside, and convenience store soda cups everywhere. The inside of the house smells like burned Spam, and it's all I can do to keep from gagging.

Apparently, Ms. Suban isn't big on keeping house. She closes the door and leads us into the living room then plops down into the well-worn grooves in the couch with a loud groan. Other than one battered and threadbare recliner, there is no other furniture in the room. But then, she didn't invite us to sit, anyway, so whatever.

"So?" she asks. "What do you want?"

"Your son is Gary Suban, ma'am?"

"You know that already, too, or you wouldn't be standin' there," she snaps.

"Where is your son now, Ms. Suban?" Astra asks.

"How the hell should I know?"

"Does he stay here?" I ask.

"From time to time."

I walk the perimeter of the living room, looking at the collection of knick-knacks on the shelves of a beaten and battered pressboard bookcase. There are a few picture frames with photos of a younger Ms. Suban, along with Gary, and a woman I assume is his sister, Gina. Interestingly enough, there are no pictures of their father.

"When was the last time he was here, Ms. Suban?" I ask.

She shrugs. "Maybe a month ago. What did he do this time?"

"We need to talk to him," Astra says. "He's a suspect in some very serious crimes."

Ms. Suban's eyes immediately well with tears, and her face flushes red almost instantly. She sniffs loudly and runs the back of her hand across her eyes, trying to wipe away the tears. As gruff, ill mannered, and asocial as she is, it seems as if she loves her son very much. Which is kind of sweet, I guess.

"Ms. Suban, it's imperative we locate your son immediately," I say.

"Tell me what he did."

I exchange a look with Astra and give her a nod. Astra turns to her with a grim expression coloring her face.

"Your son is a suspect in a series of armed robberies, assaults, and murders, Ms. Suban."

The older woman's eyes widen as a horror-stricken expression crosses her face. She shakes her head, as if denying it makes it any less true. Tears race down her cheeks as she looks at me. I can see her begging me with her eyes to tell her this isn't true. Unable to do it, I look down at the ground instead.

"I'm sorry, Ms. Suban, but we really need to find Gary."

"He was always a good boy. He was always so kind and considerate. He took care of me," she says. "But when he came back from the war, he was different. He kind of lost his way. He changed. But he was still a good boy and never would have hurt anybody."

Astra and I exchange another look. Ms. Suban seems to sink even further into the sofa, looking down at her hands, which are clasped in her lap. She looks utterly miserable. Heartbroken. She finally raises her head and looked at me.

"Are you sure it's him?" she asks. "Are you sure it's my Gary who's done these things you're sayin' he did?"

I nod. "I'm afraid so, Ms. Suban. I'm sorry," I say.

She shakes her head and her expression changes. It shifts from forlorn and miserable to dark and angry. Her eyes narrow and she clenches her jaw.

"It's that woman he took up with. My Gary wouldn't have done any of this stuff if not for her," she hisses. "I never liked her. Not from the start. He brung her around her once and I just got a bad vibe from her. Told Gary she wasn't welcome around here no more. But he never woulda done none of this stuff if not for her."

Astra gives me a subtle smile of triumph. Ms. Suban just confirmed her theory and I know she's got to be beating her chest. Metaphorically, of course. But that confirmation sends a white-hot bolt of electricity shooting through me all the same.

"Ms. Suban, what is this woman's name?" I ask.

"Sammy, maybe? Or no, it's Sasha," she says, thinking hard about it and finally nodding, looking back up at us with a turbulent mix of emotions in her eyes. "Yes, that's it. It's Sasha. I'm sure of it."

"Sasha what, Ms. Suban?" Astra asks. "What is Sasha's last name?"

She shakes her head. "I don't know."

"Ms. Suban, do you have a way of contacting Gary?"

She nods. "Well, yeah."

"Alright. Then I need you to call Gary," I tell her. "I need you to tell Gary that you need to see him."

Ms. Suban is horrified. She looks at me and shakes her head. "I can't do that. That's my son. I can't betray him like that."

"Ms. Suban, you need to understand that your son is going to be hunted. Law enforcement officers will be looking for him. And if one of them gets to him, I can't guarantee his safety."

She looks at me with wide eyes, her face contorted with fear. "You can't let them kill him. Please, you can't let them kill my son."

"Ms. Suban, we have no control over local law enforcement. We think the best and safest thing to do is for you to call your son so we can handle this ourselves," Astra says.

The woman lets out a choked gasp. "Please, you can't let them hurt my son."

"That's up to you, Ms. Suban," Astra presses. "If you call Gary and have him meet you somewhere, we'll take him into custody peacefully. We will do our very best to resolve the situation without hurting him. But you have to work with us, Ms. Suban."

"You can either work with us to bring your son in safely," I add. "Or you can let Gary take his chances with the local PD. It's up to you, Ms. Suban."

She looks at me with fear and pain in her eyes. But I know we have her. I know it's an impossible decision for her to make. There's some small part of me that feels terrible for putting her in that position. But it's the only way we're going to get him, so it's not as if we have much of a choice, either.

Astra picks up Ms. Suban's cellphone and hands it to her. She holds it in her trembling hands, staring at it as if it's a loaded weapon. But she makes no move to make the call.

"Please, Ms. Suban," I push. "We want to bring Gary in alive and unhurt. Help us make that happen."

She sighs heavily and finally puts in the call, then puts it on speaker so we can hear. The call is connected and then begins to ring. Gary picks it up on the third ring.

"Mom, you alright?"

"I'm fine, honey. But we need to talk," she starts.

"What's going on?"

Ms. Suban looks up at me and I shake my head, silently telling her not to give us away. She lowers her gaze and looks back down at her phone.

"The cops came by here, Gary. They said you done some terrible things," she says. "Is it true? Did you do the things they say you done?"

There's a long pause on the line. I can tell that Gary's thinking about it and is reluctant to lie to his mom.

"You done those things, didn't you, Gary?"

"Yeah, Mom. I did those things."

"Why, honey? Why are you doin' them things?"

"I–I don't know."

"I want to talk about this with you, but right now, we don't have time," Ms. Suban says. "Right now, we need to get you out of town. We need to get you out of here for awhile."

"How are we gonna do that, Mom?"

"I've got some money. Not a lot, but some –"

"I can't take your money, Mom."

"You can and you will," she snaps. "You have to go until this heat is off you, Gary."

There's another long pause on the line. It goes on so long I start to wonder if he hasn't hung up the call. But then I hear a car horn from the other end of the line. I hear a heavy sigh and look over at Astra. She's as on edge as I am right now. We're so close. So close, and all it will take is for Ms. Suban to shout a warning to bring this all tumbling down and send her son on the run. And if he goes on the run, we may never find him.

"Alright, Mom. Thank you," he says quietly.

"I'll bring you the money and your passport, just in case. You may not need it but better safe than sorry," she tells him. "Just tell me where to meet you and pass it off."

Astra and I exchange a small smile. We're close. So very close to ending this guy's reign of terror.

"Um...How about the Westfield Mall, Mom?"

"You got it, Gary. You got it," she says, tears in her eyes. "I love you, son."

"I love you too, Mom."

She disconnects the line and claps her hands to her mouth, collapsing in a sea of silent tears.

THIRTY-ONE

Westfield Outdoor Mall; Downtown Seattle

I KEY MY MIC. "Does anybody have eyes yet?"

The tac team that's positioned around the courtyard check in with negatives all around. No sign of Gary Suban just yet. I have my eyes on his mother, who's sitting at a table in front of a coffee house, waiting for him. The crowd is somewhat sparse and there's not a ton of foot traffic, which is both good and bad. It means there aren't as many civilians we have to worry about getting caught up in our fight. But it also makes it hard to blend in.

I've already had to tell the tac team to lose the paramilitary gear and opt for civilian clothing. I can pick my people out of the scant crowd, and I just hope that Gary can't. I take a drink of the coffee in my hand and casually flip through the rack of blouses as I keep my eye on Gary's mother.

"Contact," Astra's voice comes through my earpiece. "Target inbound, approaching from the east. He's got a guest with him."

"All teams stand ready. But stay loose," I whisper. "Don't tip him off. We don't want to spook him, guys."

The team keys their mics, signaling their acknowledgement. I watch as a large man emerges from the crowd. It's the same man from the surveillance photos, and he looks even more massive than he did in the pictures.

"Twenty yards from the position," I say. "Keep cool, folks."

I hold the blouse up as if I'm inspecting it while surreptitiously keeping an eye on our target. Gary keeps walking and then I see the Amazon walking along with him. She's probably very close to six feet tall and has legs for days. She's got enticing curves, long blonde hair, honey golden skin, and she seems to glide rather than walk. She's a stunning woman, no question about it.

Gary's still about fifteen yards from where his mom is sitting, and he suddenly stops. As if he's a prey animal that caught the scent of a predator on the breeze, he tenses and starts to look around. I didn't think any of my tac team was that obvious, but something must have alerted Gary to their presence, because he's suddenly on edge.

He leans over and says something to the blonde. Immediately, she walks away from him and starts moving quickly through the crowd. I quickly key my comm.

"Astra, she's coming your way. Take her," I order. "All teams move in on primary target. Take him down, take him down."

All at once, there is a flurry of movement as the tac team begins to circle him. But Gary is a man of action and isn't going to stand there waiting to be taken. A high-pitched keening wail erupts from the crowd, and it takes me a minute to realize it's Gary's mother. Her scream fades, but then she starts yelling at him to surrender, then starts screaming at my tac team to not hurt her son.

Gary's already moving though. I watch in horror as this massive juggernaut of a man takes off at a run. He lowers his shoulder and bodies one of my guys out of his way. The crowd in the mall stars screaming and running to get out of Gary's way, not wanting to get trampled. My tac team is in pursuit, but Gary's fast for a man his size, and they're caught up in the throng of scrambling people. He is easily outpacing my tac team, but he's headed straight for me.

I drop the shirt I'm holding and go charging straight toward him. I know there's nothing I'm going to be able to do to slow him down. He's way too big. He will run straight through me as if I'm made of paper. I need to be smarter than he is, or I'm going to lose him.

I close on Gary and see his eyes shift toward me. Though it's tempting to draw my weapon and put a round through his leg, there are just too many civilians around. It's too much of a risk. So, as I move to within ten yards of him, coming at him from an angle, I grab a chair as I run, then fling it as hard as I can at his legs.

Gary sees it coming, though, and tries to hurdle the chair. But his foot catches the chair, and that's all it takes to knock him off balance. He hits the ground hard and it drives the breath from his lungs with a loud "oof." But he's back on his feet in the blink of an eye. I close in on him. Admittedly, I hadn't thought he'd get up so quickly; I can't avoid the fist as he drives it into my stomach.

The breath explodes from my body. I stagger backward, seeing flashes of light bursting behind my eyes. I croak, gasping for breath, as Gary takes a step toward me, his face etched with rage. He moves quickly, far too quickly for me to keep up in my current condition, and his fist connects with my cheek. As my head snaps to the side, my face erupts in the purest agony I've ever felt.

Gary grabs a handful of my hair and pulls me upright again. My eyes are watering, my face is throbbing, and I still haven't caught my breath yet. He delivers another devastating blow to my face and my mouth is instantly filled with the metallic taste of my blood. I stagger back a few steps, but my ankle clips a chair and down I go, landing hard on my butt.

Gary is coming for me. My eyes are focused on the long blade in his hand, the razor-sharp edge of it glinting in the dull light of the afternoon. As he closes the distance between us, the edge of that blade drawing ever nearer, I piston my leg out and slam it into his knee with as much strength as I can muster.

My foot connects with his kneecap and it buckles. Gary lets out a howl of agony so loud, it almost makes the ground shake beneath me. His leg gives out under him and he topples to the ground. Hatred and rage on his face, his leg bent at an awkward angle, Gary starts dragging himself toward me, so I get to my feet, standing above him, my weapon pointed directly at his forehead.

"Drop the knife," I bark.

Gary, his face a mask of rage, lunges for me. I dance backward, but I'm not quick enough. The edge of his blade slices along my thigh, opening a shallow gash. I grit my teeth and hiss as pain lights me up. My thigh is instantly on fire.

But Gary isn't done. He tries lunging for me again, but rather than dance backward this time, I move forward, bringing my knee forward as well. It catches Gary just under the chin, slamming into him so hard, his teeth clack as his jaw slams shut. A groan passes his lips as his head knocks back sharply.

He collapses to the ground in a heap and I move in quickly to cuff him. My tac team chooses that moment to come running up, weapons at the ready. My face and leg both throbbing with pain, and struggling to catch my breath, I look at them with disbelief in my eyes.

"Great timing," I exhale. "Really. Great timing."

THIRTY-TWO

Interrogation Room #2; Seattle Field Office

"YOU OKAY?" Astra asks.

I nod. "I'm fine. Patched up and good to go."

"That's a nice shiner you've got."

"It's a badge of honor," I offer. "I beat him."

She smiles. "That you did."

Astra and I stand in the control room looking through the two-way mirror into the interrogation room. Gary is seated at the table, his hands shackled to a bar that's bolted to the middle of the table, which is bolted to the floor. He's just sitting there with his eyes closed, almost in a meditative state.

"We need a confession," Astra says.

I nod. "We do."

"We've got jack in the way of physical evidence."

"I think we've got even less than that."

"Think you can break him?" she asks.

I look at the man and try to see into him. The way he's

sitting there, seemingly at peace, makes me think he's... relieved.

"I do," I say. "Think you can handle Sasha?"

We both turn around and look through the window into the other interrogation room. She's seated at her table, shackled just like Gary. But unlike Gary, she seems amused by the whole process. She's not taking it seriously and doesn't seem to think she's got anything to worry about. That worries me. It's as if she knows we don't have anything on her and is just running out the clock.

"Do you think we jumped too early?" Astra asks. "Should we have waited before we scooped them up?"

The first seeds of doubt start to take root within me. For the first time since this all started, I'm second-guessing myself. But then I see the faces of the victims. I see Lacey Mansour's body splayed out and torn open. That firms my resolve, because if we had waited, who knows how many more people would be hurt? How many more would be killed while we waited for these two to make a mistake and give us some physical evidence?

No. We were always going to wind up at this point. We were always going to need to get a confession out of them. They're both too smart. Too good. They know how to cover their tracks and how to conceal their crimes. If we'd waited, more people would have died. There's no doubt in my mind.

"No, I think we scooped them up when we needed to. We saved lives by getting them off the street," I tell her.

"Unless we have to put them back on the street."

I look at her. "I guess we have to make sure that doesn't happen."

I pick up the files that are sitting on the table and look over at the tech. "Audio and visual good to go?"

He nods. "Good to go."

"Great."

I open the door, step into the interrogation room, and close the door firmly behind me. I walk to the table and set my things down, then take a seat across from him. Gary opens his eyes and looks at me. I see him looking at the black eye he gave me, and for a moment, I see a flash of regret in his face.

"Sorry about the eye," he starts, his voice deep and gruff.

"Sorry about the jaw," I counter.

The chains around his wrist rattle as he raises his hands and rubs his jaw. A slow smile crosses his face.

"It was a good shot," he says.

"It was a desperation shot," I admit.

"Couldn't tell."

"Would you like your Miranda rights read to you again?"

He shakes his head. "Nope."

"Would you like to invoke your right to counsel?"

"Nope."

"So, you're speaking to me of your own free will?"

"Yep."

"Great. So, why'd you do it?" I ask. "Ten people. You killed ten people."

He looks down at the table as if he's trying to find an explanation that even he can understand. But he gives his head a small shake and he looks up.

"I didn't kill ten people," he says.

"Let's not do that, Gary. Let's be honest with one another."

A small smile curls his lips as he looks at me. But then he looks down at the shackles on his hands, as if only just now noticing them.

"We have you at Lacey Mansour's place the night she was murdered," I say.

I first take the picture of Lacey's ravaged body and set it down on the table. Gary doesn't even look at it, but I can see the disgust in his micro-expressions. He's ashamed of it. It was probably that he was caught up in the moment, egged on by Sasha, and committed atrocities that in his normal state, he'd never even consider.

I pull out the next picture, the still photo from his snuff film. In it, Lacey's agonized, terrified face is crystal clear. Also, although his face is blurred out, his gloved hand around her throat is clear as day. As is his jacket, which is clearly visible in hanging from the chair behind them. I tap on it to emphasize it.

"We've got you, Gary," I say. "That's you and that's your jacket."

"If you say so."

"You're going away for life."

"Okay."

"How about Tanya Abbas?" I ask, whipping out her photos and spreading them out. "Shelby Morton? Sandy Davis? You raped them on camera, cut them open, and then killed them. And then you uploaded the videos to a snuff site to help other people get their jollies."

One by one, I show him all the photos of the victims. He doesn't react.

"How about Peter Huffman? Employee at EZ-4U Payday Loans. You left a boot print on his face."

He grumbles in irritation, but doesn't say anything.

"You know what I think?" I ask.

"I have a feeling you're going to tell me, whether I want to hear it or not."

I give him a grin. "The disadvantage of being a captive audience," I say. "But what I think is that you didn't want to kill. You didn't want to hurt anybody. I think Sasha was the one inciting and encouraging the violence."

His gaze falls to the top of the table and he goes silent on me, which tells me I hit the nail on the head.

"For three years, you hit check cashing places without a

whiff of actual violence," I say. "And then, all of a sudden, you start beating and killing people."

"Guess I'm defective."

"Nah. It's Sasha. She's the one making you do this," I say. "This isn't you. Murder. That's not your thing."

"You don't know me."

"I know enough," I say. "What is it about her, Gary? How did she get you to kill?"

"She didn't get me to do anything I didn't want to do in the first place."

"So you wanted to murder ten people?"

He falls silent again and runs his hand over the smooth metal surface of the tabletop, studiously ignoring me. I look at him. Study him closely. I know I need a confession, but I haven't moved the needle a bit in that direction yet. I need to find his pressure point. I need to find that one button I can press that will make him do whatever I want. And that's when it hits me. It's so obvious and has been staring me in the face this whole time.

"Where did you meet Sasha?" I ask.

He doesn't say anything, but I can see a tension and tightness in his shoulders. He's good at controlling his features, though. Good at controlling his emotions and himself. This is the Gary who spent three years knocking over check cashing stores. He's calm and perfectly in control. This is the real Gary. The Gary of the last two years is the one that's false. The Gary of the past two years is a construction built by Sasha. I know it is as well as I know my own name.

"You're going to prison for a long time, Gary," I tell him. "Sasha too. And you will never see each other again. How do you feel about that?"

"Sasha isn't going to prison."

"She is, actually. She may not get as many years as you do,

simply because she wasn't the one making the killing blows, but she was an active part of it," I explain. "She'll be charged with a whole slew of crimes. And you know what? She'll be doing a lot of years in prison. I figure she'll be old and gray by the time she gets out. But hey, maybe she'll still remember to come see you. Assuming she remembers you at all."

"Sasha is not going to prison," he repeats.

"Oh, but she is."

His jaw is clenched tight enough to shatter stone and his face is turning red. Sasha is his pressure point. He'll obviously do anything he can to protect her. Somehow, she got this man to worship her. His love for her is devout and unconditional. That's as plain as day. But it makes me wonder how she did it. How in the world did she make this man abandon any sense of self and make him willing to kill for her? Not only kill for her, but take the full weight of it for her too?

"Did you ever stop to think that she was using you, Gary? Using you for her purposes?"

"You don't know what you're talking about."

"No? Why were you the only one on camera then? Why did those videos get uploaded to the Internet?" I ask. "She's the one who obviously gets off on the violence and death. The one who really gets off on the blood and the killing. But you're the one taking the full weight for it."

He cocks his head and looks at me as if I'm suddenly speaking Mandarin. He shakes his head, denying my words, but for a moment there, he didn't look so sure. But then his expression changed and the sense of worship he feels for her came roaring back.

"It doesn't matter. I've got all I need to put you both away for a very long time –"

"Leave her alone. She didn't do anything."

"That's not what the law says."

"Fine. You want a confession? Is that what you want?"

"I want the truth," I say.

"The truth is Sasha didn't do anything. That's the truth."

"But see, it's not. Even if she didn't hurt anyone, she was still there committing the robberies with you. She was still an accessory to each one of your crimes."

He sits back in his seat and looks at me, his eyes burning with rage. I know I should be happy to get a confession and call it a day. It's more than I walked in here with. It's what I needed, as we don't have much in the way of physical evidence. But I hate the idea that Sasha is going to walk away scot-free, while Gary is taking the full weight of it for her.

In a perfect world, they'd both be going away for the rest of their lives. But life isn't perfect, and so we muddle by, doing the best we can. And in this case, although I'd like to take Dr. Frankenstein down, the best I can do is take Frankenstein's monster off the streets. After all, it was Gary who murdered ten people and hurt many, many more.

"Alright, Gary. You want to take the full weight for her? Then do it. I get paid either way," I say.

"So, I have your word that if I give you my confession, you'll leave her alone and she won't do any prison time?"

It's actually the lack of evidence that will guarantee her lack of prison time, but I'm not going to say that to him. We have almost nothing on Gary and even less on her. I hate the idea that she's not going to do a day in prison, but there's nothing I can do.

"I guarantee you that she won't do time for the murders," I say. Technically it's true, even if I do somehow snag her on accessory to murder.

"And you'll turn her loose. Today."

"I'll turn her loose when we're all done here. You have my word."

"Fine. Give me a pad of paper and a pen and I'll write it all out for you."

I pull a pad of paper and pen out of my bag and slide them over to him. He picks up the pen and starts to write as I sit here and stew about the outcome of this.

"Is she worth it? Giving up the rest of your life the way you are," I say. "Is she really worth it?"

"I take it you've never been in love. Never found that one who makes you whole and fixes all those broken spots inside of you," he says. "I pity you, Agent. That's sad."

"What's sad is trading your life for somebody else's."

He shrugs. "For the chance to live and love the way she showed me is possible, it's all worth it."

I sit back in my seat and watch him writing out his confession. It might as well be the bill of sale for his soul. I pity this man. The love he thinks he had is nothing more than an illusion. A manipulative game played by a woman who is a master at her craft.

Gary's life is effectively over. And if I don't nail her, Sasha will just move on to the next man who will satiate her need for violence and death.

THIRTY-THREE

SHE'S EVEN MORE beautiful up close than from a distance. She's five-eleven, with white-blonde hair that falls to the middle of the back and eyes so blue they're almost silver. Full lips, full hips, full breasts, and curves for days. She's almost as gorgeous as Astra is. Almost.

Sasha is sitting at the table, shackled to it just like Gary. But unlike Gary, she's smiling at me when I walk in. I drop my things on the table and take a seat. This is all a game for her and she's enjoying herself. And she's enjoying herself because she knows she's winning.

"Girl, whatever you have between your legs must be magic," I start.

She laughs and shrugs. "I suppose so."

"I mean, you convinced a man to kill for you."

"I didn't convince anyone do to any such thing."

Her voice is smooth and sweet, cultured and refined, with a hint of Georgia honey to it. She looks at me with a feigned innocence, but behind her eyes, I can see she knows exactly what I'm talking about. What's more, she likes that I know what she did. And she loves the fact that even though I know what she did, I can't touch her.

"How many times have you done this? Convinced somebody to help you fulfill your sick, twisted little fantasies?" I ask.

"Oh, every man I've been with has fulfilled my fantasies. We are sensual creatures, and we should enjoy every inch of our bodies. We should never be ashamed of taking our pleasure where we can. Don't you agree?" she purrs. "But I've never convinced anybody to do anything they didn't want to, nor anything that hurt anybody else."

"Huh. So, it's a coincidence, then, that you were taken into custody in the presence of a man who has murdered ten people and beaten many others. A man who recorded not just his sexual assaults, but his murders as well?" I ask.

"I never knew that Gary had this dark side to him," she frowns. "Believe me, I'm just as shocked and horrified as you are."

"Right. Because you're not the kind of twisted sicko who gets off on watching people being beaten and murdered."

She gives me a sensual smile. "I admit to having tastes and fantasies that might make most people look askance at me. But let me assure you, murder is not one of my kinks, Agent."

I don't know why I'm sitting here talking to her. I've got nothing. No evidence. Nothing tying her directly to the scenes of either the murders or the robberies. The absolute best I can do is the corner of blonde hair on camera at the Stargazer Motel, and even then, that only confirms that she checked into the motel with him.

If I really pulled that string as hard as I could, I could possibly get her on accessory to armed robbery at the Bellevue case thanks to the keycard, and the slight possibility that Jeffrey

Searles' testimony might clear up. But that would be torn to shreds by every half-competent lawyer on the West Coast. I've got absolutely nothing. She is, for all intents and purposes, untouchable. As galling as that is.

At this point, I can only assume I'm talking to her out of curiosity. She's unlike any of these monsters I've hunted before. I hate to admit it, but there is something compelling about her. She has her own sort of gravitational pull and I want to understand it.

"So, how many other lives have you ruined like this?" I ask.

"Ruined? I don't know what you're talking about."

"Gary's going away for life, Sasha. He's writing out his confession now," I say. "Before he met you –"

"Before he met me, he was a sad man who had lost any sort of passion for life. He was a ghost, just drifting through the world," she replies. "Because of me, he got to taste life again. He got to feel that lust for life he used to feel. Excitement. Passion. Love. He got to feel those things again because of me."

"And now he'll never feel anything but life in an eight-by-eight cell – also because of you," I counter.

"What is it you want from me, Agent Wilder?"

"What do I want? I want you to step up, do the right thing and confess to your crimes," I say. "What do I expect? That you're going to remain a manipulative, murderous, evil woman who wouldn't know what the right thing was if it walked up and smacked you in the mouth."

She laughed softly. "Why do you hate me so much, Agent Wilder?"

"You mean, other than that you're a killer? I'm kind of finicky about people like that."

"I can assure you that I've never killed a single person in all my life," she replies. "Hand to God, I've never hurt, let alone killed a person in my life."

"So, do you just cruise around, looking for the weakest, most co-dependent people you can find? Do you just look for the most emotionally vulnerable?" I go on.

"I don't know what you're talking about," she frowns again, her big eyelashes fluttering. God, I want to smack that expression off her face. "We all have our baggage and issues," she reasons. "We are all damaged."

"Agreed. But it takes a predator like you to bring out the worst in somebody," I say. "It takes a predator like you to bring out the worst in another."

"I'm hardly a predator."

"Not from where I'm sitting."

"So, are you just going to sit here and hurl insults at me all day?" she asks. "Or is there another purpose for this charming tête-à-tête?"

"Oh, I figured I'd give you a chance to gloat that you're going to be walking out of here."

"I'm not much for gloating."

We sit in silence for a moment, our gazes fused together, both of us locked in a battle of wills. The cop and the criminal. The innocent and the guilty.

"So it really doesn't bother you that these men go to prison for you?"

"As I said, they're not doing anything for me, Agent Wilder. Believe it or not, there are some bad people in this world. And they fool everybody. Including those of us involved with these monsters."

I turn and look at the mirror behind me. "Cut audio and visual please."

I give it a moment and hear the beep of the camera shutting down, then turn back to Sasha. I purse my lips and look at her for a long moment. My curiosity is working overtime right now. I want to know what makes her tick. Why she is the way she is and why she does the things she does. I think gaining some understanding of her can only help me both personally and professionally. It could be another tool to put in my profiling toolbox.

"So, it's just us girls now," I say.

She leans forward in her seat. "And what is it you want to know, Agent Wilder?"

"I want to know why you do this. Why do you take a man like Gary Suban and turn him into a killer? Is it the power rush? Is it because you just enjoy watching people suffer that much? What is it?"

A faint grin crosses her lips as she looks at me. She's cagey and probably thinks I'm trying to trap her. It's a reasonable fear, given she's sitting in an interrogation room with her hands shackled to the table. I get up and pull the keys out of my pocket and unlock the shackles, dropping them onto the table with a loud clatter. She raises her eyes to mine.

"So, is that it? I'm not under arrest anymore?" she asks.

"You know I have nothing to charge you with. No matter what I did, Gary wouldn't roll on you," I say. "His devotion is absolute. You're like Jim Jones with breasts and he'll never speak against you, not even when he's staring down the barrel of a life sentence. So, you win."

She laughs softly. "Gary is a good man."

"Satisfy my curiosity, Sasha. Tell me why you do it. Why do you turn guys like Gary into killers? Is it purely sexual? Or is there more to it?"

"Well, hypothetically speaking, having absolute power and control over somebody is the ultimate aphrodisiac," she says. "Making them cater to your every want and whim, regardless of how....*unusual*....it might be, is absolutely intoxicating. Hypothetically speaking."

"But what is it about the violence that excites you? Why does death turn you on?"

"I'm not saying it does. But when you're with somebody who is so absolutely devoted to you that they'll do literally anything for you – it's a wonderful feeling. And addicting."

"And how many Garys were there before him?"

Her laughter is rich and smoky. "Have you ever been in love, Agent Wilder?"

I shrug. "I don't really have time for love right now," I reply. "Have you ever been in love?"

"I've loved all of my boys," she replies. "Each of them holds a special place in my heart and always will."

"But you see them as disposable."

"Everything in this world is disposable."

"Then I'd say that's not really love," I argue. "True love isn't disposable. True love is giving yourself over to somebody. Being vulnerable with that person. Trusting him or her. True love is not about dominance. It's not about having someone kill for you."

"Wouldn't you agree that mutual pleasure is a component of love and relationships?"

"Well...yes. Of course."

"What you need to remember is that we all have different opinions of what is pleasurable," she says. "As I said before, I freely admit that what brings me pleasure is different than with most. And I'm sure many would find it distasteful. But this is my life, and I spent too many years subjugating my own wants and desires to somebody else. I spent too many years being subordinate to somebody else. Not anymore. It is my time now. And I would encourage you to seek out those things and people who bring you pleasure. I would encourage you to indulge in your fantasies and do those things that make you feel good. We only go around once, Agent Wilder. Might as well have a good time."

What she's saying sounds so simple and so basic. It's common sense. And yet, to see it so easily adapted to such evil, monstrous purposes gives me pause. What she's making me see is that the lines between devotion and obsession, pleasure and pain, as well as love and control, are incredibly fine.

"Well, this has been fun," she says as she gets to her feet.

"Are you really going to just leave Gary in prison? Are you really just going to let him take the weight for you?"

"It's an unfortunate situation. It's sad. But it's time to move on. There are new adventures to have, new people to meet, and new loves to find," she says.

Sasha gives me a smile and then, without another word, turns and glides out of the interrogation room, leaving me alone with my thoughts.

"I'll catch you later," I say to the empty room.

THIRTY-FOUR

THE BULLPEN IS EMPTY, the lights are off, and all is perfectly quiet and still. And I'm sitting in my office, dwelling on Sasha's words. I've been playing and replaying our conversation a thousand times over, hoping to find some sort of wisdom, or at least a lesson worth learning. But all I got was self-serving garbage.

I know I shouldn't have expected anything more. And I didn't, not really. I'm not sure exactly what it was I was looking for by having a conversation with Sasha. The only reason I can think of is that I'm always trying to better understand myself.

And maybe, loath as I am to admit, I was trying to understand what it is to love. To have a relationship. It's no secret that when it comes to love and romance, I'm woefully lacking. It's something I don't understand. Never have.

But having somebody like Mark in my life is making me want to learn. To be better. I want to be as good to him as he is to me. I don't want what we have to be the sort of one-sided, only-my-pleasure matters, kind of affair that seems to be the hallmark of Sasha's relationships. I was hoping for some sort of insight, even if that insight was only learning to do the opposite of what she did. But I learned very little.

And I hate to admit it, but even knowing what an absolute monster she is, I still found Sasha to be a fascinating creature. No, she's not somebody I'd want to hang out with. She's evil, plain and simple. But I'd be lying if I said there isn't something I find intensely interesting about her. As much as I didn't want to, and as hard as I tried to reject her for being the monster she is, I wasn't able to do it. I'm not able to deny that pull she has.

Of course, that is probably why and how she finds these men who worship her. Who fall under her spell and subjugate themselves to her. They fall under that natural magnetism she has. She's like a black hole, and all who fall into her orbit get sucked in. It's obsession. It's not love.

And perhaps the one thing I learned that I wish I could un-learn, is that given my reaction to her – which mirrored that of her men, though to a lesser degree – I must be lacking. There must be some missing pieces inside me that, for whatever reason, I felt she could fill. I find that disturbing. It shows that I still have a lot of work to do on myself.

"Why the long face, Wilder?"

I look up to find SAC Rosalinda Espinoza – Rosie to most of us – standing in my office doorway. She's got a bottle of scotch in one hand, two glasses in the other. She gives me a smile and comes in, dropping down into the chair across from me, then sets the glasses down on my desk and pours us each a couple of fingers.

She pushes the glass across to me and I scoop it up and raise it to her. She returns the gesture and we both take a drink. I sit back in my seat and stare down into the glass, running through everything that happened today.

"This is good," I say.

"Of course, it is. You know I don't drink the cheap crap."

We share a laugh and I drain my glass. Rosie promptly refills it. She settles back in her seat and looks at me.

"Why do you look so glum?" she asks. "You had a big win today."

I shake my head. "It was a medium-sized win, if anything. Sasha Harris walked away, remember?"

"Well, now that she's on our radar, we will eventually catch her."

"And we'll have the same outcome we had today," I say. "She's careful. She uses the obsessions these men have for her to fulfill her darkest desires. I mean, sure, we all have our kinks, I guess. But who in the hell gets off on watching people die?"

"Monsters," she says. "And that's why we do what we do – to take those monsters out of circulation."

"Yeah, if we're actually able to do that."

"Don't beat yourself up, Blake. There's nothing you could have done," Rosie says.

"Maybe we jumped too soon. Maybe we should have let this play out a little longer."

"And if you'd done that, the likelihood is that we'd be looking at several more bodies," Rosie counters. "Blake, you and your team did a great job. You connected cases nobody else did. Not in five years. And because of that good work, you guys took a monster off the street."

"But I'm stuck on the one who got away."

"And that's a worry for another day. Do you really think Sasha is going to find the right guy at the right time to carry on her work anytime soon?"

"I know she'll be trying," I say.

"'Trying' being the operative word there," she says. "When

and if she succeeds at some point, we now know what we're looking for. And that's thanks to you and your team."

I open my mouth to reply, but she cuts me off with a gesture, making me laugh. That's one thing about Rosie, she doesn't have to say a word to get her point across.

"Take the W, Blake," she says. "Your team did exceptional work. Truly."

"I appreciate that, Rosie."

"The Director thinks so too."

I look up. "The Director, huh?"

She nods. "Oh, he's being kept apprised of your team's work. And suffice it to say, he's genuinely impressed."

"Thanks for that," I say. "I appreciate your going to bat for the team."

"I believe in what you guys are doing. And I champion your team because you guys never fail to make me look good."

A companionable silence descends over us as I sip at my drink, my mind still spinning with a thousand different thoughts.

"What's on your mind, Blake?"

I shrug. "I just don't understand it all. I don't understand how somebody could do that to another person just because somebody else told you to do it."

"You remember being a kid? What if someone told you to jump off a bridge, would you do it?"

"Course not."

"What if it was someone you loved? And I mean, really loved. Someone you couldn't go without. Someone you'd rather die than be away from, someone you trusted and loved more than life itself. What if they told you to do it?"

"I don't know. I can't say I've ever felt that kind of trust in anyone."

Even as I say the words, I'm second-guessing myself. Do I

trust Mark in that way? I trusted him enough to tell him about Claude Rosen. But does that mean I trust him that deeply? And if I don't, does that mean I don't truly love him? But of course, what Gary feels for Sasha is not real love. That's obsession.

Is there a difference at all? I shake my head and stare at my drink. This stuff really is strong. "I think that if you loved someone that much, that person wouldn't ask you to do such a thing, because he or she would love you in return and would want the best for you. And yet, Gary thinks he loves her."

"Maybe he's so damaged he truly believes he does. He felt so broken by the world that he could only find solace in her. That's how cult leaders operate."

"It's something a predator like Sasha wouldn't miss."

"Those predators are all the same. Cult leaders, pedophiles, rapists – they can always smell the weakest person. They can smell the one person in a crowd that they can use. The one person who will most easily fall under their sway and give themselves over to them."

Does my reaction to Sasha mean I'm weak? Easy pickings for a predator? I pride myself on my strength. I've always felt that growing up the way I did thickened my skin and toughened me up. I work hard in what is a boy's club, and I have to be tough to make it here. But the instant somebody with the charisma and magnetism that Sasha has comes knocking, all of a sudden, I'm putty. Or something close to it.

"You alright?" Rosie asks.

I nod. "Yeah, I'm good. Just got a lot on my mind."

"Anything you want to talk about?"

I shake my head. "No, I'm good. But thank you."

"Sure thing," she says. "And you know my door is always open if you want to talk. About anything."

"I appreciate that, Rosie."

She grins. "Gotta keep you mentally healthy so you can keep making me look good," she says. "I figure I'm going to need to stand on your shoulders, and the results your team gets to climb into the Director's chair."

"Yeah? You going for it?"

She shrugs but smiles. "No idea. I can't deny there's something appealing about it. But I just don't know that I can do the politics side of it."

"I get that. Politics is not my thing, either."

"Yeah, we're both usually a little too blunt and outspoken."

"Amen," I say and laugh.

Rosie gets to her feet and drains the last of her drink. "Well, I should be gettin' on. Just wanted to congratulate you on a big W today – and it is a big W. Don't diminish it. Savor it."

I snap her a salute. "Yes ma'am."

Rosie chuckles as she heads out of my office, then out of the CDAU altogether, leaving me alone once more. I glance at my watch and see that it's getting late. I drain the last of my drink and set the glass down before packing up my bag and heading out for the night.

THIRTY-FIVE

Arrington Investigations; Downtown Seattle

THE ELEVATOR DOORS slide open and I step into the lobby of Paxton's office. The place is empty and most of the lights are out. The only light I can see is coming from the Fishbowl – the glass walled conference room – but that light is muted thanks to the smoked glass. I can see Paxton inside, though, and he's on the phone, so I walk over.

I open the door and poke my head inside and he looks up. Paxton gives me a smile and waves me in, so I step inside and take a seat at the table across from him. There's a large computer screen mounted to the wall, showing the Mariners and Angels game, though the sound has been turned down. Paxton wraps up his call and sets the phone down on the table, then looks up at me.

"Thanks for coming by," he says.

"No problem," I reply. "Where is everybody? I thought you guys were a twenty-four-hour operation."

He chuckles. "Nick's working a case, and it's date night for Brodie and Marcy," he says. "I'm the night shift."

I laugh softly as he sits back in his set and runs a hand over his face. I can see that something's troubling him and I automatically think it has to do with Claude Rosen. Ordinarily, Pax will meet me somewhere we can get a drink; his usual spot is a bar that was built from the bones of an old church. It's sacrilegious as hell, but I can't lie, it's got a fun vibe. I'm curious why he wanted to meet here tonight.

"Everything alright?" I ask.

"Yeah, yeah. I think," he says.

"What's going on, Pax?"

"Brodie got done with his deep dive on your Claude Rosen."

Sometimes, I hate being right – especially when he looks as grim and sounds as foreboding as he does right now.

"Yeah, I told you, though, I don't know anybody named Claude Rosen."

"That's because he doesn't exist."

"Right, I think I told you that."

He nods. "Sure. But there are ways to hide yourself, even online. If you know what you're doing, you can make yourself a ghost. This is according to Brodie, and as he's a tech-God, I tend to believe him,' he said. "Anyway, he worked his magic and found that there is literally nobody named Claude Rosen. He's fictitious."

My stomach roils and I shudder, even though I knew that already. But there's something about the way Pax is presenting this that makes it sound even more ominous.

"How much did you know about what your parents did?" he asks.

"I told you, they never talked to me about it," I say. "I knew nothing. They totally compartmentalized their job from home life. Kit and I were always insulated from their work world. Why do you ask?"

He shakes his head. "I don't know. But Brodie was able to track down who Claude Rosen really is – don't ask me how. He tried explaining something technical to me once and it made zero sense to me," he says. "Anyway, Claude Rosen's real name is Steven Corden –"

"He was our neighbor when I was growing up. I used to call him Uncle Steve. Nicest guy ever," I exclaim. "He was a big part of our lives when we were growing up. But why would he have information about my parents' murder? I mean, he was a schoolteacher."

"Actually, he wasn't," Paxton says.

I cock my head. "What? Of course, he was. He taught eleventh grade history at our local high school."

"Okay, this is going to get weird, so prepare yourself."

"For what?"

"Claude Rosen is one of Steven Corden's aliases. Not a very good one, as it turns out. There's no history or credit or anything. It's a cutout."

"Why would Mr. Corden have aliases and cutouts?"

"Because he's not who you think he is, Blake."

I look at him for a long moment, cold worms of fear wriggling around in my belly. That feeling of dread presses down on me even harder. I try to snuff out my fear and sit up straighter. There has to be a mistake. Brodie must have been on somebody else's trail. It has to be a mistake.

"Alright. So who is Mr. Corden, then?"

"He's a retired CIA covert field operative," Paxton says. "He was a spy, Blake."

I look at him for a long minute as those worms wriggle harder and my throat grows dry. As if reading my thoughts, Paxton slides a bottle of water across the table to me. I uncap it and take a long swallow, giving myself a beat to try and turn my world right side up again.

Mr. Corden was always the nicest guy, and he seemed to never be without a smile. I remember that he always had a kind word to say. He was a widower and had no kids of his own, so he was over at our place for dinner several times a week. I remember he used to enjoy dressing up as Santa around Christmastime, and always went over the top in decorating his house at Halloween. And he always, always gave out the full-sized candy bars.

That is a CIA spook? Seriously?

I shake my head. "Brodie had to make a mistake. There is no way Mr. Corden was a spy. If you knew him, you'd see that it isn't possible."

Paxton laughs ruefully. "It's the people who are the least likely spies who are the best spies. Nobody suspects the high school teacher, or the nice neighbor. The more invisible the person, the better spy he makes."

"No way. This has to be a mistake."

"Perhaps. But Brodie doesn't usually make mistakes like that."

I open my mouth to reply but close it again. He's right. Brodie is the best I've ever seen on a computer, and if I could have poached him away for my unit, I would have. But he's loyal to Pax, and I really doubt he would have come to work for the federal government, anyway. But still, the idea that Mr. Corden was a spy is so far-fetched, it's laughable.

I try to stop my mind from spinning. The revelation that he is supposedly a CIA spook is kind of overshadowing everything else. That it's Mr. Corden trying to reach out to me should be good news. It's not some strange man I don't know and have never heard of, it's Mr. Corden. That should be cause for a giant sigh of relief, right?

"I think that's good news, then," I say. "I mean, it's somebody I know well. Nothing to be scared of now. Right?"

"Maybe. But I personally still worry. I mean, this guy – who may or may not actually be a CIA spook – comes to you almost twenty years after the fact and wants to share this supposedly explosive information about your parents," he replies. "Yeah, that doesn't sound suspicious as hell at all."

I laugh softly. "Okay, fine, put that way, it sounds a little fishy, I guess. But still, I'm just relieved it's somebody I know."

Paxton purses his lips and he leans forward, clasping his hands in front of him, looking like the harbinger of doom. His expression is serious, and in that moment, I know I'm not going to like whatever he's about to say.

"I don't think you should meet him," he says.

I'm taken aback by his words for a moment and then I get a bit testy. "I'd think you, of all people, would understand and be sympathetic about getting answers."

"I do understand, and I am sympathetic, Blake. But the difference between your situation and mine is that I don't have ex-spooks, false identities, and mysterious men contacting me after twenty years – all in all, I'd say the danger level with your situation is a lot higher than mine."

A rueful laugh escapes me, and I shake my head. Once again, put that way, my situation sounds a lot worse than I imagined.

"Look, I'm the last person to ever tell you to stop pushing for answers or for the truth," Pax presses. "I'd be pretty hypocritical if I did. But when you start mixing in the NSA, CIA, and suggestions of conspiracy, things can start getting really deep, really quick. Things can get dangerous, Blake."

I drink down the last of the water and screw the cap back on, giving myself time to think. I've never been a big believer in conspiracies or mysterious men in black showing up to drag

people away in the middle of the night. But I know my parents
were murdered. And I know it wasn't a home invasion robbery
gone bad, as the local PD ruled. With facts like that in
evidence, it's hard to deny that there is a conspiracy afoot.

What I don't know is the nature of that conspiracy. I don't
know who's involved or why my parents had to be killed. What
did they know? What did they do? But Paxton's not wrong.
When the alphabet agencies start getting involved, things can
get murky and dangerous.

I've worked so long and so hard with Dr. Reinhart to get
past the murders of my parents. I was in a really good place in
my head. Or at least, a better place than I had been previously.
I'd found a sense of peace within myself, and the deaths of my
parents and abduction of my sister no longer ruled my life. I
was at a point where I could think of my family and not
instantly launch the emotional roller coaster. I could actually
think of them and recall the happiness and the good times,
rather than the heartache and misery that followed.

Going to meet with Mr. Corden would be violently ripping
the bandage off. It would likely tear the fresh skin that's grown
across the wound and make it bleed again. If I meet with him, it
sounds as if I'll be diving into conspiracy theories headfirst.
And is that what I want in my life right now? Do I want to roll
back all the progress I've made with Dr. Reinhart? Do I want to
do that to myself?

But the other side of that coin is my responsibility to my
family. Long ago, I vowed that I would find who killed them
and bring that person or persons to justice. I vowed that I
would find out what happened to Kit, and if at all possible,
bring her home. I made promises to my family that I would do
whatever I could to solve their murders and make the people
who did it pay dearly for it.

I'd been a kid at the time I made those vows. I'm sure that

my folks are looking down on me and they'd forgive me if I didn't uphold a child's vow. Especially if it put me in danger. I have no doubt that my folks would never want me to put myself in a position where I might be hurt or killed trying to solve their murders.

They were always pragmatic in life, and I have no doubt they would tell me that they are dead and gone and nothing is going to change that simple fact. I have no doubt they'd say whether or not their murders are solved doesn't much matter to them. Unraveling the mystery of their deaths wouldn't bring them back. Nothing I do can change that.

The fact of the matter is that the only thing solving their murders will do is make me feel better. That's it.

There is also a side of this argument I haven't though of. It only just occurred to me because I'm so caught up in my parents' deaths. It's as if I'm wearing blinders to anything else. And the thing that occurred to me is that if there is a conspiracy, and there are people in positions of power carrying out extrajudicial executions – otherwise known as murders – unraveling the mystery of my parents' deaths could topple them. If I could get proof of this conspiracy, I could expose them. And casting sunshine on these shadowy figures would help cleanse our government of evildoers. That has to be counted as a good thing, right?

"I don't know what to do, Pax. I want to find out the truth. I want to know who killed my folks and abducted my sister," I tell him.

"I hear a 'but' coming."

"But I don't want this thing to blow up in my face," I say. "I don't want to be looking over my shoulder for the rest of my life."

He presses his lips tightly together and shakes his head. "I'm afraid that you might not be able to have one without the other. If this Corden guy is right, and he really does have proof of a conspiracy, they will do anything they can to keep that buried – even committing cold blooded murder."

His words send a chill through me and leave me feeling confused.

"When are you supposed to meet him?" he asks.

"Tomorrow night."

He nods. "If you decide to go ahead with the meeting, I'm coming with you, Blake. That's non-negotiable. I'm not letting you walk into an ambush."

"Thanks, Pax."

He nods. "We're family and I've got your back. Always," he says. "And whatever you decide, I support you."

"You are the best and I appreciate you," I smile. "I'll let you know what I decide."

"I'll be ready."

THIRTY-SIX

Wilder Residence; The Emerald Pines Luxury Apartments, Downtown Seattle

"Hey, you."

I drop my bag and keys onto the table, then step through the entryway and into the apartment to find Mark reclining on the couch reading a book. He sits up as I drop down onto the couch beside him.

"You're late tonight. Everything okay?" he asks.

I nod. "Yeah, I'm fine. It's just been a day."

He laughs softly and pulls me down onto the couch with him. I lay my head on his chest, taking comfort in the strong, steady sound of his heartbeat. I nuzzle against him closer, relishing the feeling of being so close to him.

As I lay with him, I think about Sasha and her view of relationships. I think about Gary and his view of love. The way they both warped and distorted what it is to love somebody makes me pity them. I realize now, that lying here curled up against somebody you care for after a rough day, having him just listen to and comfort you – this is what love feels like. It's not obsessive. It's not manipulative. It's just being with each other and opening your heart to each other.

I guess I did learn something from Sasha today. And that's what love is not.

"I saw Pax on the way home from work," I start.

"Yeah? How's he doing?"

"He's good," I reply. "He found out who my mystery man is. Or rather, Brodie did."

"Do I want to know how?"

"Definitely not."

Mark laughs softly, and it sounds like a strange echo in his chest. He strokes my hair, just giving me the time I need to talk to him – or not. But I want to because love is also sharing yourself. It's being open and vulnerable. It's trusting the other person.

"Turns out this Claude Rosen is actually my old neighbor, Steven Corden. He was always around when I was growing up. He was the nicest man ever," I say.

"So how does he have proof of this conspiracy against your family?"

"Because he is apparently ex-CIA," I explain. "In all those years we lived next door to each other, I never knew – never even suspected – that he was a government spook."

Mark laughs again. "I'll go out on a limb and say he wouldn't be a very good spy if you knew or suspected that he was a spy."

That makes me smile and laugh a little. I trace lazy figure eights on his taut stomach with the tip of my finger.

"What are you going to do?" he asks.

I shake my head. "I have no idea. I'm still trying to wrap my head around the idea that kindly Mr. Corden was a CIA operative. I mean, that's so wild."

"Sounds like it," he replies. "When's the meet?"

"Tomorrow night," I tell him.

"Are you going?"

"I don't know."

"If you do, I'm going with you."

"Thanks, but I've apparently already got an army at my back," I say. "Pax and Astra have already said they're not going to let me go without them. I'm half sure Pax put a tracker on my car somewhere just in case I try to give him the slip."

He laughs. "Shouldn't I be the one out there protecting my woman?"

"How very caveman of you," I reply, smiling widely.

"Be nice or I'll club you over the head and drag you back to my cave."

"That could be fun."

He laughs as I roll over onto my side and prop myself up on an elbow, then lean down and place a gentle kiss on his lips. I pull back and he's smiling at me.

"Is this supposed to distract me from the fact that you don't want me in your army?"

I give him a smile. "Is it working?"

"Maybe. Try again."

I lean down and kiss him again then pull back.

"It's a little bit better. We may need to work on it a bit more."

I laugh and shake my head. "It's not that I don't appreciate your wanting to be there. I do. It's just that, I mean, if it came down to it, Paxton and Astra can both kill without giving it a second thought. And you've got such a good heart, I would hate to think of what taking a life would do to you. I'd be afraid you wouldn't be able to live with yourself after that."

"I'm tougher than I look, you know."

"I know you are. But your gift is healing. Not killing," I say.

"And to be honest, I haven't decided whether I'm going yet or not."

"Why's that?"

"I don't know if I want to open up that can of worms again," I tell him.

"Well, you know where I stand on the issue," he says. "Personally, I think you'd be better off if you just left it alone."

"I know. I'm torn, though. Part of me doesn't want to undo all of the progress I've made with Dr. Reinhart," I say. "The other part wants to find my parents' killers."

"Yeah, but you don't know for sure that this Corden guy has information to help you do that."

"What else could it be?"

He shrugs. "No idea. It just seems really weird that almost twenty years later, he pops up, pretends to be somebody else, and has this mysterious information."

"But what if he's using an alias because he's on the run, too? What if these things that are in motion that he mentioned have forced him underground?"

Mark laughs softly. "This all sounds like a Jason Bourne movie or something. Conspiracies and cabals, secret information, aliases..."

I frown. I don't think he's taking this as seriously as he should. I don't find this to be a joking matter. Not at all.

"Answer me this: why would Mr. Corden try to lure me out somewhere isolated to kill me, when he could just sneak into the apartment in the middle of the night and kill me here?"

"Maybe he's not sure he could sneak in?"

I roll my eyes. "He was CIA. A covert operator. I'm pretty sure a door lock wouldn't slow him down much."

Mark purses his lips. "Okay, that's a good point. But why would he show up twenty years after the fact? Wouldn't they have been able to eliminate you early on?"

"Maybe they think that as I've gotten older, I've come to know more. Maybe they don't know but don't want to take a chance. I'm a loose end, so maybe they want to cut out any loose ends."

"I still keep coming back to the fact that it's twenty years later. It just doesn't make sense."

"Something's changed, obviously," I say. "He did say there are things now in motion. I read that as being recent."

"Maybe," Mark acknowledges. "I just think this all sounds crazy."

"If my parents hadn't been mysteriously murdered, I might, too," I say. "But I know that conspiracies exist. And this is one I want to solve."

"Sounds as though you've made up your mind already."

I laugh softly. "Sounds more as if you've talked me into it."

We curl up together in silence for a little while, both of us lost in our thoughts. I appreciate how worried about me he is. I know he wants to keep me from getting too deep into this and possibly getting hurt. Or just being disappointed when none of this conspiracy talk pans out. He's trying to protect me from myself, and I love him for that.

"Where are you meeting him?" he asks.

"The Cascades RV Park," I reply.

Mark tries to choke back a laugh, but he can't hold it and suddenly erupts into loud guffaws. I sit up as he rolls into a ball, holding his stomach as he laughs hysterically. I just watch him, trying to hold back my irritation.

"I don't know what you're finding so funny, but I can assure you it's really not that funny."

"It's hilarious," he gasps.

I sigh and lean back against the couch, waiting for him to laugh himself out. He does so a couple minutes later and sits back on the couch next to me. He's still chuckling, though, and wiping his tears of mirth from his face.

"Sorry. I wasn't laughing at you," he says.

"Kind of sounded as if you were."

"I swear I wasn't," he says. "I was just picturing this CIA superspy tooling around the country in an RV," he explains. "I figured he'd be cruising in an Aston Martin or a Maserati. An RV just doesn't send the right message, I don't think."

"I said he was retired," I snap.

He slips an arm around my shoulders and pulls me to him, then places a gentle kiss atop my head. I nuzzle a little closer to him.

"I'm sorry," he whispers. "It just struck me funny to think of 007 rolling around in an RV."

"You're awful," I say, feeling my irritation draining away.

"Whatever you decide to do, I'm with you, Blake," he says. "If my role is to be here to patch you up after all the shooting's over, so be it. Just know I'll do anything you need to help. Anything at all."

Gary Suban flashes into my mind again. I find myself wondering if that's similar to what he said to Sasha when he pledged himself to her. I give my head small a shake, trying to rid myself of those kinds of thoughts. That case is closed, and I want to move on from it. I had a weird moment when I thought having a conversation with Sasha would be a good idea, but being here, in Mark's arms, is all I need. It's all I want.

And as I nuzzle closer to him, I realize it's all I'll ever want. And that I've never been happier than I am right now.

THIRTY-SEVEN

Chapter Thirty-Seven

CASCADES RV PARK; *Seattle, WA*

"Mr. Corden?" I call out. My voice echoes across the small pound. "Hello?"

The night is dark and ominous. Thick clouds the color of slate clog the sky and a cool wind stirs the leaves on the ground and the branches in the trees above. Mr. Corden's RV is the only visible one in the grounds. There's a fire ring, but when I hold my hand over it, I don't feel a lick of warmth. There's been no fire built in the pit today.

I stand up and look around, wondering where he's gone. "Mr. Corden, it's Blake! Hello?"

All I hear is my voice echoing around the grounds again, but I get no answer. I look back to the car and see the pair of shadowy silhouettes inside – I agreed to let Pax and Astra come so long as they stayed in the car while I was talking to Mr.

Corden. But with an foreboding feeling building inside of me, I'm starting to get a little nervous.

I turn on my flashlight and wave Pax and Sasha over. No sense in standing out here alone. The overhead light in Paxton's Escalade goes on as they climb out of the car and walk over to where I'm standing.

"What's going on?" Pax asks.

"I don't know where he is," I tell them.

"This doesn't look good," Astra comments.

I turn back to the RV. There are no lights on inside, and when I touched the front engine compartment, it was stone cold, so Mr. Corden's been here a while.

"Have you tried the door?" Pax asks.

"Well, no. I knocked but he didn't answer."

"And you didn't try to open it?" Astra presses.

I shrug. "I thought it might be rude. Especially if he were in there."

"Well, at this point I think we need to open it up," Pax says. "Just to make sure he's not in there and needs help or something."

"Yeah, that makes sense."

I walk over and grab the door handle. It pops and the door opens. I look back at Pax and Astra, feeling like an idiot. I reach inside and flip on the light and climb the three steps into the cabin.

"Oh my God," I mutter. "Pax, Astra. You guys better get in here."

The RV rocks as they both climb in behind me. I move deeper into the RV, flipping on lights as I go. The place is trashed. Everything that was in the cupboards is now scattered all over the floor. Dishes have been shattered, shards of glass litter the floor, and the small appliances have been smashed and broken into pieces. Everything in disarray.

I pull my service weapon and head to the rear of the RV to where the bedroom is located. I yank back the accordion door and breathe a sigh of relief when I don't see Mr. Corden in there. The place is empty, but like the front of the RV, everything is trashed. Drawers have been pulled out and the things in the closet are strewn on the floor.

"This doesn't look good, Blake," Pax says.

"Somebody was looking for something," Astra adds.

It really doesn't look good, and as I stand among the wreckage of Mr. Corden's RV, I become absolutely certain we're not going to find him alive. We might not find him at all. I walk out of the RV and take a deep breath, inhaling the earthy, musky scent of the woods around us and try to block out the bad, negative feelings that are stealing over me.

"What in the hell is going on," Astra mutters.

"I think we have a conspiracy," I say.

"Maybe not," Paxton says, trying to sound reasonable. "It could be a random robbery."

"It wasn't," I say.

"How do you know?"

"There were expensive things all around in the cabin of the RV. A Rolex sat on shelf above the sink. Mr. Corden's money clip – stuffed with cash – sat on the nightstand back in the bedroom and a dozen other high -value things sat around. Whoever busted into Mr. Corden's RV was looking for something, and it wasn't trinkets."

Astra slips her phone out of her pocket and dials 9-1-1. She takes a few steps away and presses the phone to her ear. I turn to Paxton and frown.

"So much for that ambush," I mutter.

"Could still happen," he replies. "Keep your eyes open."

"It's going to take the cops a little time to get up here," Astra announces.

"In the meantime, we need to see if we can find Mr. Corden," I say.

We branch out in different directions and scour the entire campground, but there's no sign of Mr. Corden anywhere. It's as if the earth opened and just swallowed him whole. We meet at the RV again and I can't speak for the two of them, but I'm starting to freak out a little bit. Something bad happened here, but I have no idea what it was.

"What in the hell happened out here?" I ask.

Pax shakes his head. "No idea. But it seems certain it wasn't anything good."

"So, what are we thinking? Was this a CIA hit squad?" Astra postulates. "I mean, if he's ex-CIA, could they have gotten word he was going off the reservation and decided to not let him?"

"Makes as much sense as anything else to me at this point," I say.

"Let's not let our imaginations run away with us just yet," Pax says evenly.

"How is this a case of our imaginations running away with us?" I ask. "I mean, the CIA has a long history of disappearing people."

Paxton laughs softly. "And random strangers have an even longer history of ransacking and disappearing tourists."

"Don't patronize me, Pax. A random robbery? That's exactly what they said about my parents' murder."

"Blake, I didn't –"

"If this was about Veronica, you wouldn't be laughing it off right now," I cut him off. "I appreciate your back-up, but this is my investigation. My life. Please let me follow this.

"I'm sorry."

I cross my arms over my chest and pace around the ground outside the door of the RV. It's getting chilly as the night stretches on, and I'm tempted to start a fire for warmth. I look around, and that's when I notice the logs and kindling spread all around the pit. It looks as if Mr. Corden was surprised and was taken as he started a fire.

A current of grief ripples through my heart as I wonder what became of him. Mr. Corden is a good man. He doesn't deserve whatever's become of him. And I'm not naïve. I don't think he's alive. Maybe the bleak mood I'm in has me thinking worst case scenario, but I'm betting that whoever took him has already killed him.

I stand up with my arms crossed over my chest again and look out across the pond. The trees on the other side are little more than dark shadows with their boughs dipping low, some of them hanging in the water. There's a foggy mist curling around the surface of the water and it's smooth and peaceful.

But when the moon peeks out from behind the clouds for just a moment, the silvery light rains down over the land, casting the world in a monochromatic light. And it's then that I see a lumpy form caught up amongst the reeds at the edge of the pond.

"Oh, God," I whisper.

My heart is beating so hard, I'm sure it's leaving bruises on the inside of my chest as I start to run toward the water's edge.

"Pax! Astra!" I call out.

I hear their footsteps pound on the ground behind me as I rush toward the pond. And when I get to the edge, a choked cry passes my lips when I see what's in the reeds. Mr. Corden. He's lying on his back, his body limp, his face an unnatural shade of white. There are two holes in the center of his forehead, and his eyes are wide, bulging, and unblinking. He's got that faraway glaze of death on his face, and a permanent expression of surprise.

Pax's arm is around me and he turns me away from the

water. He nods to Astra, who takes over. She walks me back toward the RV and I feel a cold numbness spreading out from the center of me.

"Get a fire started, Astra," Pax calls.

I cast a look over my shoulder and see Paxton dragging Mr. Corden's body out of the water and a shuddering sob passes my lips. My entire body is trembling, and I hear Astra's voice, but it's as if I'm hearing it from underwater. It's just a muffled murmuring. Astra sits me down on one of the logs that are positioned around the firepit, and she immediately gets a fire going.

I watch as the flames dance and writhe in the stone pit, casting flickering shadows all around us. Astra is sitting next to me, my hand in hers. Paxton comes back from the edge of the pond and sits down on the log across from us. None of us speaks, all of us lost in our own thoughts.

As I sit there, staring into the flames, there are two questions that continue rattling around in my mind: who could have killed Mr. Corden? And who knew he was out here?

Did somebody know he was meeting with me? Given how careful he is, how could somebody have known this was where we were meeting? None of this makes sense to me. Could it really have just been a random attack? Or was this another piece of the conspiracy? Did somebody tumble onto the fact that Mr. Corden was going to pass along some information to me? Was his phone tapped?

As the last question passes through my mind, I freeze. Ice water flows through my veins and I feel myself trembling. If Mr. Corden was going to pass along information to me – where did the information go?

I jump to my feet and dash to the RV, both Paxton and Astra calling after me. I think it's safe to say, given the condition of the interior, that the killers were looking for it. Vigorously.

"What are you doing?" Paxton asks.

"I'm looking for the information Mr. Corden was going to pass on," I say.

Pax spreads his hands out wide. "I think it's safe to say whoever was here probably got it."

I shake my head. "I doubt the entire place would be trashed if they found what they were looking for. This isn't just gratuitous violence. They were searching."

"That's possible, sure –"

"And second, Mr. Corden was being so careful, he was bordering on paranoid. He would have kept it hidden until he was ready to give it to me," I say.

I shuffle through the papers on the ground and start opening draws and cupboards, throwing everything on the ground at my feet. I stop for a moment and look around. My mind floats back to a time when I was with my dad and we were in Mr. Corden's garage. I'd been bored and was looking around when I stumbled upon a drawer in his worktable. I opened it and something about the bottom of drawer didn't look right to me. I recall that I'd reached in and pulled on a loose piece of wood in the drawer.

It had been a false bottom, of course. My father scolded me for being so nosy. I'd apologized, but Mr. Corden had laughed and said my natural curiosity was going to take me places. Right now, I just want it to take me to the information he was going to give me. I start over and begin checking all the drawers. Perhaps catching on to what I'm doing, Paxton starts looking for false bottoms in the drawers as well.

"Blake."

I turn and see him holding a manila envelope. My name is scrawled in neat black letters across the front, and I get a chill. It feels as if the dead are speaking to me. I take the envelope from Pax and open it up. It's a file folder, so I slip it out and drop the envelope. Pax sidles over and stands next to me. My heart fluttering wildly, I look up at him.

"It's why we're here. Take a look."

I clear my throat and open the file – and am immediately gripped by confusion. The first few sheets of paper are dossiers of two sitting Supreme Court Justices. The third piece of paper is entirely blank, save for one word: *bichu*. It's a foreign word, but I'm not sure which language just yet. I look over at Pax.

"Recognize the language?"

He shakes his head. "I have no clue."

"Maybe Astra knows."

We head for the door, and I've just stepped into the doorway and started to descend the stairs when the shots ring out. The sharp cracks are so loud in the silence of the woods, it sounds like a cannon going off. I hear a slug tear into the flesh of the RV and feel it shudder.

"Get down!"

I hear Paxton's voice before I feel his hand in the middle of my back, shoving me down. I hit the dirt, the sudden fall so unexpected, it drives the air out of me. More shots ring out from the other side of the pond and I see Pax and Astra scrambling for cover. A minute later, they're in position and are returning fire. I roll over onto my back and shove the file into the waistband of my pants, then find cover for myself. I squeeze off a few shots only to realize the enemy is no longer firing.

I glance over at Pax and Astra. The sudden silence is oppressive, and I imagine a squad of black-clad commandos circling around behind us, looking to do to us what they did to Mr. Corden. I look around and see nothing. A moment later, the high-pitched whining of a motorcycle engine firing up shatters the silence. I exchange looks with Pax and Astra, but it's on the other side of the pond. He'll be long gone before we get there. Through the gaps in the foliage on that side, I see the glowing red in the darkness, and then the sound of the motor-cycle starts to fade as the gunman takes off.

"What in the hell was that?" I ask.

"A conspiracy, it seems," Paxton replies.

The red and blue flashing lights of the police cars rolling in is a comforting and welcome sight. Or as comforting and welcome as it can be. I have a feeling I'm not going to be very comfortable for a long while.

THIRTY-EIGHT

THE MOTORCYCLE BOUNCED JARRINGLY on the dirt road and the trees pressed close to either side of the trail were darkened shadows. The world passed by him in a blur. He hit a pothole so hard, it made his teeth clack together almost painfully, and he let out a string of curses. He steered around another hole and did his best to mitigate those he couldn't go around. He looked behind himself, checking to make sure he was still alone, even though he knew there would be no way they could be following him.

He still couldn't believe he'd yakked that first shot. He'd had the crosshairs on the center of Paxton's forehead, but just before he squeezed the trigger, something touched the back of his neck, making him jump. He was already squeezing the trigger and it was too late. He yakked the shot. Once they knew he was out there, it was all over, and he'd had to go. So, he'd laid down some fire and then got out of there.

He'd completed his primary mission – which was to eliminate Corden. He was unable to complete his secondary mission, which was to find the packet Corden was supposed to be passing on to Blake. But if he hadn't been able to find it, she wouldn't be able to, either. The primary mission was the most important – keep Corden from speaking to Blake. Corden had reams of information, and it would be a tremendous blow to his employer if he'd been allowed to spill the tea. Everything had been fine until Corden had grown a conscience.

As a result of that, his employer hadn't wanted Corden anywhere near Blake. Things were already in motion, and they had to be allowed to run their course. There was too much at stake to leave things to chance now. Blake was a wild card to them. His employer believed she knew much more than she was letting on. And in this business, you didn't take shortcuts or hope for the best. You eliminated the threat immediately. As Mr. Corden had just discovered.

He knew he should have taken out Blake. He knew that when his employer found out she was still alive, he wouldn't be happy. But he couldn't bring himself to do it. There was a time he would have squeezed the trigger, dropped her, and gone about his day without a second thought. But that time had passed, and things now were... complicated. He'd tried, but he couldn't force himself to do it. He'd have to find some other way to make his employer happy by ensuring her silence and stifling her curiosity.

He followed the road out of the woods and raced down the darkened highway toward the cabin where he'd left his car. He knew Blake and her group were going to be tied up with the local LEOs for a while yet. Finding a body was a time-consuming thing when it came to answering the multitude of questions the cops would have for them. But he still wanted to be far, far away from there well before the cops released them.

He turned down the small access road that ran parallel to the property, then cut the engine and coasted for a while. The bike came to a stop at the edge of the property, so he walked it the rest of the way, storing it in the shed where he'd gotten it. He locked the shed and went into the cabin to clean up and change his clothes. When he was done, he came back out to the dining room and opened up his laptop and logged onto their secure server.

As the connection was made, he felt a flutter in his gut. The mission was a success, but not a complete success. And his employer was not the type you wanted to disappoint.

SitRep...

He quickly typed out his message and hit send. *Primary mission successful. Threat is eliminated. Secondary mission uncertain. Package was not on site.*

Secondary target?

This is where he grew nervous. If his employer determined that he had been compromised or that he had become unreliable, it would be a problem, and then he would suddenly become a loose end himself. And his employer did not tolerate loose ends.

He keyed in his message and sent it. *Unnecessary to eliminate second target. Package not on site. Best to avoid more attention from LEOs who believe attack was random robbery gone wrong.*

We worry you have been compromised.

He let out a long breath and composed his answer. *Situation well in hand. Nothing has been compromised. Still on mission.*

See that you are. We do not tolerate failure.

The dialog box closed, and he let out a breath as he shut down the computer. He was worried, though, simply because they were apparently concerned enough to wonder aloud whether he'd been compromised or not. That was almost as good as saying they were going to greenlight him. Almost. He believed he still had some wiggle room, though.

But it was going to become increasingly important that he handle Blake better and do all he could to steer her away from the path she was walking. It was imperative for both of them if they wanted to live. And he very much wanted to live. After all, she had given him a reason to.

Mark Walton left the cabin and got into his SUV, started it, and pulled out. He wanted to be home long before Blake arrived.

EPILOGUE

I T 'S A BEAUTIFUL DAY. The sky is a stunning shade of blue, filled with large, fluffy white clouds. The air is fresh and crisp and the cool breeze is refreshing. All around me, children are laughing and playing, and people are enjoying their picnic lunches. It's tranquil. Peaceful. Idyllic. I don't get out enough.

I walk through the park and walk into the playground. I sit down on the swing and hold onto the chains as I kick my legs, building up momentum. I love that feeling of weightlessness I get at the height of my swing, that moment where I just hang there, right before my swing takes me backward.

After a little while, I slow my momentum and get off the swing. I haven't been on a swing set for a long time. Not since I was a kid. The nostalgia welling up within me is thick and over-whelming. Walking out of the playground area, I try to push away those feelings. They don't serve me now, so there's no sense in dwelling on them.

I walk through the park and sit down beneath a tree. Resting my back against the wide, rough trunk, I survey the

park before me. I watch as a couple of kids stand off to the side
flying kites. I watch a group of kids playing football. But then
my gaze settles on a family about fifty yards away from me.

The father is tall and has dark hair, and the mother is small
and petite with blonde hair. They have two kids – two little
girls. They're playing together on the blanket, laughing and
squealing with each other. It tickles the memories within me.
Dredges up things I haven't thought about for a long, long time.

And it brings a sad smile to my face.

I watch the family enjoying their picnic. They look like
such a happy little family. The parents look as if they're in love
and love their children wholeheartedly. It makes me miss my
family. It's been a long time since I've felt the sort of unconditional love of a family. It's been so long I don't know that I'd
even recognize it anymore.

Life hasn't unfolded the way I thought it would when I was
a child. And there are days I wish I could go back to that time
when I was young and naïve. Those days when I was still innocent and hadn't seen a lot of the things that infect my memories
today.

I wonder what my life would have been like had things
turned out differently. If I'd had a family who loved me as
much as that mother and father I'm watching obviously love
their two little girls. I wonder what I would be today if I had
parents who'd encouraged me to reach for the stars and be
everything I wanted to be. If I'd had a family who built me up
and dared me to dream – and to chase those dreams.

I get to my feet and dust myself off, still watching that
family, doing my best to stuff down the jealousy that's surging
within me. Jealousy does nothing. It's wasted thought and
energy. Envy does nothing but diminish me. But still, even
knowing that, it's hard to not feel it when I see people who have
things I long for.

My sister is my only family now. And I haven't seen her in a very long time. But I'll be changing that. I'll be seeing her again. Soon. And hey, maybe I'll even get a chance to feel that sort of unconditional love again. Maybe.

THE END

NOTE FROM ELLE GRAY

I hope you enjoyed *Her Perfect Crime*, book 3 in the *Blake Wilder FBI Mystery Thriller* series.
My intention is to give you a thrilling adventure and an entertaining escape with each and every book.
However, I need your help to continue writing and bring you more books.

Being a new indie writer is tough.
I don't have a large budget, huge following, or any of the cutting edge marketing techniques.
So, all I kindly ask is that if you enjoyed this book, please take a moment of your time and leave me a review and maybe recommend the book to a fellow book lover or two.
This way I can continue to write all day and night and bring you more books in the *Blake Wilder* series.

By the way, if you find any typos or want to reach out to me, feel free to email me at egray@ellegraybooks.com

Your writer friend,
Elle Gray

Click here to get your copy of A Perfect Wife (Blake Wilder FBI Mystery Thriller Book 2) today.

ALSO BY ELLE GRAY

Olivia Knight FBI Mystery Thrillers

Book One - New Girl in Town

Blake Wilder FBI Mystery Thrillers

Book One - The 7 She Saw

Book Two - A Perfect Wife

Book Three - Her Perfect Crime

Book Four - The Chosen Girls

Book Five - The Secret She Kept

Book Six - The Lost Girls

Book Seven - The Lost Sister

A Pax Arrington Mystery

Free Prequel - Deadly Pursuit

Book One - I See You

Book Two - Her Last Call

Book Three - Woman In The Water

Book Four - A Wife's Secret